{ DELPHINE PUBLICATIONS PRESENTS }

A HUSTLAZ DREAM
PART 1

JASMIN JOHNSTON

A Hustlaz Dream Part 1

Delphine Publications focuses on bringing a reality check to the genre urban literature.

All stories are a work of fiction from the authors and are not meant to depict, portray, or represent any particular person.

Names, characters, places, and incidents are either the product of the author's imagination or are used fictitiously, and any resemblances to an actual person living or dead are entirely coincidental.

A Hustlaz Dream Part 1 © 2013 Jasmine Johnston

All rights reserved. No part of this publication may be reproduced, stored in or introduced into a retrieval system, or transmitted, in any form, or by any means (electronic, mechanical, photocopying, recording, or otherwise), without the prior written permission of both the copyright owner and the above publisher of this book.

ISBN 13 - 978-0996084475

Cover Design: Odd Ball Designs

Layout: Write On Promotions

Published by Delphine Publications

www.DelphinePublications.com

Printed in the United States of America

Dedication

I would like to thank God for his many blessings and unconditional love.

This book is dedicated to my beautiful mother, Wanda Johnston whose life's experiences helped lace my boots so I wouldn't trip along the way. To my sister's Nikita Brown and Jolisa Brown, you've showed the love and support I needed in my triumphs and failure's, hugs and kisses forever!

To my grandfather Earl Brown, Sr. Thank you for always being there for all of us!

To my sister's Patricia Davis, Shaina Langford and Danielle Langford, I love ya!

To my loves that have supported me along the way: Nicole Triplett, Twavida Plummer, Bryan "Dubb" Walker, Jason Johnston, Carey Clethen, Leeanna Riggins, Alesia Riggins, Lori Riggins, Adrian Brown, Gerald Brown, John Lain, Niki Wade, Ramona Fefe, Angela Jones, Robert Jones, Rosita Jones, Shavonna Brown.

Special thanks to the team at Delphine Publications, thank you for everything!!!

And last but not least, shout out to Arlono 'Zo' Banks, without you I wouldn't have noticed this light at the end of my dark tunnel. I love you more than life, and best believe when those bars bend I will be at the gates with open arms. Love you forever and a day!

A Hustlaz Dream

July 15, 2009

"Dearly beloved, we are gathered here today..." Rev. Huddleston's voice bellowed through the sanctuary's surround sound speakers.

'Ohh my goodness, look at me! I am actually standing at the altar, getting married to the love of my life... Is this a dream, should I pinch myself because this can't be happening to me? Look at him, standing there looking like he just jumped out of a Men's health magazine. So sexy and he's all mine, finally. I've only been waiting on this day for what, 7 long years? My dreams have totally become a reality, thank you Lord!

Well I'm not going to lie, there's been quite a few hiccups in between, as far as dealing with the skanks and groupies. I refer to them as groupies because my man is a hood star. Not only is his money longer than the 880 freeway, but he has a swagger that's outta this world. The hood rat chicks from around the way look at him as if he were royalty, a king. But wake up bitches, I am his queen and shall receive my crown in the next few minutes.

Rev. Huddleson cleared his throat.

'Ohh shit, I'm daydreamin', and they're all waiting on me,' she thought. Looking around, she saw the congregation with their eyes glued to her.

Once eye contact was made the Pastor continued.

"Jai'Myiah Amonya Liggins, do you take Zeh'Shon to be your lawfully wedded husband, to have and to hold, through sickness and health, until death do you part?" He repeated in a sluggish tone.

"Yes! I do," She replied anxiously.

"And do you, Zeh'Shon Montiece Banks, take Jai'Myiah to be your lawfully wedded wife, to have and to hold, through sickness and health until death do you part?"

"I do," he said with a smile on his face like he held the winning lottery ticket.

Rev. Huddleston closed his bible and spoke. "By the power vested in me, I now pronounce you husb---"

RAAGGGA-TA-TATT-TATT.

Four loud shots filled the church like a thunderstorm. Confused screams danced through the building like the guns after smoke, tapping the stained glass windows and ceiling. Guests began to scatter like the running of the bulls. Some stopped, dropped and rolled for cover while others ran like hell to the nearest corner screaming to the high heavens.

'Why does it feel like my chest is on fire? Oh my GOD look at my dress, it looks like somebody threw ketchup all over me... wait... why am I so tired?'

"Baby, baby. Myah! Don't leave me, baby. Please don't go. I need you, I love you so much. Please, please," cried Zeh'Shon. "Somebody call the ambulance, tell them to hurry the fuck up!"

'I love you too baby! Why am I laying on the floor with all these people surrounding me? Help me up, baby. Why can't I move my leg? Let me find out if Prada uses cement in its products.

Zariah, I hear you girl, I love you, too best friend. Don't let me die, help me y'all! Why is my chest so hot, and the rest of my body feeling so cold? I gotta... I gotta take a nap, I'm so sleepy.

Outside of the house of God, a car door slammed. Tires screeched loudly while burning rubber from the curb, followed by an ambulance blaring its sirens. A few wedding goers hit the door in pursuit of the fleeing vehicle, but were a second too late. The shooter was long gone.

CHAPTER 1

The waiting room at Kaiser Hospital in Oakland, CA, was packed with Jai'Myiah's friends and family members. Some were in groups huddled together and praying for positive news, while others held discussions trying to figure out who could've done something so evil.

Zeh'Shon sat in the far corner of the room in a zombie-like state. His heart was too heavy to communicate with anyone, so the well-wishers gave him space and sympathized from the sidelines. Seated as still as a log, he stared blankly at the white plastered wall, only seeing blurred lines.

Kaiser's waiting area was very spacious. There was enough room to allow patients and their loved ones space to move around without feeling cramped, yet the suffocation of gloom was felt. Two enormous windows stood in place for walls on the right and left side of the room. About twenty or so chairs lined the area, there were also chairs placed in the center of the room.

Pictures of doctors with his/her credentials, no smoking signs, and health pamphlets adorned the walls. Two television sets held place on each side of the room, but no one cared what was showing. Six plastic plants were scattered around the area, to give a comforting feeling, but no one paid attention to them one way or the other.

The reception desk was placed a few yards away. Behind it sat a chubby black lady that kept a cellular phone glued to her ear for the most part of her shift. The strong stench of disinfectant mixed with dried rose pedals reeked off the walls of the building. Jumbled voices were heard dancing off the walls, but not one conversation was recognized.

Time trickled by slowly as the sixteenth hour of patiently waiting for the doctor's verdict approached. Most of the wedding goers had gone with promises to pray for a full and speedy recovery for Jai'Myiah. Eight of her closest loved ones quietly remained, refusing to budge until they knew the outcome of surgery.

Trish, Jai'Myiah's older sister, and Jolisa, their younger sibling, were cuddled up by the women's restroom, having cried themselves to sleep, their mouths hung agape with ashy tear coated cheeks. Wanda, Jai'Myiah's mother, was seated in the front of the television system, in a daze, looking at the screen but not focusing on the picture. Bo, Jai'Myiah's older brother, had been pacing back and forth, from the bathroom to the vending machines for the last three hours. Zeh'Shon's younger sister, Shanell, was seated directly in the middle of the room holding a lengthy conversation, clearly disregarding the no cell phone sign.

Zeh'Shon stood at the window, gazing off into the city trying to figure out the details of what just happened and who on earth had balls big enough to send fire to the person closest and dearest to him. He thought what he was going to do when he found out who was behind this foolish act. He knew he would eventually, due to the role he played in the game. He was the streets and the streets talk; it was just a matter of how soon they

A Hutlaz Dream

would begin whispering. His promise was to bring so much heat to their lives that their ancestors would feel the flame.

Niki, Zeh'Shon's mother, approached her son from behind him carrying a tray from the cafeteria, a roast beef sandwich on sourdough, a bag of chips, vitamin water and a bowl of mixed fruit.

"Here baby, try to eat this." She stretched out her short, chubby arms. "Just put a little something on your stomach. I don't want you getting sick on me," she said in a loving motherly voice.

"Nah Mama. Thanks anyway, but I can't eat right now cause I aint got no appetite," he replied, his voice was a cracked murmur.

"Zeh'Shon come here and give me a hug," she spoke grabbing hold of his arm and pulling him forward. He obediently turned and fell into his mother's opened embrace.

"Mama," Zeh'Shon cried, "What if everything ain't all right? What if Jai'Myiah don't make it, what am I gonna do? That's my heart in there mama, my wife. This shit is so fucked up, what happened?"

"I know baby, I know. All we can do at this point is pray. Her fate is in the Lord's hands. Have faith son, don't lose hope," encouraged Niki.

Zeh'Shon sobbed on his mother's shoulder for the next several minutes, pouring out emotions that not even she knew he possessed. When he finally came up for air, his eyes were blood red and her shoulder was connected to him by the snot that hung from his nose.

Niki felt terrible seeing her son in such a sensitive state, but at the moment there was nothing left to do but console him as best she could. She loved Jai'Myiah as her own seed, and his outward pain mirrored her inner, but she had to stay strong for her child's sake. Niki suggested that her son go in the restroom and try to get himself together while she went to check on Wanda.

When Zeh'Shon opened the door to the men's room, he was greeted by the strong reek of urine and musk. Fragments of toilet paper along with balled up paper towels littered the tiled floor, while water dripped from the stained sink. The slow- moving janitors needed to get a move on it and check their areas because this part of the job was not up to par, he thought to himself.

Standing in front of the smoky mirror, he gazed at his reflection. He looked like a dope fiend that had been up for more than a week straight. His eyes were as red as the lights on top of a police cruiser when activated, accented with eye lashes that sat with a upward curve. Freshly twisted Dred-locks, which had hung evenly at his shoulder blades during the ceremony, were now in a pony- tail held together by a thick rubber band. His goattee and razor sharp line up were immaculate as his thick eyebrows spread at a disorganized angle.

His handsomeness was still obvious, even with his dark brown slanted eyes swollen and puffy. Chocolate skin hugged his 6'3" 240lb frame tightly; bulging muscles were evident even through his tuxedo. His once white dress shirt was now painted with his wife's blood, the wrinkles on his sleeves and collar spoke of a rough evening. Starring at the crimson stain through the mirror's reflection caused his heart to drop for the umpteenth time.

Reaching down and twisting the knobs of the water faucet, he bent over and splashed his face a couple times. The fatigue and depression fogged his mind to the point of insanity, but he managed to remain standing. A million miles away from the place where he had everything in life figured out, he was, for once, misplaced with the element of surprise.

A Hutlaz Dream

Drying his face and hands, he heard a toilet flush. The stall door opened and out walked Bo, looking just as disheveled as his brother-in-law.

"'Sup bruh?" Bo said.

"Shit, fucked up! How you holdin' up, bruh?"

"I can't even call it right now." He said shaking his heavy head. "I mean, I can't explain how I'm feeling, that's lil sis man, hopefully the doc come wit some good news."

Zeh'Shon nodded his head in agreement while replying in a regretful voice.

"I just wish I could've done something. That's my wife in there, I'm supposed to be her protector."

"I feel somewhat like you, but we can't..." Bo got cut off by as he caught sight of the bathroom door flying open. Zariah, Jai'Myiah's best friend rushed in yelling.

"Come on y'all, the doctor want to tell us Jai'Myiah's situation."

The three of them rushed over to hear the information. The cold air pierced the naked skin of the trio, but for some strange reason Zeh'Shon had a feeling the revelation would only add to the freeze.

Upon arriving within earshot of Dr. Chan, Zeh'Shon noticed he had an odd look on his face. His gut told him that the news couldn't be anything good, but he was still optimistic. The family huddled around the small man who couldn't be any taller than 5'0, or weigh any more than 90 lbs. soaking wet.

"You are the family of Jai'Myiah Liggins, correct?" asked Dr. Chan.

"Yes" voices replied in unison.

"Banks, Jai'Myiah Banks is her name, we were married today," stated Zeh'Shon matter-a-factly.

"Banks," Dr. Chan corrected. "I do apologize. We just came out of surgery. Mrs. Banks made it. Unfortunately, we will not be able to tell if the surgery was 100% successful until 72 hours has passed. Jai'Myiah has suffered three gunshot wounds, one to the chest cavity that miraculously missed her heart by merely millimeters. The second went through her abdomen and lodged itself directly by her spine. We did not remove this bullet for fear that Mrs. Banks may end up paralyzed for life. The third and final bullet went into her left cheek and came out of her right ear."

The family shed tears and let out soft agonizing moans. Dr. Chan continued, "Her brain has quite a bit of swelling, and she is not strong enough to breathe on her own. My suggestion is that you all go home and get a little rest. All we can--"

" What the fuck you mean, go home? I wanna see my baby," yelled Wanda, her face saturated with tears.

"Mama, please calm down," begged Jolisa, her face just as wet as everyone else's.

With a sorrowful expression on his face, Dr. Chan replied, "All you can do as a family is converse with your higher power. My staff and I have done the very best we could, now we have to see if this young lady is indeed a fighter. My prayers are with you, good night."

With that said, Dr. Chan walked briskly down the hallway, leaving the family standing in the middle of the floor in shock and utter disbelief.

Wanda broke into uncontrollable sobs, her son Bo holding her up while at the same time directing her towards the exit doors. The rest of the family followed suit, all sharing looks of defeat and bewilderment. As everyone got into their respective

A Hutlaz Dream

cars, Zeh'Shon stood motionless on the sidewalk looking at nothing in particular.

"Zeh, come on let me give you a ride, you can stay with me tonight," said Niki, breaking the surge of his thoughts while rubbing his back in a circular motion.

"Just give me a ride to my car, I need to handle something," he whispered.

While in the car, Niki strained to talk her son out of whatever it was that he planned to do, but the wise words landed on deaf ears and she knew it. His mind was made up. With the stubbornness that her son possessed she knew there was nothing she could do to prevent it.

Riding down the I-580 towards East Oakland, Zeh'Shon reached into his pocket to retrieve his phone.

Ring, Ring. Zo answered on the second ring.

"What's the word?" asked Zeh'Shon.

"Nothing right now, but you know I'm working on it, got my ear to the ground."

"Meet me at the spot in 15". Zeh'Shon ordered.

" Aiight, one." The line went dead.

"Get off on High St." Zeh'Shon said to his mother.

Noticing that her words weren't registering in his brain, she reluctantly complied with the request. Nothing ceased to amaze her as she drove down High St. and watched the nightly activities that transpired. Young boys posted on the block, waiting on the next customer to come and buy whatever product they were selling. She took notice that almost every hustler wore blue jeans, white t-shirts, and either Jordans or white Nikes. Their hair was worn in dread locks or bald fades, some with black sweatshirts, others with their arms tucked in the sleeves of their shirt to keep warm in the cold night. 'This must be the uniform of the streets,' she thought to herself.

Dope fiends or "knocks" as they were referred to in Oakland, wandered around aimlessly in search of their next hit. Some smokers were absolute mental cases as they strode through the concrete jungle cursing at the sky, and holding full conversations with the voices in their heads.

"Make a right on Lyon, Mama," Zeh'Shon spoke, snapping Niki out of her thoughts. As the car cascaded up the short hill he continued, "Right here."

She pulled over to a set of rundown pink apartments and placed the gear in park.

Before she was able to get a word out of her mouth, Zeh'Shon planted a kiss on her right cheek and got out of the car. Saddened, she watched as he closed to door to the 2014 Toyota Camry that her dear son purchased for her as a birthday gift.

She watched as he walked over to a tan Cadillac Escalade and climbed into the passenger seat. Seeing his childhood friend occupying the driver's seat, she knew that he was safe, at least for the time being. Tooting her horn followed by a brief wave she made a U-turn and drove off, heading home to 92nd and Birch. "Dear God, protect my child and save Jai'Mayah!" She pleaded before turning the radio's dial to KBLX.

***

A Hutlaz Dream

"Ay blood," said Zeh'Shon as he closed the door. "I don't give ah fuck what you gotta do, but I need whoever did this shit found A. S. A. P., whoever it was just declared war on the whole family."

"I'm already on it my nigga, I got you." Said Zo.

"Take me to the house, but first stop at School St. Market."

After a quick walk thru of the liquor store on 35th and School St., they made purchases then proceeded to Zeh'Shon's residence. Music played at a normal octave as they cruised, each man connected to his own points of view. Twenty-five minutes after taking the Monument Blvd. exit in Concord, they pulled up to Zeh'Shon's four bedroom, two-story home.

"Hit me," Zeh'Shon said to remind Zo to call as soon as he heard anything.

"Fasho," Zo replied as he watched his friend disappear into the bushes that lined the house. He cranked up his radio before pulling off, and headed to the block to see what was shaking.

Chapter 2

Zeh'Shon fumbled with his keys for a few seconds before finding the right one to let himself in. Upon entering his domain, he flicked the light switch that lit up the entire foyer. Closing the door, he locked it and stepped over to the tiny ADT box on the wall to deactivate the alarm system. A funny feeling came over him as he sensed how empty the house felt without Jai'Myiah's loving presence in the vicinity.

Seeking comfort, he decided to crack open the bottle of Remy Martin that he clutched tightly in his left hand. He hoped that the potent liquid would somewhat ease his pain. He put the bottle to his lips and took three thirsty gulps, never minding the burn in his throat that advanced to his chest. The feeling could hardly compare to the burn his heart was enduring at that moment.

Walking towards the staircase, he opted to take a hot shower before trying to put something on his stomach. Sluggishly hiking up the white carpeted stairs, he continued to drink while tip-toeing to his destination. Upon entering his master bedroom he made a bee line straight for the bathroom for some necessary relief.

Turning on the shower to the hottest temperature his body could stand, he removed his blood coated clothes and stepped in. The high pressure pumping through the shower head flowed rapidly, giving off a much needed massage. He hadn't realized the pain in his back from sitting on the hard and uncomfortable hospital chairs for so many hours.

A Hutlaz Dream

As the steady stream poured over his body, steam engulfed the large room imitating a sauna. The mist opened up his congested chest as he breathed deeply. At that moment, his reality had truly set in and hit as hard as a ton of bricks. He couldn't remember shedding tears since a kid, but at that moment he broke down and cried uncontrollably.

Out of all of the females that he'd ran through over the years, none had ever gotten to his heart, or even close for that matter, as Jai'Myiah had. He had made a vow to himself in his younger years to never trust a woman. He lived by the mottos "Bitches aint Shit" and "A bitch is a bitch and a hoe is a slut", those were the general pages printed in his book of life. He'd always remembered that line from Ice Cube's "A bitch is a bitch" song on N.W.A's Greatest Hits album.

Somehow Jai'Myiah broke down the wall that had been cemented with bricks around his heart. He tried denying the feelings that he'd felt for this woman in the beginning stages of their relationship, but couldn't help the way she got to him. Every time he was graced with her presence, her smile alone could light up a haunted palace.

Zeh'Shon couldn't contain his tears as he was overwhelmed with thoughts of losing her. Out of his 29 years on earth, he couldn't recall experiencing such despair.

He knew that he was far from perfect, and admits to putting Jai'Myiah through more than her share of bullshit, but she stuck by his side no matter what. His ride or die chick that wasn't easily broken and for more reasons than that, he respected her gangsta.

She was never the jealous type, and understood that the game her man played a part in required other broads for the purpose of increasing the bankroll. She felt by him having them, her job was a hell of a lot lighter so she sat back and reaped the benefits. No need for her being on the front line jeopardizing her freedom. Plus, blue or yellow baggy jail uniforms weren't a good look on her. She had been there and done that.

Though Zeh'Shon occasionally lied to his girl about sexual encounters he had with a few of these women, Jai'Myiah was no fool. She knew what was up from the jump but felt that as long as her man came home at night and didn't bring home any type of diseases or babies, she was content with his infidelities. She would never admit that out loud, but she was managed.

As the shower continued Zeh'Shon reminisced on the night they'd met.

Mid-October 2002.

Zeh'Shon contacted his partner Zo to set up a meeting at the club Sweet Jimmy's, located on 17th and San Pablo at 10 that night to go over the plan that they had of robbing a couple of cats from West Oakland. They'd heard from one of Zo's "bitches" that these dudes were playing with a little bit of change and flossing in the hood like it was all good.

When 10:20 arrived, Zeh'Shon glanced down at his diamond bezel wrist watch. "This nigga can't never be on time fa shit." he said.

Looking up, he saw Zo coming through the door talking to a couple of females simultaneously. He stood up and waved to hurry his partner along. He wasn't too fond of the club scene but decided to meet here because of his mistrust of cell phones. His apartment was out of the question, due to the fact that the nosey chick he was shacked up with couldn't be fully trusted either. Plus

A Hutlaz Dream

she had been picking fights with him about the chick that had phoned a few days prior.

"What's up, nigga? Yo mackin' ass sweat bitches 24-7. You hella late, I was 'bout to cut in the next10-15 minutes," said Zeh'Shon with a grin on his face.

"My bad, my nigga you know how I do. I came across a couple bitches that was reckless eyeballin', feel me? I had to let 'em know I'm 'bout my loot and if they wanted to play on the winning team," he said pointing to himself. "I need my money on time."

Zeh'Shon shook his head and smiled while taking a sip of his Patron margarita.

"Let's get down to it. My bitch said these two niggaz from Ghost Town named Jason and Wigy, been fuckin' wit the paper game kinda tough. She say they been sending bitches outta town to go up in banks and shit and withdraw money from cash advances, payday advances. I don't remember what type of advances to keep it real, but them hoes be comin' out them banks wit a few geez a piece. When they get back in town they be cashin' these niggaz out.

From what I heard these niggaz is softer than cotton candy. My bitch claim they be goin' to clubs buyin' out the bars in shit, advertising they wealth, so I got her club hoppin' as we speak. She know to buzz if she see one or the both of them dudes. Shit it might be tonight, it might not, just be ready. This might be the lick we need to step our game up."

"Nigga you know, I stay ready." said Zeh'Shon with a smirk plastered on his face.

The men made small talk for the next thirty minutes about other dealings as well as the current gossip in the Town, who shot John and who got locked up. As E-40's song Block Boy ended, he noticed a dark skinned girl approach a chick with a caramel complexion that was sitting alongside the bar with a blue drink that he supposed was an Adios.

"Zo," spoke Zeh'Shon over the bass of the drums.

"What's up my nigga?"

"You see them broads sittin' together in the middle of the bar, a dark one and a brown one? You know them?"

"Let me see," He said stretching his neck. "I don't know the dark bitch, but the light one, that's the nigga Bo lil sister."

"Bo?" he responded questionably.

"The nigga from Seminary, over there wit Scrilla Mike and them. The crazy nigga wit the shit, he the one with that outta town line on the pistols."

"Ohh yeah, I heard of the nigga."

"But yeah, the little broad name is Jakyah, Myah or something. I heard she go get it, she be in the city." (San Francisco) in the T.L. (Tenderloin, downtown S.F., well known drug area). " I got my Puerto Rican bitch out there spittin' rocks and she told me 'bout how she tried to recruit the broad a few times, but the bitch aint bitin' the bait."

"Is that right?"

"Hell yeah."

"Well I'm 'bout to go see what's up wit her right quick." Zeh'Shon said standing from his seat.

"I'ma roll wit you, let me see what's up wit the black one. I need another chocolate hoe anyway to hit the block at night. Put her ass in a black hoody so she could blend in with the darkness, police won't harass the bitch as much while she gettin' my dough, since they won't be able to spot the bitch."

Zeh'Shon snickered at his confident friend saying, "You'sa fool."

A Hutlaz Dream

"Naw nigga, I'm just so serious about my dough," he said with the smile that he was famous for.

Approaching the bar, Zeh'Shon took notice of the girls' appearances. The darker chick, later to become known as Zariah, stood about 5'2", 120 lbs. With facial features resembling those of the singer Rihanna, she was considered attractive, but not drop dead gorgeous. She sported a short haircut with a blue highlight running through the front which gave her an exotic, with just a touch of hood, look. The blue Apple Bottom jumpsuit she wore hugged her curves in all the right places; however when he noticed that she'd chosen a gold watch with silver earrings he shifted his gaze.

'She bootsy', he thought to himself. Not really caring what she had on, he just felt that if she couldn't accessorize correctly then she would probably be a failure at conducting business as well. She wouldn't have been beneficial to his game plan, so he had no use for her.

The light skinned chick, introduced as Jai'Myiah, was your average looking female, not drop dead gorgeous, but far from ugly. She had hazel doe shaped eyes and looked as though some of her ancestors were of Asian descent. She wore her hair in a straight flat iron that hung down to her shoulders with a slight curl. Standing 5'6" from the ground, she weighed in at approximately 145 lbs. Jai'Myiah wasn't built as thick as her friend with the endless curves. Zariah's ass was referred to as an 'apple bottom', but Jai'Myiah's would've probably been considered an 'apple slice'. Regardless of this fact, she still had a cute shape.

Nonetheless, Zeh'Shon wasn't really worried about her ability to break the scale on a 1-10 meter. The job he had in mind didn't require being eligible to win America's Next Top Model. The black velour sweat suit and matching baby doll shoes were acceptable, being that the club wasn't really strict on dress code.

Taking in both their appearances, Zeh'Shon thought of the girls as typical hood rats. 'Ima pop at the light skinned one first, but if I play my cards right I might just knock both of them, more money in my pocket. I have a couple different positions I'm hiring for anyway. Let me holla at this broad'

"What's up ladies, how y'all doin'?" asked Zeh'Shon.

"I'm okay," said Jai'Myiah

"Shit we over here chillin', what's up wit y'all?" replied Zariah.

"Damn baby girl, do you have to be so aggressive when a mathafucka ask you a simple question?" asked Zo with a puzzled look on his face.

At that moment, Zeh'Shon knew that he wouldn't waste his time trying to reel Zariah in, he could tell she would be a hand full by her attitude alone. He would probably have to physically reprimand her on a regular basis about his money and he wasn't even that kind of dude.

"Check this out, y'all came over here, don't get at me like that," said Zariah. "What's up, is y'all buyin' drinks or what?"

"Bitch, you crazy as fuck, I wouldn't buy yo bum ass a glass of ice water if it was free. Fuck you!" said Zo.

"That was probably on your wish list before you walked ya ratchet ass over here," said Zariah while starting to walk back to the dance floor. "Come on, Myah let's go dance, these niggas is too disrespectful for me."

"Girl, you know I don't dance plus I'm still sippin' this drank, go 'head. I'll be here when you're finished. I'm almost ready to go anyway," Jai'Myiah spoke.

A Hutlaz Dream

"Okay, I'll be close by if these niggas get outta line and you need help," She replied seriously.

Zeh'Shon looked on with disgust as she strolled off. He then turned his attention back to Jai'Myiah and made small talk to break the ice and have her open to consider his job offer, or so he thought.

"What's your name, lil mama?" he inquired.

"Jai'Myiah, and you?"

"Okay, okay, I'm Zeh'Shon," he announced. "What's up wit you, what you into?"

"What do you mean by that?"

"Ohh, my bad. What do your daily activities consist of? Work, school, hustle?" he said being more specific.

"I do a little bit of this, a little bit of that, nothin' too heavy." She said taking a sip of her beverage that had now became watered down due to the melting ice.

"Like that huh? Do you mind being a little more specific?"

"Well, actually I do. I'm not really comfortable with meeting people and giving a full run down of my life. I don't know you from a can of paint and am not quite sure of your agenda," she stated.

"I feel that, but I'm harmless," He assured her, feeling that maybe a change in atmosphere would help loosen her up. He changed the subject. "What's up you hungry? We 'bout head to the little breakfast spot around the corner and grab something to eat."

"Naw, I'm okay. As a matter fact I'm about to get up outta here, got a busy day tomorrow."

"I can dig it. Well let's exchange numbers, maybe we can link up in the near future to finish this conversation," Zeh'Shon implied.

"That's cool," said Jai'Myiah

They stored each other's phone numbers in their individual cell phones, and said that they'd keep in touch. Jai'Myiah then took the black coach bag that was laid on her lap and swung it over her left shoulder, said her good-byes, and disappeared into the crowd of dancers to find Zariah so that they could bounce.

***

Thoughts of his wife made Zeh'Shon smile through his tears. Being in the shower for 45 minutes, he decided to lather up and get out. His head was so light when he stepped out of the tub that he thought it would fly off. The liquor had him in a stupor and for the first time in hours, he was feeling good.

After tending to the rest of his hygiene, Zeh'Shon laid down on his Eastern king sized bed to relax. Five minutes of tossing and turning underneath the triple down comforter was all it took for him to get up and head towards the bedroom door. He decided to sleep on the couch in the living room that night. There was no way could he get comfortable in the bed that he shared with Jai'Myiah, knowing that she was laid up in the hospital and barely clinging to life.

Making his way down stairs, bottle in hand, he took a swig. Nearing the end of the staircase, he missed the last two and tumbled down, somehow managing not to spill a drop of Remy. Drunk as a skunk, at this point, he still found the living oom. He grabbed the remote and plopped down on the couch. He turned the radio to 106.1 KMEL only to hear Jai'Myiah's favorite song 'Love' by Keyshia Cole. Millions of memories flooded his mind like a tsunami. Taking another mouthful he spoke to the ceiling, "Baby, I love you! You gone make it. I swear to God Jai'Myiah, please make it."

A Hutlaz Dream

His mind raced back to 2002 once again...

It had been a couple of weeks since the club, he hadn't heard from the chick that he'd met, but he wasn't mad, it was sweat off a duck's back to him. He still resumed daily operations of keeping his hustle flowing, she probably wasn't ready to meet his level anyway. He sped through life all gas no breaks, and obviously she wasn't meant to keep up.

A week after the conversation that he had with Zo, they caught them niggas slippin', ran up to their houses and stripped them for all their cash and valuables. At that point, they were fifty thousand a piece richer. Zo was right about them being suckas, because they gave it up quick like a young hoe-bitch on E.14th St.

The paper game was something that Zeh'Shon promised himself to look into, he figured if those chumps were chewing like that off that paper shit, he wanted in. Not your average everyday stick up kid, being that he moved ounces on a few East Oakland blocks, anything from weed, ecstasy, cocaine, and heroine, he still never passed up a sweet lick for extra money.

Speaking of the chick from the club, Zeh'Shon spotted her slamming the driver door to a 1998 dark purple Buick Regal on twenty inch rims; she looked pissed with an unpleasant grimace on her face. His first thoughts were to keep going, saying to himself, she had a chance to get down with a boss and missed out. Having drove a few more blocks down the street, he turned around. He was just cruising the area anyway, headed to check his trap house. 'It's only 8:30 in the morning, I'll do that shit later', he told himself. Rolling up, he heard her having a conversation on the phone.

"Man, my fuckin' car just stopped on me... Where? On School St. ... I'm hella late, where you at?... Work?, aiight never mind. I'ma just hop on the bus. I'll leave the car here for now and come back and get it later. This raggedy ass scrapper, I shouldn't have bought this bucket in the first place.... Alright Trish, I'll holla later," Jai'Myiah said right before closing her phone.

"Lil mama, you need a ride somewhere?" asked Zeh'Shon.

She walked up slowly to get a closer look at the person that occupied the green candy painted GS300 Lexus. "Ohh hey," said Jai'Myiah remembering his face from the club. "Zeh?" she said trying to remember his name.

"Zeh'Shon," he replied.

"Zeh'Shon, right. I'm bad with names don't trip, but yeah I do need a ride real bad. My car just broke down and I'm late for school."

'School?' he thought. "Yeah, hop in."

"Aiight, let me grab my stuff." As she switched back to the Regal to grab her books he couldn't help but watch her ass, which in the jeans she wore made her look slightly thicker than she seemed at the club that night.

Not the type to think with his small head, he didn't really focus on her strut. With plans to accomplish his mission, he got his mind on the situation at hand, because if it wasn't about dollars, it just wasn't him.

Jai'Myiah slid onto the soft leather seats and got comfortable before closing the door and strapping on her seat belt. "So what school you go to, Laney College?" asked Zeh'Shon.

"No not yet, maybe next year. I go to Skyline," she answered.

"High school? Damn how old are you?"

"17," she replied.

A Hutlaz Dream

"Damn, you just a baby! And you was all in the club trying to act grown," he said smiling.

"A baby is what I'm not, and I was at the club on business, my folks work the door so I didn't need I.D. How old are you?"

"22."

"Wow, and I'm a baby?" she said grinning. "You aint that much older."

"Baby girl, I'm an OG in these streets, you better ask about me," he claimed. "But you say you was on business, what you into?"

"I told you I do a lil bit of this, and lil bit of that."

"Ohh, we gonna stay on that, huh?"

"I hustle in the city."

"So you're a rock star?"

"I wouldn't say all that. I do what I gotta do to keep my head above water, feel me?"

"Yeah, I can dig it. But on some real shit, you sound like my kind of people. I think we would make a great team."

'Here he goes with this. I done heard it all before', thought Jai'Myiah, as they drove up the steep hill nearing the school house.

"Check this out," she started." I've been hustling for the last three years, not by choice, but because I gotta take care of my fam. No disrespect to you, but I'm not in this shit to run bundles for niggas, I hustle for me."

'Damn, she shut me down quick', he thought. 'But I aint trippin'. One monkey can't stop my show.'

Pulling up and stopping in front of Skyline High School, Jai'Myiah got out. Bending down, she spoke through the opened window.

"I appreciate the ride. I should still have your number in my phone, is it cool if I called you sometime to discuss prices? I usually push 'bout three zips a day, and if the numbers are right and the quality good I'ma fuck wit you. My line has been flakin' lately anyway." She said. Zips are referred to as ounces in the Bay Area.

"Yeah, do that. I got it fa cheap."

"Fa sho." she replied while throwing her back pack over her shoulder and heading in the direction of the school's entrance. 'Well', he said to himself. 'If she aint go get no money for me, at least she can spend some with me.' Thinking of money, he headed over to 102nd and Walnut to check his bitch Omari for being short with his paper the night before.

Over the course of the next several months he and Jai'Myiah became good friends. She bought no less than two ounces a day and he gave her a playa price that she couldn't beat. The dope fiends in the city said it was cream, so she spent with him faithfully. They started off as business partners and eventually developed a friendship.

Zeh'Shon would find himself calling her phone just to check on her at times, making sure that she was alright and didn't need anything. He found out about her family history and felt for the girl. Her mom was a smoker that was out there bad, doing any and everything to chase the white dragon. She took responsibility of caring for her younger sister, Jolisa. Bo, the other brother stayed in the streets 24/7, he was more of a jacker than a hustler. He had been shot twice at the age of 19 in a robbery gone wrong. Her older sister, Trish, lived in North Oakland, she came around every now and then, but was mainly concerned with herself and wasn't as family oriented as Jai'Myiah.

Zeh'Shon would also call and ask her opinion on different things and she would give it to him straight with no chase. He

A Hutlaz Dream

respected her mind and came to the point where he started feeling her beyond business. She wasn't game goofy like most of the broads in the hood. She was ambitious and he took notice that if she wanted something she went for it, a go getter, and he liked that. She handled business and had more heart than most of the dudes he'd known.

They found themselves in each other's company more often than necessary. He'd come by the house and bring food for the family, sometimes even movies, and just chill with her until either she would have to get to the money or his phone would ring for trades.

The chicks that he had handling his business on a regular would catch attitudes from time to time about the lack of attention he showed or the amount of time spent with them, but being the boss he was he would check those attitudes at the door and let it be known that if they weren't feeling the program they were free to leave. But as he already knew, they weren't going anywhere.

Jai'Myiah was really feeling Zeh'Shon, the sexual attraction she had for him grew stronger as the days passed. Not wanting to be the one to make the first move, she opted to sit in the cut and allow nature to take its course.

Seven months had nearly passed since Zeh'Shon had given her the ride to school. Her birthday was rapidly approaching, May 9th wasmerely a week away. She was hardly excited about turning the big 1-8. Most kids her age couldn't wait to turn 18. For them, that meant freedom and gave them the ability to do things that they couldn't do the year before. Their parents would be officially cutting off the leash that they had linked to them, or at least loosening their grip. But that wasn't Jai'Myiah's case, she had been "grown" for a number of years already. Even though she wasn't legal in the government's eyes, she had been forced to take on adult responsibilities at an early age. Her mother didn't give a damn if she was coming or going, as long as when she came back she wasn't empty handed.

Jai'Myiah sometimes wondered how her life would be if her mother wasn't strung out on crack and cared for her offspring like common mothers did. Although her situation wasn't normal, she decided not to spend much time sulking about what could've or should've been, she realized early on that is it what it is.

No special plans were made to celebrate her born day. Zariah phoned stating that she wanted to treat her to a night on the town, starting with a club in San Francisco called the Mission Rock and ending with a boat ride around the Pier. Not one to be a party pooper, she sadly declined. She wasn't really up for that type of function. Most years she just looked at it as another day, but Zeh'Shon thought differently.

Tuesday May 9, 2003

As Jai'Myiah came out of the brown house located on 62nd and Hayes that her mother rented through section 8 (she may as well say that she rented it through her mother's section 8, since she paid all of the bills there) when Zeh'Shon pulled up.

"Happy birthday, baby girl," he said as he handed her a card along with a dozen of long stemmed white roses.

"Aww, you shouldn't have, thank-you," she replied with a shy blush flushing her cheeks, "What are you doing out and about so early?" It was 7:30 am.

"Well, you know what they say, the early bird gets the worm? Well, I'm like the alley cat waiting to get the bird," he retorted. "You on your way to school?"

A Hutlaz Dream

"Yeah, after I drop Jolisa off at Elmhurst, she claims she missed the bus," she said.

"Come on I'll take y'all."

"And how am I supposed to get home if I don't drive?" she asked.

"I'ma come and get you, duh," he said and playfully rolled his eyes. "It's your birthday and I want to take you out to eat, if that's okay. I mean I'm not trying to impose if you had other plans."

"Naw, that sounds cool with me," she replied desperately trying to hide the excitement in her voice. "Let me go in here and put these in some water and tell this little girl to come on."

"Alright, take your time," he said as he parked his car behind Jai'Myiah's purple scrapper and killed his engine.

"Come on, Jolisa." She yelled from the kitchen while she filled a clear vase with water and deposited the beautiful smelling flowers into it. She rushed down the hallway to her room to set them on her dresser and read the card before going back outside. She placed the flowers in the middle of the dresser and ripped the envelope open.

The outside of the card was plain pink with 'Happy Birthday' written in yellow letters. As soon as she opened the card, her mouth hit the floor. Starring back at her was ten crisp hundred dollar bills. She moved the money to the side and read the writing, 'Happy birthday baby girl have a wonderful day, you deserve it, much love Zeh'Shon'. She smiled but her focus redirected when she saw Jolisa standing in the doorway.

"What the fuck you smiling for?" Jai'Myiah's 12-year-old sister rudely inquired.

"You better watch your mouth lil girl, you aint grown, don't you ever forget that," she scolded with her finger pointed in the youngster's face. Being that their mother cared less about them and Jolisa was at the age of influence, she thought it was cute to talk like she was grown.

"I'm sorry Myah," said Jolisa with her head down. "Happy birthday sister, I love you."

"Never say you are sorry! Just apologize, okay?"

"Okay"

"Thanks for the birthday wish, now let's go, Zeh'Shon is going to give us a ride."

She then stood the card on her dresser and placed the thousand dollars in her pocket with intentions of giving it back as soon as Jolisa was dropped off.

They got in the car and strapped up for safety before pulling off. The block that Jai'Myiah lived on seemed dead at this hour. 'I guess dope fiends have to take a smoke break from time to time,' she thought to herself.

"Myah," said Jolisa from the back seat.

"What's up?"

"Can you give me some lunch money, please?"

"Lunch money, what happened to the $20 that I gave you yesterday for lunch? Money doesn't grow on trees, what you thought? Here," she said, pulling a ten dollar bill from her pocket, "and I better not find out you buying weed with my dough."

"Thank-you," said Jolisa reaching for the ten and looking disappointed that it wasn't a dub, because as soon as they dropped her off she was going to walk around the corner to 96th and Cherry and buy a bag of purple before going to class.

Zeh'Shon pulled up to the middle school and let Jolisa out. She got out in a rush and slammed the door without as much as a

A Hutlaz Dream

'Thank-you'. Zeh'Shon smiled while shaking his head before pulling back off into traffic. He hated riding down 98th in the early morning, E. Morris Cox Elementary School was located directly across the street from Elmhurst Middle, so driving cautiously was mandatory. With a zillion kids running around he knew at any given moment one might shoot out into the middle of the street thinking that he or she was made of steel.

"Zeh'Shon, I need to give this back to you," Jai'Myiah said digging into her front pocket and retrieving the thousand dollars, trying to hand it over.

"Naw that's you, baby girl," he responded. "You can't keep your guard up all the time. You have to be able to accept gifts from time to time. I want you to do something nice for yourself, I don't want anything in return, I promise."

Jai'Myiah stared at the money like she was going to insist that he take it back, but instead folded it back in half and placed it in her pocket.

"Thank-you," started Zeh'Shon, "Now this is the plan, I want you to kick it with me today, all day. I got something special planned."

"But I have to go to school."

"Man, miss me with that, it's your birthday. All the parenting, hustling, and school work you've been doing you deserve a day off," he stated. "So you rollin' wit me or not?"

"I guess," she replied smiling since he put it like that.

"Alright, that's more like it. Now where you want to go get something to eat at? Cause you know what they say, breakfast is the most important part of the day." he smiled.

"Al's sounds good."

Jasmin Johnston

"Damn, I guess it's true, great minds do think alike. I just had a taste for Al's." Zeh'Shon sat back in his seat after grabbing the half-smoked blunt out of the ash tray and lighting it.

"This my song," claimed Jai'Myiah as she turned up the radio's volume a few notches, and let Goapele's song 'Closer to my dreams' song pour out of the speakers.

After dining at Al's on Seminary, Zeh'Shon had to check a couple of his traps before proceeding with the day's activities. Three hours and about ten different spots later, Jai'Myiah was thinking that she should have just followed her first mind and took her butt to school. Graduation was next month and she knew she didn't have any business playing hookey for a day to ride around Oakland.

Just as the thoughts slipped her mind, Zeh'Shon was heading back to the car. Upon taking a seat, his phone started ringing. She didn't really care, but boredom caused Jai'Myiah's gaze to shift to his caller I.D. The name on screen said Omari.

Every time Jai'Myiah was in Zeh'Shon's presence his phone blew up, constantly. It seemed as though he conducted business twenty five hours a day, eight days a week.

"Yeah," he answered. "What the fuck you mean, bitch, where I'm at? Did you handle that business? I need that done with Olympic speed. Hurry up!" he said and closed his phone.

Jai'Myiah couldn't help but shake her head and look out of the window, smiling. She couldn't believe how nice he treated her, and how disrespectful he could be to others.

"What?" he asked.

"Nothing, you're crazy."

"I'm not crazy, it's just these dumb, punk rock ass hoes I be havin' to deal wit to keep my dollars stackin', it could be a headache at times," he said looking down at the phone that had

A Hutlaz Dream

started to buzz again. Instead of answering, he pushed the power button to turn the phone completely off.

"I'm taking the rest of the day off," he said tossing the phone in the glove compartment and closing it.

They made small talk while heading over the Bay Bridge towards San Francisco. Finally having a chance of being a passenger, Jai'Myiah looked over at the water and took in the scenery. The skyscrapers that stood high in the distance told of a life she'd probably never have the opportunity to live. The business that was conducted behind those glass walls were out of the league of a hood rat such as herself.

Needless to say they had a ball that day, Zeh'Shon took her on a shopping spree and spared no expense. Even items she objected to due to the price tag, he paid her no attention. If he saw something he thought was nice and would look cute on her, he took it to the register and had the clerk ring him up.

This was something new to Zeh'Shon, he had never bought anything for a female besides his mother and younger sister. But for some reason he was having fun seeing Jai'Myiah's eyes light up in every store they visited. He really didn't understand what he was going through but he was really starting to feel her, and the crazy part was they hadn't even had sex.

After hitting almost every store on Stockton, Geary and neighboring streets, including Gucci, Louis Vuitton, Salvatore Farragamo, and Tiffany's, they were exhausted. Before moving on to their next destination, they decided to stop and grab a polish dog from a street vendor. All that shopping and walking from place to place had caused them to work up an appetite.

They then went on to purchase tickets for the San Francisco city sightseeing tour bus and jumped on. They ended up visiting pier 39, Fisherman's Warf, and a number of other sites that

Jai'Myiah had often heard of but never visited. She came across the bridge on a daily basis to hustle, but never had the time to venture off into the city and see what it really had to offer. She was having a ball and feeling like a tourist.

When they got back to the location where the bus picked them up, it was 8:45 p.m. They were overloaded with shopping bags and countless souvenirs as a reminder of this precious day. Reaching the parking garage and placing their purchased items in the trunk they fell into the coziness of the seats with a sigh of relief. Feeling like they had just pulled a twelve hour shift they immediately let their heads relax with an exhale. Looking over at Zeh'Shon, Jai'Myiah spoke.

"Thank-you for today, I really enjoyed myself."

"It's good lil' mama, but don't thank me yet because the day is hardly over," he said smiling.

'Damn', thought Jai'Myiah. 'He is surely full of surprises; I haven't ever met anyone like him, walking around portraying this hard core gangsta image.' She never would've thought he had a heart.

After driving up the steep hill on California St., he pulled into a garage and parked the car. Getting out and walking 100 feet or so they stopped, she looked up and saw the sign that read Crustaceans.

"So this is the place that I've heard so much about?"

"You've never been here?"

"Nope, everybody aint able," she said sarcastically, looking him up and down grinning.

"Come on, let's go," he said grabbing her hand and leading the way into the five star restaurant.

"Table for two?" asked the waiter.

"Yes."

A Hutlaz Dream

"Sir, do you mind putting this on?" asked the waiter handing Zeh'Shon a blue button up shirt. "We have a dress code here, no t-shirts."

"My bad, I forgot all about that." He said extending his hand and accepting the loaned button up. Jai'Myiah was dressed appropriately in her Roc-a-Wear ensemble.

Waiting for the food to arrive, Zeh'Shon ordered two coffee warmers and waters with lemon. The warmers consisted of coffee and a shot of cognac, whipped cream and a bit off cinnamon to serve as decoration. Throwing them back fast, they ordered another round. They then began to laugh and joke with each other about hilarious incidents that they had encountered in life, nothing negative at that moment, simply the highlights of their individual journeys.

When the food was delivered, Jai'Myiah felt that she had already had a taste of heaven today and this was just the icing on the cake. As if she were living a piece of someone else's life, she pinched herself to make sure it was tangible.

Laid out before her was her order of Pan Roasted Hailbut, Papaya Salad with Calamari, and a bowl of garlic noodles. Zeh'Shon went for the Saigon Beer, and for an appetizer they had crab and Crustacean Shrimp toast and crab puffs.

Through the course of dinner, Zeh'Shon looked up and said,"Jai'Myiah, I'm really, really feeling you, ma. I don't know what it is about you, or what you did to me, but you got a nigga open. I ain't never felt this way about a female in my life. I enjoy your company, fa real. I know you're aware of how I get down and you've witnessed my phone conversations, but those broads don't mean shit to me. The sole purpose of them being around is to bring my dough and nothing more. I don't want anything from you, except for maybe one thing."

Shocked by his confession she replied, "And what's that?"

"For you to give me that shot, you know, be my back bone. I need a chick like you on my side. I found a friend in you and in this game I'm playin', you don't come across too many of them."

She really didn't know how to respond to his revelation, but somehow managed to say, "I've been feeling you for a minute as well, let's do it." He smiled and continued eating.

Before leaving they drank two more coffee warmers, and had dessert. They were stuffed and also a little tipsy on their return to the car.

Jai'Myiah thought that for sure that the day was over. This was by far the best birthday of her life; she didn't want the night to ever come to an end. She soon realized it hadn't yet.

They pulled up to the Waldorf-Astoria hotel and parked.

"Come on," said Zeh'Shon as he opened the door and let his fresh pair of Jordan's hit the pavement in San Francisco's Financial District. Totally baffled, she complied but moved at a turtle's pace. Zeh'Shon tossed his keys to the valet driver before reaching into the trunk and pulling out a Louis Vuitton duffel bag, and a gift wrapped box. He then went to the front desk to check in. I was then thatshe came to find out that he had this room reserved for a week. He got the key and they took the elevator to the eighth floor.

When Zeh'Shon opened the door to the room, Jai'Myiah just stood in the doorway for a few minutes like she was star struck. Wandering through the room, she touched everything in sight. She couldn't believe that she was actually in a room at the "W". She rushed to the window to take a peek. She had to admit that the view was truly breathtaking and she looked at all the bright

A Hutlaz Dream

towers that lit up the night sky. Zeh'Shon approached from behind carrying the gift box.

"I hope you like this." He whispered in her ear. She took it and sat on the bed to open it. Zeh'Shon then went in the bathroom and started running a bubble bath in the Jacuzzi styled bathtub for his young princess.

Opening the box, she was surprised to find a dark purple satin camisole with matching underwear that was just her size. There were also a few beautifully fragranced hygiene items, such as soaps, lotions, deodorants, and body sprays.

Emerging from the bathroom Zeh'Shon continued to the living room section of the suite and poured two glasses of Moet that had been chilling in a bucket of ice on the coffee table.

"Here you go, baby girl." She gladly accepted the bubbly champagne and swallowed its contents in two gulps.

"What's wrong, you nervous?" inquired Zeh'Shon.

"Light weight," she replied, nodding her head rapidly.

"You don't have anything to be nervous for baby girl, from here on out it's me and you. There will be many more days like this," he said then kissed her juicy lips. Holding her breath, she attempted to reciprocate the love as best she could with a trembling jaw.

Jai'Myiah came up for air first, then immediately grabbed her Victoria's secret box excused herself and headed towards the bathroom. Undressed and in the tub, she turned on the jets, laid back and let the alcohol she'd consumed take over and help her receive the much needed recreation.

Minutes later, she opened her eyes abruptly upon hearing the door open. Standing in the nude was Zeh'Shon holding up a wash cloth.

"I came to help you wash your back, baby girl," he said cleverly.

Jai'Myiah's chin loosened and eyes bulged at the sight of him. He had the most attractive body that she'd ever seen or imagined. His body from his neck down to his waist line flavored that of the rapper 50 Cent, but she didn't have anyone to compare the lower half with. His manhood hung low, stretching in length to the middle of his thigh and the width was that of a large cucumber. 'Ohh shit! Where does he plan on putting all that?' she silently said to herself.

He walked over and sat on the edge of the tub. Dipping the hand that held the rag into the water, he gripped the bottle of body wash with his free hand and squirted and ample amount before closing is fist and began soaping up the rag. He motioned for her to come closer as he then commenced to lather her entire body. She had a gorgeous figure, was blemish free, and had enough ass and titties to make any man's mouth water. As he continued washing her body, his erection throbbed so hard between his legs that he had to stand up. Completing that task, he turned on the shower to rinse her off. He then held up an oversized towel for her to step into andhe slowly dried her off.

Picking her up and sitting her on the counter top, he kissed her mouth hungrily. He skipped the foreplay because he felt as though he was about to bust already. He slid his dick between her lips and felt she was wetter than Niagara Falls. He slid in very slowly and deliberately, due to the fact that she was tighter than a Chinese man's eyes. He chose to take his time and savor each second. Jai'Myiah moaned with a painful look on her face.

"You okay, baby girl?" asked Zeh'Shon concerned.

"Yeah, I'm fine," she lied. She really felt like a baseball bat was being shoved inside of her. He continued gently and when he

A Hutlaz Dream

reached the bottom of her love tunnel, he let out a deep sigh and exclaimed, "Damn Jai'Myiah, you got some good pussy."

Moments later the pain subsided, whirling into pleasure, and she let her head rest against the giant mirror. She closed her eyes for the ride of her life. He put it down so swell, she cried out in ecstasy and clinched her lids tightly, before reaching the biggest climax she'd ever endured. Zeh'Shon reached his peak a second or two later. With heavy breathing and perspiration coating their bodies, they stared at one another, lost in the ambiance of their love making. They remained in this position for just enough time to catch their breath and regulate their heart beat. Zeh'Shon then took her to the bed area and they made magic for the remainder of the night and well into the next morning before clonking out...

Snapping out of his resonant stage, Zeh'Shon took another sip of the Remy. Keyshia Cole contiued to sing, "Love, never knew what I was missin', but I knew once we start kissin', I found love...." He then drifted off into an alcohol induced coma.

Chapter 3

BAM BAM BAM BAM... BAM BAM BAM.

Somebody was beating on the door like the law enforcement agency.

"What the fuck?" said Zeh'Shon, startled out of his sleep by the constant rapping on the wooden door. He sat up and leaned back on the cushions. He remained in that position for a while because his head felt extremely heavy due to the light hangover that he inherited from the previous night. Getting himself together, he lethargically made way to the door to curse whoever was on the other side. When he opened the door, the sunlight nearly blinded him, it was bright as a neon sign.

"Zeh, what's up my nigga, you aiight?" asked Zo as he side stepped by his friend to gain access to the inside of the house.

"Yeah I'm good. What time is it?" he asked while rubbing his head. He felt as if he had just gotten slapped in the face with a wrecking ball.

"Nigga, it's 3:30 in the afternoon, I called ya phone a couple times, but it kept going straight to voicemail. Then, ya moms just called me 'bout 30 minutes ago and told me to come check on yo ass."

"Is that right? I call her in a minute, I'm 'bout to hop in some water then probably shoot to the hospital."

A Hutlaz Dream

"Alright daddy-o, hit me if you need me," Zo said as he exited the house. "I'm 'bout to strike to Berkeley and slide up on this bitch to see what's up with my money from the work she put in last night."

"Fa sho." Said Zeh'Shon giving his partner a fist pound and a head nod. He watched as Zo jumped in his silver Jaguar and sped off. He then resumed his position on the couch, only this time he kicked his feet up on the coffee table and placed a hand in his boxers. He knew his mother was concerned about him, but he didn't feel up to talking to anyone on the phone just yet, he'd just woken up and his mind was still distorted. He stared blankly at the wall as he remembered the time he thought Jai'Myiah would leave him.

February 8, 2006

Jai'Myiah and Zeh'Shon had been living together for three years, few weeks after her 18th birthday. His graduation gift to her was a nice two bedroom apartment in Emeryville, right off San Pablo St. on the other end of the Pak'n Save parking lot.

Standing barefoot in her kitchen, Jai'Myiah stood at the sink washing the last of the dishes left behind from breakfast. Zeh'Shon was out running streets somewhere, and her best friend Zariah was in the living room dancing to Mac Dre's song 'Thizz dance', which blasted loudly from the entertainment system. Jai'Myiah laughed at her friend as she stepped along to the late rapper's lyrics. The vibration of her phone caught her eye from the counter top. Drying her hands she looked at the caller I.D and noticed the incoming caller was blocked.

"Zariah turn that down some, my phone is ringing…Hello," she asked after the radio was turned down enough to hear the person on the other end.

"This Jai'Myiah?" The caller asked rudely.

"Yep, who is this?"

"Don't worry 'bout all that bitch, I just wanted you to know that you been dealing with my man for far too long, and I'm really starting to get upset."

"Aww, is that so? All I want to know is what gave you the audacity to call this phone? Bitch, you callin' me like I'm the other bitch. Don't get it twisted…" she was heated, but kept it cool. "Here's a reality check for you, you're just a worker, believe that!" Zariah came in the kitchen so she could hear a little better.

"Whatever bitch, that's why he was at my house all night last night!"

"Congratulations" Jai'Myiah replied, "but know this and don't ever forget, I allow my nigga to cat off with you bum bitches from time to time, but he knows exactly where home is. You project hoes are hilarious to me. I suggest you find a hobby or something with your desperate ass…Ohh yeah, and you're the person I should be thanking for the new Lexus truck that I received the other day, I know you probably played a big part in contributing to the cost," said Jai'Myiah as she smiled knowing that she had struck a nerve with that one.

"Whatever, bitch, all I gotta say is watch yo' back," the caller threatened.

"Most definitely, I stay ready so I don't ever have to get ready, know that! You just make sure you watch your front 'cause that's what Zeh'Shon is going to come for when he hears this," said Jai'Myiah as she closed her cell phone, ending the call. She then filled in Zariah as she was curiously and anxiously waiting to hear

A Hutlaz Dream

more about the incident that had just transpired. Jai'Myiah informed her about what the chick said then made a call to Zeh'Shon.

"What's up, baby?" he answered, traffic was heard in the background so he was more than likely on the block playing umpire.

"You need to keep your bitches in check," she said.

"Huh?" Zeh'Shon replied dumbfounded, he was caught off guard. She ran down the scenario and waited on his response, but it took him a minute to process the information. He was so infuriated that he had no idea what to say.

"What's wrong, cat got ya tongue?"

"Naw baby, that's crazy, but ay luv that you know what it is wit' me and these other bitches, strictly business. You're not mad are you? I'm 'bout to go put my foot in this hoe ass as we speak, and cut her water off."

Jai'Myiah knew good and well that it wasn't just business, but she played along anyway.

"No, I'm not mad. I'm just a 'lil upset that I have to change this number, cause I'm not about to play on the phone with these nerds."

"Baby, you don't have to change a thing. I can guarantee that this will never happen again, I promise."

"Yeah, whatever you say. You make sure that next time you cat off, them hoes don't have access to your phone."

"Baby--" Zeh'Shon started to say, but was cut off when the line went dead. "Fuck!" he yelled as he hopped in his whip and mashed the gas to get to Omari's apartment as quickly as possible.

He had other bitches, but he knew that they would never try his patience in that way. Omari had been known to try that in the past with other chicks. He gave her a pass in the past, but this time she was going to learn.

He parked the car so fast upon arriving at his destination that he took up two spaces and ran up the stairs to the second level of the green and white apartment complex. 'BOOM BOOM BOOM', echoed in the air as he pounded on the metal screen door of the apartment.

"Open up the door, punk rock," he demanded before realizing that he had a spare key to the padlock on his key chain. Fumbling with the keys, he found the right one after two attempts, and let himself in. He made a mental note to make this quick because with all the noise he'd just made, some nosey neighbor was bound to come out and investigate.

"Omari, bitch, I know yo' stupid ass is in here, come out, ain't no need in prolongin' this ass whoppin'. You know you was dead wrong and outta pocket for callin' a number that was in my phone," he yelled as he walked towards the bedroom in the run-down apartment. The shack was in shambles. Filthy clothes were thrown across the living room floor and couch. There were dirty dishes piled a mile high in the kitchen sink. The living room table held a soda can that had been turned into an ashtray and was so full you could see the cigarette butts coming out of the top. The entire place reeked of stale marijuana.

Rushing into the room that she normally slept in, he didn't see her. He charged the bathroom door so hard it nearly flew off the hinges, but still she was not there. Finally he went to the spare bedroom. He busted open the door to the room, and there he saw Omari standing by the closet door crying. He had no sympathy for all the dramatics, she brought this unneeded situation on herself. He ran up on her and tried to slap fire from her. She fell to the floor on impact and was greeted by a kick in the stomach so hard

A Hutlaz Dream

that you would've thought he was trying out for the Oakland Raiders. A piercing scream echoed through the barely furnished place and engulfed his ears like a pair of Dr. Dre head phones.

"Why the fuck you have to go out your way and start trouble?" he asked while pulling her up by her multi-colored quick weave. "You hear me talkin' to you, bitch?" She nodded. "Then answer the question before I stomp a mud hole in yo' bootsy ass."

She looked up scared to death, but surprising herself, words escaped her mouth like a flood. "I love you, Zeh'Shon and I would think after all I do for you, all the money I give you, you would love me and be with me. But you chose her, you on some square shit wit that bitch." 'SMACK', Zeh'Shon hit her again.

"Bitch, who could you possibly think you are? You claim to be in love knowing good and well we ain't never been on that type of time, strictly business. You better get your mind right. You know what I think? I think I fucked up by fuckin' you. I thought you could handle a friendly fuck from time to time, but you proved me wrong once again."

Omari stood there crying and holding her face while starring down at the worn out brown carpet. "You know what bitch? I'm cool on you. You couldn't handle your position and play your part, so it's a wrap. I need a team player, a bitch that's goal oriented, not a weak ass bitch like you." He said and started to head towards the door. "And don't call my phone, we done, fineto!"

"No!" Omari yelled. " Please daddy, I'm sorry, please don't leave me, I'll do anything." She cried hysterically, "Please daddy."

She pleaded on deaf ears because Zeh'Shon had made it back to his vehicle and all that was heard next was burning rubber as he peeled outta the parking lot.

For the next two hours, Zeh'Shon rode the East Oakland streets trying to find a way to explain himself to his girl. He thought of going to buy her a gift, but quickly dismissed that notion. Jai'Myiah wasn't the type of person you could just shower with gifts when things hit the fan to make everything alright. He had to approach the situation like a man, and whatever she chose to do he would have to respect, because he shouldn't have been slipping and fallen asleep in Motel 6 with the bitch without his phone on him anyway.

Drawing him from his thoughts the phone rang, it was Sharice. He had her selling Oxycodone by the boat load in the Bay Area and bordering cities. "What's up Reece?" he said.

"Hey daddy, I just wanted to check in, I got $16,000 for you, and I still got 500 of them thangs left."

"Is that right?"

"I wanted to know if you wanted to meet up with me to get this before I head back out to finish the rest?"

"Naw, just go put that up and finish handling your business. Hit me when you get back in the house."

"Alright, are you okay daddy?"

"Yeah, bitch damn, I'm just tired, go finish and call me later," he said and hung up. The broads that he had in his life were starting to become very nerve racking. As of lately, he was starting to feel as though he may need to take a vacation in the near future.

Parking in his stall, he got out of his car and headed toward the elevator while preparing himself for the tongue lashing that he was destined to get. He unlocked the door to his apartment and was greeted by the fresh scent of the glade plug ins that Jai'Myiah seemed to keep an endless supply of. After leaving

A Hutlaz Dream

Omari's ghetto-fied cubby hole, he was happy that he had a woman that kept a clean and fresh house.

Jai'Myiah was seated on the black chaise lounge staring at the television, not even acknowledging his presence as he entered the living room. He took a seat on the couch.

"Jai'Myiah," he stated, but stopped when she looked over at him with tear filled eyes. He dropped his head in his hands and rubbed his temples before continuing. "Baby girl, I really apologize for that bullshit that happened today, and on my mama that will never happen again." She couldn't hold back the tears any longer.

"Zeh'Shon, I thought you loved me."

"I do love you baby, to death."

"Well for some reason, I'm not really feeling the love. You know what, I know you deal with other broads and I know they pay you, I also know that you sleep with them even though your favorite line is 'Baby, it's strictly business', but come on now I'm no dummy, even still I don't ever throw your infidelities in your face. I try to remain that ride or die, down with you through whatever type chick that you fell in love with. But when you call and let me know you won't make it home at night due to "business" and the following day I get a call from one of your "bitches" letting me know you were laid up all night doing God knows what, how do you expect me to feel? I'm not about to sit around and accept that, straight up!"

"Baby I understand everything you're saying, and I apologize, but please give me one more chance." He then got up from his seat and put his arms tightly around her as she quietly sobbed. That night, she refused to come to bed with him, claiming that she needed to stay on the couch so she could get her mind together.

For the next three days, he walked on eggshells around her, catering to her every want and need. Every time she would call, he would stop whatever he was doing and rush to her aid. It didn't matter if all she wanted was something to eat and didn't feel like driving, he was on the way. She felt bad at first, but those feelings quickly turned to enjoyment from seeing him sweat.

Chapter 4

Zeh'Shon got up from the couch in his living room and decided to get dressed and head over to Kaiser to check the news and see if Jai'Myiah was making any progress. He located the cell phone that he dropped by the bathroom door the previous night and powered it on, as soon as he did it rang.

"Hey moms," he answered. It was Jai'Myiah's mother Wanda.

"Baby boy, how you feeling?" she asked concerned.

"I'm trying to get it together, how you doin'?"

"Not too good, but I'm praying on it," she sighed." I'm on my way to go see Jai'Myiah."

"I was just getting dressed, 'bout to head up that way also."

"Okay baby, we'll see you in a minute."

"Alright moms."

They hung up, Zeh'Shon quickly dressed and left the house for the hospital. He decided to take his wife's car, for some reason he felt by taking it he would feel her presence. He hadn't really noticed how short she was compared to him until he sat in the driver's seat and had to adjust it before he could pull his legs in. He cranked the engine and started bobbing his head to local rapper D.Lo's song 'No Hoe'. He smiled thinking about how much Jai'Myiah loved that song. He jumped on the 680 freeway with the navigation system pointed toward Oakland.

When he got off the elevator on the I.C.U floor, he noticed Wanda and Jolisa sitting outside of Jai'Myiah's door crying. He walked up and gave each of them a hug.

"It's not a pretty sight, but go on in there," claimed Wanda with a muffled tear filled voice. Taking a deep breath, he twisted the door handle and stepped in. Nothing in the world could've prepared him for the sight that lay before him. Jai'Myiah had what looked to be at least ten machines hooked up to her, there were tubes and wires coming from everywhere. She wasn't breathing on her own, so one of the machines was a respirator. Her head was bandaged in thick layers of gauze as she lay there with a limp frame.

"Baby girl, I love you, please pull through. Fa me," he pleaded, praying to God that she could hear him. "I swear to God, I'm going to kill whoever did this to you…I gotta go now, I can't see you like this." He said walking out of the room and closing the door behind him softly.

"I gotta go moms," he said to Wanda who was sitting with her hands cupped over her face as he started heading towards the elevator.

"Zeh'Shon wait, the doctor should be on his way back now, he just left to go and get Jai'Myiah's chart."

Taking a seat next to Jolisa, Zeh'Shon sat with the family and waited on Dr. Chan for what seemed like hours, but was only minutes. All he could think about was getting out of there before he truly lost it.

"Good afternoon," greeted Dr. Chan as he approached the threesome. "I have some news that isn't too great at this time," he said flipping through the pages in the thick manila folder that he clutched in his hands. "Unfortunately, Jai'Myiah has slipped into a coma and she also suffered a miscarriage after surgery." he said.

A Hutlaz Dream

When Zeh'Shon heard those words he got up and walked away. "Zeh'Shon, Zeh'Shon, come back," cried Jolisa, but he kept walking. That blow hit him hard and he sensed that he was near the point of a nervous breakdown. He couldn't deal with the fact that another one of his seeds were lost.

Jumping into Jai'Myiah's candy burgundy Lexus SC 430 he peeled out of the parking lot. He fumbled through the car's ashtray desperately looking for a black and mild. "Damn, Jai'Myiah don't even smoke blacks," he said out loud. Not having any luck finding tobacco, he came across a half of blunt. Jai'Myiah wasn't a weed head but did indulge on occasion. He put the 'dubbie' to his lips and inhaled deeply, the purple herbs instantly took effect.

He drove like a bat out of hell trying to put distance between his self and the hospital. He wound up sitting in front of his mother's house on 92nd and Birch. He sucked the blunt as if his life depended on it. As his mind wandered back to the time that he'd found the secret that Jai'Myiah called herself trying to hide from him.

December 3, 2006

This was a big day for Jai'Myiah. After receiving her business license in June, she told Zeh'Shon of her childhood dream of opening a liquor store and laundry mat. He didn't understand why she wanted to do some shit like that but he never vocalized his thought. He went along with the plan and told her to find out where she wanted to open them and to get all the paper work necessary. He encouraged her and stated he would put the money up to make it happen.

She found two small buildings for lease and filled out all the papers for them, one sat on 82nd and Bancroft the other on

53rd and Foothill. She chose the location on 82nd to be home to the laundry mat, and felt the liquor store would do well on 53rd, since traffic was always heavy on that side of town. Even with the fierce competition, being that Oakland had liquor stores and laundry mats on damn near every corner, she felt her business would be lucrative due to the fact that she planned to have lower prices and great customer service.

She scheduled the grand opening for December 3rd. The day came quickly and the store had a beautiful turn out. Having everything on sale at half the price of nearby establishments, the school kids came by in bunches to stock up on goodies to last them through the week. The laundry mat also had customers lined up outside the door for the special they offered of pay to wash with free dryer time plus complementary single load boxes of washing detergent.

Over the years Jai'Myiah's mother Wanda had gotten her life together, and her future appeared bright. Due to the tragic murder of her partner in crime Sandra, she got a reality check and got back on the right track, vowing to never use drugs or alcohol again. The autopsy report and grueling photographs of her mutilated compadre wiped the sleep out of Wanda's eye, promoting her transition to a new life. Rumor had it that Sandra was kidnapped by a group of drug dealers who tortured her to death by continuously burning her with a hot crack pipe from her face to her vaginal area. Crack being their drug of choice left Wanda traumatized by the glass object.

Wanda was able to resist the temptations of any mood or mind altering drug after this incident and vowed to remain clean by any means necessary. It was her legacy to be a productive member of society and role model to her family and others in the

A Hutlaz Dream

struggle. She was determined to change the old adage of 'once and addict, always an addict'.

Seeing that her mother was now responsible, Jai'Myiah put her in charge of the liquor store. She had a plan for her younger sister Jolisa to help, but she was too busy running the streets and chasing the young 'D boys' to focus on anything positive. She also wanted her older sister Trish to be a part of the new family business since she was between jobs and dependent solely on her government issued welfare check, but she figured she was too good to work for her little sister. Jai'Myiah didn't see it that way, but that is how it was going to be.

The businesses flourished, and it only took a month and a half to make back the capital they'd used to open them plus a cool profit. Everything had been going better than planned and felt too good to be true. Jai'Myiah smiled to herself as she made it home about 6 p.m. on January 6, 2007.

When she entered into the house, she noticed that Zeh'Shon was seated on one of the wooden bar stools in the kitchen sipping on a glass of Remy, with the rest of the bottle on the counter top within reach. He was fully clothed as if he'd just gotten home, eyebrows held a slight arch as if he'd been stressed from a long day. Scattered in front of him were a group of documents.

"What's up baby?" she greeted while placing her purse on the kitchen table and shifting through the mail. Zeh'Shon didn't respond so she stopped and looked at him because she knew damn well he'd heard her. "Hello," she said waving her hand in front of him, "What's wrong with you?"

"So you just weren't going to tell me, huh?" he murmured, tight lipped.

"What are you talking about Zeh'Shon?"

"This is what the fuck I'm talkin' 'bout," he yelled and flung a bunch of papers from the hospital in her face. She gathered them off the floor and stood in shock. 'How did he find these?' she asked herself, or better yet how was she going to explain. The look on his face said that he was hurt beyond explanation.

"Baby, listen," started Jai'Myiah.

"Fuck listenin', it aint shit you can say to me, or try to clarify a reason for takin' it upon yourself to abort my baby," he yelled, "aint that a bitch? What? I aint got no say around this muthafucka?"

"Baby, please," she begged.

"What?" he yelled, looking at her as if she had shit on her face.

"I know I'm wrong, I should've gotten your opinion, but with everything that's been going on lately, and how busy we've both been... With me trying to start up these new businesses, and you running the streets, I just thought it was the right thing."

"Well since you so 'smart', and always 'thinkin', I'ma let you do it on your own from now on, I'm out." he said while grabbing his coat and leaving out the front door and letting it slam behind him.

Jai'Myiah didn't run after him to beg him to stay because she knew she was dead wrong. She should have informed him of her pregnancy, but to be honest she wasn't ready to bring a baby into the world. She vowed to herself at a young age that she wasn't going to have a baby unless she was married and well established. Zeh'Shon claimed to love her but what if one day he picked up and decided to leave her for something better? She couldn't accept the 'baby mama' title. Or even worse, God forbid something happened to Zeh'Shon, but what if it did and she was left with nothing and

A Hutlaz Dream

ended up having to push her baby in a stroller and wait for a bus somewhere to get to her destination. She couldn't fathom that.

Over the course of the next two days, she was an emotional wreck. Crying tears of regret, she thought of what the future held. Things weren't looking too good for the home team, being that Zeh'Shon hadn't been home or answered any of her calls. Willing to stay strong for the sake of her businesses, she made it through as best she could, but she felt as though she was on the brink of a meltdown. The smile she held in place for the public told nothing of her dying insides.

Zeh'Shon's memory loss finally subsided on the third day, the ripping and running the streets played out quickly but felt a lesson had to be taught. Nearly home, he whipped around a few corners and drove below the speed limit, he had to make sure that he had made the right decision to return.

He arrived home only to find the love of his life sprawled out on the living room floor sleeping soundly. A half empty bottle of promethazine and codeine was visible, accompanied by an empty half pint of Remy bottle, four swisher sweet cigar wrappers, and an eighth of weed scattered across the coffee table. She must've been high as a kite before she passed out.

The sight of his girlfriend in that state angered him, but being that he decided to come home with forgiveness in his heart, he cleaned up the litter that remained from her solo party, picked her up and carried her to bed. With drool running down the side of her mouth, Zeh'Shon had to check her pulse to make sure she still had a heart beat because she didn't move a muscle as he undressed her and tucked her into the warm covers, before doing the same to his self.

Tap... tap...tap.

Zeh'Shon was snatched from his trance by a constant tapping on the passenger window. He looked up only to see his younger sibling Shanell smiling at him.

"Get your big headed self out of the car," he heard her say through the window.

Shanell was a hand full and a half when she was younger. Taking on the fatherly role, Zeh'Shon was the only one to keep her in line and on the right track for the most part. When he was out hustling, he could never give the game his full attention being that he got called constantly by his mother saying, 'You better come get this little tramp before I kill her.' During those days, he hardly ever walked around with two feet on the ground being that one was almost always in Shanell's hind parts.

Not only did he have to take up his biological father's slack by basically raising himself and taking a huge part in Shanell's upbringing, he had to play 'Daddy' to Shanell's 6 1/2 year old son, Montiece.

He got out of the car and the siblings embraced. "Mama ain't home from work yet. You alright, Zeh'?"

"Yeah I'm good," he lied. Shanell knew her brother like the tracks in her hair, she knew he was hurting so she tried to lift his spirits.

"Montiece made two touchdowns today when they played against the Oakland Dynamites," she said with the smile of a proud parent plastered on her face.

"Is that right? Where my lil' nigga at?"

"Next door playing video games with Adrian and Gerald bad ass. You wanna hit the weed?"

"Purple?"

"And you know this, man!" She replied trying to sound like Smokey on 'Friday'.

A Hutlaz Dream

"Shit might as well, fire it up," he said. Over the years he had calmed down on his smoking habit, but since he had just smoked in the car, he thought 'what the hell'.

Shanell broke the trees down, emptied the tobacco from the swisher before refilling it with weed, rolling it, licking it, and then adding fire. She hit it twice and passed the ganja to her left.

Chapter 5

Zo drove his tan Escalade down Hagenburger Rd. on his way to drop four of his workers off at the airport. He was driving like he raced for Nascar trying to rid the car of its occupants and get the chicks out of his hair. Dealing with too many females at one time could become a headache. Four women with four different personalities, plus the additional two in his head, was not a good look. He maneuvered the SUV through traffic with precision while Too Short's 'Blow the whistle' CD played softly in the background.

"Kianni and Shavonna, y'all stuffed up?" he asked the two sitting in the far back seats.

"Yes," they replied in unison.

He was sending the two runners to Alaska with two hundred Oxycodone pills apiece; there they are sold for a hundred dollars a pill. Before leaving the house he had both of the girls put the pills in sandwich bags and wrap them in saran wrap before stuffing them in their vaginas. By stashing them in their personal safe deposit boxes, they wouldn't go to jail for trying to smuggle drugs. Since 9/11 Oakland International Airport's security had gotten tighter, so he made sure to take no unnecessary risks, he wasn't in the business of taking losses. "Barbie and Moet, where are you ladies minds at?" he questioned his two prostitutes.

"On your money, daddy," said Moet from the middle row.

A Hutlaz Dream

Barbie, who was sitting in the passenger seat, rolled her eyes. SMACK. "Fuck is your problem, bitch?" he snapped, waking Barbie's game up with a pimp slap to the jaw.

"Ain't nothing my problem," she said rubbing the spot on her cheek that instantly turned red.

"Yeah, I thought not, now y'all go out there and act like y'all got a job to do. Don't be out there partying and fuckin' around, because if I have to come out there you know it's not going to be no social call, got that?

"Yes."

He was sending Barbie and Moet to Manhattan to post their ads on Craigslist and Erosguide.com. Moet was a fairly new comer to the squad. She was an 18 year-old petite Filipino that the tricks just went crazy over. Before Moet got down with the team, Barbie made the most dough amongst the hoes. She was a cute white girl, looked like one of those playboy bunnies, but these days she'd been having to hustle twice as hard to keep up with Moet. She held quite a bit of pent up animosity toward her wife-n-law, but told herself to hold her tongue until they graced the rotten apple.

Pulling up to the JetBlue drop off section, he pulled over to let the hookers out.

"Alright ladies, have a safe trip and call me when you touch down."

"Okay." They said while grabbing their luggage and stepping out. He then pulled up a few hundred feet to let Shavonna and Kianni out.

"Y'all straight, got ya I.D's and tickets, right?"

"Yeah, we cool."

"Alright, call me."

"Okay." They grabbed their bags and were barely out of the truck good before he started pulling away from the curb, causing Kianni to stumble slightly before catching the curb on her shin. Without an apology, he simply shook his head as if it was the girl's fault.

Picking up the freshly rolled blunt out of the ashtray he was about to light it until he looked up and saw a police officer staring in his direction. The front window didn't have tints, so the officer was able to see Zo's facial expression clearly. "Damn dick heads always wanna size a nigga up." He said aloud, "Cracker just mad my rims cost more than his monthly salary."

Moving along with traffic, he continued to hold the marijuana. As soon as he was outta the pig's eyesight, he flicked the lighter and cranked up the radio's volume and let Too Short bump. "One things fa sho, you will get called a bitch…BITCH!" he sang along while puffing on a fat stick of grapes. Feeling the vibration of the phone in his lap he began steering with his knee since he didn't want to put the blunt out.

"Yeah?" he answered with a heavy exhale of smoke.

"What's up daddy, I'm ready for you."

"Who dis?"

"Kenatta," said the caller sounding annoyed.

"Don't get no attitude, bitch. You the one calling from all these strange ass numbers, how I'm supposed to know?"

"My bad daddy, I'm done and was wondering if you wanted me to jump on BART and come out there?"

"How much you got?"

"$5,200"

"Alright, come on get off on the Fruitvale station, hurry up," he said closing the phone.

A Hutlaz Dream

Now if you were to see Kenatta, you would honestly know that Zo didn't discriminate on the looks of the females that he dealt with. This one looked like a straight monkey. Black as night and weighing in at a whooping 220 lbs., standing 5'8", she was considered a big ugly bitch. The gap in her teeth was big enough to damn near slide her tongue through, and if she didn't have a razor handy everyday, she was bound to have a 5 o'clock shadow under her chin. She was a ghetto ass hot mess from the Hunter's Point section of San Francisco. Zo never minded her appearance because every time he gave her some work, she got the job done and brought the money back with little to no complaints.

He had her selling rocks in the mission district of the city. He was pleased with the fact that she knew all the 'knocks', so she ran through bundles with ease, and also in a timely manner. She also never called for assistance if she had a problem since she was manly enough to handle them herself. He pulled up to the station 30 minutes later to see his 'baby gorilla' standing by the taxi port, looking lost. HONK, went the horn. She raised her head looking like Wanda from In Living Color. 'Damn this bitch is hurt', he said to himself. She walked to the truck in an outfit that looked like it cost no more than $10 altogether. With a bright yellow fitted shirt, black leggings, yellow flip flops and yellow accessories. He thought to himself, 'she must be smoking some of the product I give her, cuz anybody in they right mind wouldn't come out the house looking like that on purpose.'

"What's up, daddy?" Kenetta said.

"What's up good?" he said not wanting to look in her face.

"Here you go," she said placing a plastic shopping bag filled with money on his lap. That was the one thing he hated about block money, it was always ones, fives, tens, and twenties. So it looked like a bunch of money but when you actually count it, it wasn't shit.

    Pulling away from the station, they headed in the direction of his trap house on 74th and Holly St. There he would pick up two ounces of coke for the broad, and send her back on her way.

    "Daddy, I'm stressed out... I think I need some dick in my throat," she said.

    Damn near throwing up in his mouth, he almost lost control of the wheel at the same time. She always had to say something off the wall with her ugly self and the funny part was that she had no shame. Taking a peek at her out the corner of his eye, he looked down at the dash board as if an excuse would magically appear. It didn't. He reached in his pocket and felt around in search of a condom. After locating one he thought, 'What the hell, if this is what he had to do to keep her motivated then so be it. She did just come and pay a nigga so go 'head, but if he didn't have a magnum she wouldn't of had a snow ball's chance in hell at putting those crusty soup coolers on his little man.

    He pulled over in the back of the check cashing parking lot and pulled out his third leg. Without another word exchanged, she immediately began slobbing, slurping, and deep throating like there was no tomorrow. "Damn baby, you missed me?"

    "mmm hmmm." she mumbled never taking the meat out of her mouth. The way she hummed on him sent chills from his brain cells all the way to his toe nails. Just as he was about to erupt, his phone went off. He was going to press ignore at first, but looked at the name. It said Blow, his antennae's went up because this call had to be important.

    "What's up lil daddy?" Zo inquired.

    "Ay nigga, meet me in the North ASAP, I just got word about that wedding shit."

A Hutlaz Dream

"I'm on my way," he stated hanging up and pushing the wildebeest off of him at the same time.

"You gotta go bitch, I'll come bring you that work later."

"Can I have $100, I need to pay my cable?"

"Here bitch, bye," he said tossing over two twenties. He put her out right there and burned rubber heading towards the freeway.

Making it to Dorsey's Locker on 53rd and Shattuck, the 15 minute drive was made in eight flat, if it wasn't for the Sunday driving break dancing in front of him at the exit he would've made it in 5. On the way over he tried getting in contact with Zeh'Shon, but continued to get his voicemail. 'Fuck it'.

Pulling into the parking lot, he noticed Blow's burnt orange candy painted 1998 Lexus S E 400 coupe sitting on 26" rims in the far corner. "These young niggaz is something else, he done paid more for the rims then the actual car," he laughed pulling alongside of it. Blow raised the door and got out. "No this nigga don't have the nerve to have butterfly doors on that piece of shit." Blow opened the door and hopped in clipping his chuckle.

"Check me out."

"What's the word?" said Zo

"My baby mama called not too long ago telling me that she was at this little bar in Vallejo last night called The Coconut Grove. Her and her bitches overheard these square looking ass niggaz talking 'bout a wedding that got shot up at Acts Full Gospel church the other day. So my BM said she listened harder and she heard the tall lanky Herman the monster lookin' cat talkin' 'bout how he pulled the trigger and how everybody hit the floor. So she said she walked over to get a closer look and introduce herself. Long story short, the nigga name is Kleezy, he 'bout 6'5" with light eyes. She said she got the nigga number cuz he tried to holla, so whenever you ready just say the word, I got you."

"Kleezy is what you said his name was?"

"Yup."

"I know a few dudes that live out in Vallejo, I'ma check into that, but for the time being have ya baby mama start callin' and conversing with the nigga, find out his movements, so I can get at the nigga."

"Aiigh blood, I got you, I'll hit you!" Blow got out and jumped in his car. He turned the stereo up so loud, Zo figured it had to be turned to max bumping old school Luniz 'I got five on it '. He must've had urgent plans by the way peeled out of the parking lot like he was in a high speed chase. Zo shook his head at the youngsta's actions and pulled out heading east bound.

Scrolling through his phone book he stopped at the highlighted name and pressed the send key. After the second ring he heard a raspy voice.

"Hello?"

'yeah he got the same number', thought Zo, he hadn't used it in so long.

"Dirty Rome, what's crackin' play boy?"

"Zo?" asked Rome surprised.

"Yeah, nigga it's me."

"Long time, no hear from."

"Ay, you in the 'V'? I need to slide out that way and holla at you for a minute."

"Yeah, I'm out here, come on. Hit me when you get close to the bridge so I can give you directions."

"Alright, give me thirty minutes, one."

A Hutlaz Dream

    Scrolling once again through his phone he dialed Duke's number. "Duke, where you at? I need you to ride to Vallejo wit me."

    "High St. slide thru."

    "Be ready, I'm on my way."

    When he went to pick up Duke, Tay wanted to ride as well, so he told him to jump in. A quick detour to the store for some road snacks and they were off. The traffic was moving smoothly until they got to Richmond's city limits. Cars were backed up bumper to bumper.

    "Aint this a bitch?" Zo spoke. Up ahead they saw at least a dozen highway patrol cars, four ambulances, and three damaged cars. "Probably just some hyphy ass youngsta trying to profile on the freeway," said Duke.

    As the distance from the scene closed they got a clearer picture of what more than likely occurred.

    "Damn, look at that Charger, it's full of bullet holes," spoke Tay seated in the back playing 'Round 5' on the PlayStation 3. "Somebody probably caught one of they enemies slippin', and gave they ass the full clip on the highway. It's funky out here right now and niggaz aint givin' no passes. These niggaz is trippin' now-a-days, jumpin' into this game, thinkin' shit a game, 'till they get they shit aired out."

    As traffic loosened they rode in silence, each man entertaining his own thoughts. The world must've been nearing its end, the way the young adults went wild holding no regards for neither their lives nor the ones dwelling amongst them. Nearing the Carquniez Bridge, Zo dialed Rome for directions. He was to meet him at the Butter Cup bar and grill restaurant on Sonoma Blvd.

"What's up my nigga?" they greeted each other with smiles and dapping hugs. They went into the semi vacant establishment and ordered a small bite and drinks from the bar.

"So Zo, speak to me," said Rome. "What brings you to the Valley-Jo?"

"You heard of a nigga called Kleezzy? He supposed to be from out this way somewhere?" Zo replied getting down to business. Dirty Rome looked up towards the ceiling fan as if trying to think.

"Kleezy?...Ohh yeah, square ass young nigga from the Crest, he fuck wit that music shit?" Zo shrugged. "I don't know him personally but I've seen him around the way a few times. Why what's up, y'all got beef?"

Zo ran down the story of what happened at the church and what Blow had said his chick overheard. "Is that right?" Rome said with a look of anger in his eyes. Being that Zeh'Shon was his boy as well, he was ready to find this dude Kleezy and put some heat in his life. "This chump ass nigga out here bruhggin' and don't even know about the death certificate that he signed for his self, I'ma slide thru the Crest tomorrow and holla at a couple of my young niggaz, try to find out if they can help me locate the nigga."

"Good lookin' and make sure to holla A.S.A.P. I got dudes out my way on the lookout as well. I just thought that I'd slide through this way to make sure we all on point and the nigga don't try to get ghost. I'ma get outta here and head back to the town to handle this other business," Zo spoke after swallowing the rest of his double shot of Patron Silver.

"I got you, my dude," said Dirty Rome. They embraced in a half hug once more before the foursome paid the check and headed back to familiar territory.

A Hutlaz Dream

    Zo dropped Duke and Tay back off on High St. instructing them to get the rest of the goons together just in case they had to take another drive to Vallejo soon. They parted ways a few minutes before midnight and promised to keep in touch. After calling all his workers and making sure they were busy completing the tasks that he had assigned to them with no discrepancies, he decided to go home and spend a little Q.T. with his main chick, Juanita. Before doing so he called Zeh'Shon's cell, once again getting the voicemail.

    "You have reached," recited the automated voice, "mail box number 5105558476, please leave a message at the tone."

    "Zeh'Shon, nigga this Zo why you aint answering? Hit me back 911". He jumped off I-580 heading to San Leandro.

Chapter 6

Zeh'Shon had spent the last five days sulking at his mother's house. She'd been trying to encourage him to snap out of his depression since he was powerless over the situation. He still had a life to live, and she refused to just stand by and watch her son wither away. Niki let him know that whatever happened, good or bad, was the Lord's will and he would have to accept whichever it was.

Since he had his phone off for some time now, his mother kept him posted on what the doctors said about Jai'Myiah. She informed him that Jai'Myiah had yet to awake, but the situation hadn't worsened, so that was a plus.

He took heed to his mother's advice and decided to get up and try to get back to his business. He powered on his phone and it immediately started to ring. Omari was the name that popped up on the screen.

"Yeah," he answered in a worn out tone.

"Ohh my gosh daddy, I'm so happy to hear your voice. I've been so worried about you, after calling your phone a million times. I called the hospital and the jail house, you never let me know where you lived so I couldn't look there, I was over here losing my mind," she said. "Can you please come and see me so I can give you a hug? Please?... Don't you ever do no shit like that to me again," she rambled on and on before he finally stopped her.

"You got some money for me?" he asked.

A Hutlaz Dream

"Yes baby I do, but I don't want to tell you now because it's a surprise, but I can guarantee you'll be happy with me," she giggled.

"Aiight, I'll be over there," he said and hung up. His mind raced back to the day he ended up giving Omari another chance.

December 9, 2006.

Zeh'Shon was leaving Sharice's house where he'd just finished cooking up four kilos of cocaine to be distributed on the streets when his phone rang. 'Who is this calling me from a 925 number?' he said to himself. "Yeah," he answered.

"Please don't hang up on me, I really need to talk to you," he heard the familiar voice say.

"What bitch? Didn't I tell you I wasn't dealing wit yo' childish ass no more?" he snapped angrily, "and who number is this number you callin' me from?"

"This is my folks Veronica phone, but daddy listen, my girl just put me on with this bank shit, and I hit a big lick yesterday for $50,000," she stated like an excited kid.

"Where are you? He replied instantly.

"On my way home."

"Hurry up and get there, I need that!" 'Well if this bitch wanna kiss my ass to get back under my wings, fifty stacks aint a bad start, and she claim to have a line on the paper game, it's official, I'm bout to run this bitch 'till the wheels fall off', he thought to himself.

He let himself into the apartment with the spare key, his hand rested tightly on the Glock 23 that he had on his waist line. He hadn't been dealing with Omari for a while and wanted to be prepared if she was up to something slick and tried to set him up.

When he walked in, he had to take a step back out and look at the apartment number to make sure he was at the right one. It was spotless on the inside and out of all the years he'd known Omari, he had never known her to live tidy. He was now actually able to see the patterns on the furniture and the table top in its entirety. He had to admit to being somewhat impressed. If he knew that doing what he did would have stepped her game up he would've done it years ago. He noticed she had two candles lit on the kitchen table with two bags of Red Lobster take out next to them. Doing all this spring cleaning, she could've opened a cook book in the process, he thought, smiling to himself.

"Hey daddy," said Omari, shyly entering the living room from the bedroom with a large Gucci bag on her shoulder.

"What's up?" said Zeh'Shon taking a seat on the big couch and placing his pistol in his lap just in case somebody had balls enough to come springing out of the bathroom or something, he was prepared if there were to be any surprises.

She took a seat a few inches from him and reached in her purse. Pulling out five stacks of money containing ten thousand dollars apiece she handed it all to him. He accepted it as if she was only handing him a hundred dollar bill, with no emotion.

"What else you got in that bag?" he rudely asked, as if 50 racks weren't enough.

"Umm, umm," stuttered Omari before he snatched it to take a look for himself. He rummaged through the big purse and found an additional $14,000.

"So you holding out? We ain't even bout to start back off on that foot," he stated.

"Daddy, I just need a few dollars to go on a shopping spree to step my clothes game up. I can't go in no bank and withdraw thousands wearing no hood gear," she said.

A Hutlaz Dream

"Why would you go spend cash money on clothes, when you got bogus credit cards? Come on bitch, I ain't no dummy."

He was right, she just wanted the money to continue catting off like she had been doing since she came up on this new hustle. The night before, she had gone to a strip club called 'Pink Diamond', in San Francisco and bought out the bar. She felt like a celebrity and all the attention she received helped her self-esteem to raise a couple notches.

"That's what I thought", after hearing no response, he put the $14,000 with the rest of his stash. She leaned back on the cushion with a look of disbelief plastered on her face.

"What? If you don't want me to have this I can give it all back and cut," he said manipulating her mind like he'd always done.

"No daddy, I want you to have it."

"That's what I thought, now run the game down to me."

She gave it to him blow for blow as it was told to her, from the approval codes to the name of the Mexican that made the fake identification cards. From that moment forth, it was on and crackin'.

Snapping out of his thoughts, he showered and dressed. An hour later he pulled into Omari's apartment complex and got out of his car. His phone chirped informing him he had 29 unheard voice messages. 'I'll check these in a minute.' he told himself.

"Daddy," sang Omari as he opened the front door. She threw herself into his arms and held him tight as if she hadn't seen him in years. "I missed you so much…"

"Okay, okay," he said pushing her off of him and giving himself three feet and three inches of space. He wasn't in the mood to feel smothered and all the attention was making him angry. "What you got for me?"

"Well since you're already aware of the banks being a little hot lately, I've been dealing with these credit cards. Going on nothing but shopping sprees, so come look at all merchandise I got for us!" she said leading the way to the bedroom.

'Us', he thought himself, 'yeah right, I'm taking everything.' She opened the bedroom door and stuff was piled from corner to corner. She had a number of MacBook Pro lap top computers, touch screen iPods, iPhones, desk tops, damn near every other electronic device you could think of. She had bags on top of bags of clothes for him from Macy's, Nordstrom's, Finish Line, and Foot Locker, even a couple from Neiman Marcus. Omari stood by the door smiling, basking in her accomplishments. Zeh'Shon stood by with a look that said, 'Is this it?'

"Alright, take inventory of all this shit, write it down on a piece of paper. I'ma have Sharice come by and pick it up so she could try to sell this shit on eBay."

"Sharice?" she asked with a hint of attitude coating her voice.

"Yeah bitch, Sharice, you better wipe that smug look off your face, I'm really not in the mood to beat yo' ass on my day off from being on no faggot ass jealousy hype."

"I'm not mad daddy," she said remembering the last beat down. She wasn't ready to endure round two, or worse, him leaving again.

"I'm 'bout to send her over here, so don't leave. I gotta make a few runs, but I'll try to slide back through later," he said and left out. Omari stood dumbfounded, she could do no more than shake her head at her own stupidity.

As Zeh'Shon sat in the car he called Sharice and told her, in detail, what he wanted her to do. He had damn near the same conversation with her as he had with Omari, as far as the 'I was worried about you' was concerned. She claimed to have a lot of love plus a few dollars to give to him. He gave her directions and made a promise to appear later that day. Before pulling out of the parking lot, he checked his messages. They were all mainly his workers concerned about his wellbeing, but the one message from Zo caught his attention.

RING...RING...RING

"Where you been nigga? I'm on Seminary and E.16th, slide thru," answered Zo.
"I'm on my way." Zeh'Shon hung up and got to Zo as soon as he possibly could.

Chapter 7

It would have been easier to take the streets to Seminary from 80th Ave, Zeh'Shon decided as he made his way through the Oakland city streets. Being born and raised on this side of town, he knew all the "cuts" and backstreets like the back of his hand. This enabled him to take the scenic routes as opposed to taking the main roads. He did this religiously to avoid running the risk of being pulled over by a bored or nosey cop, or being mistaken as a whooper with cheese to a hungry nigga that didn't know how much street credibility he held in the hood.

August was quickly approaching as the month of July was wrapping up its last days. The sun stood high with rays beaming brightly, not a cloud in the sky. It was hotter than a Muslim in a three piece suit selling bean pies on a corner in Hell. Thinking of which, Zeh'Shon spotted one on the corner as he sat at the stop light.

"As-salamu alaykum my brother," said brother X, walking in Zeh'Shon's direction.

"Wa `alaykumu s-salāmu wa rahmatu l-lāhi wa barakātuh," replied Zeh'Shon handing the brother a $20 bill out the window and rolled it back up. He wasn't of the Muslim religion, but his brief prison stint taught him a little of their beliefs and phrases used in greetings. As if on cue, the light changed and he pulled off. Not wanting to be rude, but not quite in the mood for the small

A Hutlaz Dream

talk is why he hit the brother off with a dub. He respected his hustle and means of enlightenment, but he had to keep it moving.

Nearing the corner of where he was to meet Zo, Zeh'Shon witnessed about ten or so kids playing in water that shot from a fire hydrant, and having a grand time without a care in the world. Parking behind the blue Dodge Mangum, Zeh'Shon got out and hopped in with Zo.

"You alright my nigga?" asked Zo after Zeh'Shon sat down and closed the door.

"I'm good," he replied while giving his friend dap. "So what's the word?"

"Well...," Zo gave him the conversation between him, Blow and Dirty Rome play by play. "I got some niggas out there studying this dude's movements, come to find out this boy is a real life J-Cat. The only reason my young niggas haven't been able to get at him is because he always surrounds his self with a group of niggas, and I don't want things to get too messy. Plus the nigga's uncle Shady's name holds a 'lil weight in the Bay. I don't want to start an all-out war at the moment, but don't get me wrong, if need be I'm cockin' back and squeezing. I was feelin' like just layin' in the cut for a minute and waitin' for the opportunity to present itself, and trust it will present itself."

Taking everything Zo said in, word for word, Zeh'Shon's blood pressure began to rise. The way he was feeling, he wanted to kill this nigga Kleezy and everything he loved right then and didn't care about any consequences. Yet he somewhat agreed on where Zo was coming from so his decision was to wait it out, but as soon as the time came he was going to set it off, all gas no mask. Plus he was well aware that stepping back from a situation will give you the perfect view.

"I'm glad to hear that we know who pulled the trigger, but I really want to know who was behind it, cause I don't know a nigga named Kleezy, so me or Myah wasn't his personal target. He probably was broke and was approached with a proposition that would put a little food in his mouth and couldn't pass it up."

"I was thinking something similar, but I think we should keep our attention focused on him for now, because soon as he get hemmed up I'ma have him singing more than slaves on a plantation."

Even though Zeh'Shon wasn't back to his typical self, mood wise, he had to crack a light smile because Zo had the tendency to throw a dash of comedy into every situation.

They ended up hanging out together and shooting the shit for the rest of the evening. Zo did everything in his power to lift his buddy's spirits, he hated seeing him all down and out. They hopped from bar to bar and took a couple trips down Oakland's most famous hoe stroll a.k.a "Hooker City," on E.14th St. Zo hollered out at numerous females on the blade and surrounding streets. Zeh'Shon watched from the passenger seat as his friend went into full pimp mode, yelling vulgar obscenities out the window. "Say, bitch come fuck wit a real nigga... I can make your wildest dream come true,"... "Ohh, you too lazy to fuck with pimpin'? Well be sure to keep up the bad work"... "I see you lookin' bitch, don't run from this pimpin', embrace it." "Turn around and see what you turnin' down..."

Zeh'Shon nearly busted an organ in his side he was cracking up so hard. He felt he held a front row seat at a Kevin Hart Comedy. They rode up on a group of prostitutes loitering beside a bus stop and Zo pulled over. When their shoes hit the pavement all of the girls scattered like bystanders of a shoot out. All that could be heard was heels on stilettos clicking against the

A Hutlaz Dream

asphalt. One girl strolled by slowly, looking to be no more than a ripe 16 years old. She wore a mini shirt with a two sizes too small tube top that hugged her under developed breasts. Her feet were secured in flip flop sandals.

"Ah hoe," Zo called out. The teenager looked up and started to move a bit faster. "Yeah, you bitch, I see you peeking. While you got on them slow shoes, I could put you in some real get money shoes, have you shinin' out here." She began trotting on in a hurried pace, occasionally looking over her shoulder to make sure this deranged pimp wasn't after her.

Since being introduced to the life of a street walker, she'd witnessed a few girls get kidnapped and put into trunks if they didn't comply with the pimps request voluntarily. As she power walked, she phoned her pimp and let him know that she was being harassed by some guys on the corner. She gave her location and hung up so she could get back to work.

Within minutes a midnight blue Cadillac Escalade EXT pulled up behind Zo's Magnum and kept the engine running. As Zo opened the driver's door, the truck's door opened and out came a dude that looked like a black Kermit the frog. "Ay playa," said Kermit. "You mind easing up on sweating my bitches, they out here to make my money!"

"That aint gonna happen, you may want to take them hoes home and give 'em the night off, cause I'm out here, and stalkin' everything walkin'."

Upon hearing the verbal confrontation, Zeh'Shon stepped back out and readied himself if something were to jump off. The Cadillac's passenger door opened as well and out climbed a light skinned pretty boy type nigga, Zo paid him no mind as he continued. "Now we can handle this like gentlemen," he stated while pulling up the bottom of his shirt exposing the chrome handle of his .40 caliber, "or we can get into some gangsta shit," he quoted a line from his favorite movie 'The Mack'.

"Come on Kapone, let's shake," pretty-boy suggested, obviously not choosing the latter, for his friend.

"Yeah nigga it's all good, I'll see you again," said Kapone backing up and gripping his door handle.

"You see me now nigga, what it do?" questioned Zo, gripping his .40, removing it and holding it at his side. "Is that a threat, cuz I don't take lightly to them."

"Naw it's good, do you," Kapone hopped in his truck and started the engine. Pretty boy was already strapped in his seat belt, visibly shaken.

The truck pulled away from the curb, but Zo waited until the occupants turned the corner and the rear lights vanished before he tucked the gun back in and hopped back in his whip. Zo immediately busted out laughing.

"You seen how scared that Rico Suave cat looked? He was 'bout to shit his self when he saw this chrome. I was damn near tempted to reach in and grab the pack of Kleenex out the glove compartment and toss it at his ass." They both shared a laugh.

For the next two hours, they rode around smoking blunt after blunt and taking a few swigs of the bottle that they'd bought. It wasn't long before all the weed and alcohol that they'd consumed had them good and medicated. As Zeh'Shon's eyes started to become weighty, he decided to head home. Zo picked up the cruising speed and delivered his friend to his car.

Heading towards the I-580 entrance, Zeh'Shon noticed his gas needle was almost on 'E'. He pulled over at the Valero gas station on MacArthur. A young cat that stood by the front entrance of the hoagie shop approached from the shadows of the lot.

A Hutlaz Dream

Grabbing the butt of his gun on instinct, Zehi'Shon gripped the handle tight, at that moment everyone was a suspect in his eyes.

"I got CDs," chimed the youngster, "five for ten and movies three for dub." Zeh'Shon relaxed after sensing that dude was harmless and removed his hand from his waist line.

"Naw I'm good," he said.

"I got that new Lil Wayne and Drake mix tape. That shit go, you should check it out," said the persistent bootlegger.

"Not right now 'lil daddy, I aint got it."

"Alright then homie. If you ever need some entertainment, I'm ya man. I be right here every day," he said walking off.

"Fa sho."

As he placed the gas nozzle in its rightful place, Zeh'Shon proceeded to pump the gas. While the car was filling up, he took in his surroundings. Across the street at the liquor store he noticed a young girl bent over talking to somebody through the window of a Pontiac Grand Prix on 26" inch rims. 'That's ridiculous', he thought. Out of nowhere came the loud sounds of Dru Down's old school song 'Pimp of the Year', echoing through the streets. The voice was so clear you would have thought Dru was rapping on the corner with a microphone. Looking around, he instantly spotted the source of the ruckus. Pulling up to the store was an old beat up van. It was so tore up that the paint was chipping and dents and dings were scattered all over the body. Whoever owned that piece of junk metal had nerve enough to put chrome rims on the bucket. To top that off, the reason the sounds were so clear was because they put a 10" speaker in the van's front grill.

Shaking his head, he said to himself, 'Well, at least the city got rid of those irritating whistle tips.' A few years prior quite a few people had whistle tips installed on their cars, where every time they would accelerate a loud whistle would blow sounding like tires screeching. Upon hearing this, drivers and pedestrians alike would take caution and make sure they weren't the next victims of an accident, only to look up and realize it was that damn whistle tip. That pissed off a lot of people in the community.

Holding the nozzle and shaking the excess gas down the tank, Zeh'Shon saw four dusty dope fiends meandering by. He questioned how someone would do a drug that made them too lazy to make sure their bodies were cleaned and well groomed on a daily basis, or have so much love for a drug that caused them to sleep walk through life. He just didn't comprehend. He felt drug addicts were weak for letting dope be the ruler of their lives. That's why he didn't feel bad for putting it out on the streets and making sales.

ne dope fiend from the bunch fell back and approached Zeh'Shon while he was getting in his car.

"Ay my man, can you spare a dolla?"

"Naw, I was just 'bout to ask you for one." The bum looked at him as if to say, 'I know this rich nigga didn't just come at me like that.' Instead he whispered, "Alright my man, you have a good night."

As Zeh'Shon pulled off he heard the smoker grunt, "Stingy muthafucka, " and saw him flip the bird through the rear view.

Zeh'Shon chuckled, he didn't feel bad in the least bit. He would've respected the dope fiend a little more had he come up and ask to wash his windows or finish pumping the gas for a few greenbacks, but no, he just flat out wanted something for nothing. Zeh'Shon felt that since he wasn't born with a silver, but more like a dirty spoon in his mouth, and had to hustle for everything he possessed, he wasn't giving no handouts, that's just the way he felt.

His phone rang, it was Sharice.

A Hutlaz Dream

"What's up Reece?" Chrisette Michele's song 'Epiphany' played loudly in the background, all that was heard was, 'Well, I think I'm just about over being your girlfriend, I'm leaving, I'm leaving…'

"Hello," he yelled.

"Ohh, hey daddy." said Sharice.

"Bitch, what's up wit all that bullshit in the background, you tryin' ta tell me somethin'?"

"No silly," she giggled. "I didn't realize you had actually answered. I anticipated leaving a message, you know that's what I've been getting a lot lately," she said sarcastically.

"Don't get cute, bitch," he stated.

"I'm not, I miss you and I thought for sure I'd see you today. You know it's been so long, I had to look at your picture on the mantel earlier because I forgot what you looked like."

"Aww, here you go," he said enjoying her sarcasm. "Listen luv, I just had a family emergency a few days ago and I've been tending to that."

"So I've heard," she replied in an annoyed tone.

"What's that supposed to mean?" he asked. She couldn't have been talking about him getting married because he hadn't told any of his broads that in fear of them jumping ship. But she could've found out because Oakland wasn't as big as it seemed. 'Fuck it' he thought, if she was mad she could cut, because whatever she didn't want to deal with another would.

"Ohh, nothing. I handled most of that business for you today. I still have a couple items left that didn't sell, but I put the word out there so they should be gone by tomorrow at the latest."

"Okay, I'll come through there tomorrow fa sho."

"I can't wait," she said like an excited child. "I'm about to go to sleep now, so tomorrow can hurry up and get here. I love you, daddy!"

"Aiight luv, I'll see you in a minute," he replied and hung up. He never used the term 'I love you' to any female except Jai'Myiah. He figured if the workers wanted to express that emotion that was their dumb ass fault.

Chapter 8

As the weeks ticked by, Zeh'Shon managed to jump back into the swing of things. He still thought of Jai'Myiah constantly, but as of late, her situation hadn't made any improvements. He made sure her business establishments were continuing to be run smoothly in her absence. Wanda stepped up and helped run the laundry mat as well.

Zeh'Shon was proud of her for taking on such responsibility. He respected her for making a 180° turn for the better. She had been a busy woman lately, with having to run back and forth between the two stores, and take on other tedious tasks that consumed her day. She still managed to stop by Kaiser each night to check on her baby before heading home, and she was sure to keep her son-in-law posted at all times.

Zeh'Shon still hadn't returned to the hospital to visit his wife since the time he'd walked out. He couldn't bear seeing her in that predicament, and if his worst nightmare came true and she were to succumb to her injuries, he didn't want to live with such an awful last memory of her.

He jumped back into his hustle head first, having to get back on top of his game. He was bumping broads left and right, and running them harder than 'Seattle Slew'. He started beef with rival drug dealers by setting up shop on their turfs with lower prices, had his chicks set fellas up, the whole nine. He was speeding at a nauseating pace, having no regards for anything or anyone.

Doing the most, Zo had to pull his coattail from time to time, not out of jealousy, but out of love. His friend was doing way too much and in order to survive out on those treacherous streets and stay dry in the rain, they had to move smarter. People were dying for less than an quarter ounce, and Zeh'Shon was in the process of taking over entire blocks by force. Zo knew he was hurting deep inside and was probably just acting out his anger, but they had to stick to their script, and follow the plan.

Meanwhile...

Wanda was at the corner store on 55th.

"Thankyou, Kendora," said Wanda to a lady that frequented the store. "You have a blessed day."
"You too, sweetie," she replied on the way out of the door, clutching her bag full goodies.

RING....RING, went Wanda's cell phone.

"Hello, may I please speak to Wanda Brown," said a man of Asian descent.
"Speaking," she answered worriedly.
"This is Dr. Chan from Kaiser Hospital. I'm calling to inform you that Mrs. Banks suffered a seizure last night, and as a result of that we've noticed minor swelling to the right side of her brain..." That was all Wanda heard before she let the phone drop and commenced to balling hysterically.
"Why, God? Why is this happening? Please help us! You said You wouldn't put more on me that I can bear when I read a

A Hutlaz Dream

chapter in Matthew. Well this pain is becoming unbearable. I need You to send a miracle, and save my baby. Answer me!" she sobbed.

Just then she broke down, and all the faith she had went out the window with the cool breeze that was circulating through the small store. She headed to the door with purpose and pushed hard. 'Just who I was looking for,' she thought as she approached the young man standing on the corner. The dark skinned gentleman was clad in dark blue baggy True Religion jeans, a pair of blue and white old school Diadora sneakers, and a white t-shirt that he appeared to be drowning in.

"Ant, come here and let me holla at you," she said.

"Listen auntie, I was not posted up in front of your store," he started to explain himself with his arms up in surrender. He tried to explain a reason for his presence, but was cut short. Wanda had approached him on numerous occasions within the past months about loitering in front of the store selling narcotics and other illegal substances. She threatened that the next time she had to tell him to vacate she would call the authorities and have them deal with him.

"Boy come here," she demanded. "Let me get a dime." She pulled a $10 bill out of her pocket.

"Come again?" asked Ant, knowing for sure he couldn't have heard these words coming out of this woman's mouth.

"You heard me, hurry up before somebody sees," she said wiping her eyes. Knowing he was in the wrong, Ant still placed his hand to his mouth and spit out a plastic covered crack rock and made the hand to hand exchange.

As Wanda rushed hurriedly back in the store, Ant felt bad for a split second. He'd known Wanda for years, and had seen first-hand how far gone she was when she was self-medicated. He was amazed at how good she had seemed to be coming along lately.

'But ohh well,' he shrugged. A dope fiend is going to always be a dope fiend at the end of the day. If the purchase hadn't been made through him she was going to walk a little further up the street and cop from someone else with a sack. Plus he wasn't hugging the corner to make a fashion statement. He was getting his rocks off, hell he had to eat too.

Upon entering the store Wanda immediately closed and locked the door, and hung the 'Closed' sign in the window. She was happy she was already in a store that was equipped with all the fixings she would need to assist in feeding the craving. She grabbed a pack of Newport shorts in the box, a Bic lighter, a box of aluminum foil to make her homemade pipe, a sponge of Brillo, and a half pint of Taaka vodka. Even though she had access to Belvedere and Grey Goose she chose to go for what she knew, the cheap stuff. The Taaka and crack were enough to numb her pain and send her first class on a flight that was far away from the present.

She took the selected items and moseyed to the office in the back of the store. Out of ear shot of her ringing cell phone, she made a spread on the desk and began getting down to business. Her son, Bo was at the front door wondering why it was closed when there were still a few hours of daylight outside. All the weed that he'd smoked gave him the munchies, so he stopped by to pick up a few free snacks. He saw his mother's car parked in the front so she couldn't have been out making a run to the bank. His antennae's rose instantly with the feeling that something wasn't right. He called to see where his baby sister was since she had an extra key.

"Sis, where you at?" asked Bo after the phone rang twice.

"On 38th getting my car washed at Hot Boys, why what's up?"

A Hutlaz Dream

"Good thing you in the area, blast to the store right quick so you can open the door, mama's car is in front but the 'Closed' sign is up."

"What? I'm on my way," Jolisa said ending the call. She wasn't sure of what to think, all she knew was that she had better get there quick. Her and her mother had a rough relationship over the years, but the situation with her sister had brought the two to a mutual understanding and now they were closer than ever before.

"Donte, that's good here, I gotta go," she said holding out two twenty dollar bills. Donte was on his knees painting 'butter' on the third tire, but stopped and rushed over to retrieve the bills since her voice sounded urgent.

"Good lookin'," he said clutching the cash as she smashed off.

Glad that she was only a few blocks away, she gunned the engine in her 2014 Buick Lacrosse, courtesy of a ballin' ass San Francisco cat by the name of Black Meezy. The engine roared as she mashed the gas, floating down Foothill Blvd. She pulled up in two minutes flat and jumped out with keys in hand. Gaining access to the entrance they both ran to the rear of the store yelling, "Mama."

Jolisa checked the bathroom and closet while Bo headed to the office.

"What the fuck?" Was all Jolisa heard before running in the direction of his voice. She reached the office and stood frozen in shock, her mouth scrubbed her chest as she looked on in fear. Right before her sat her mother with drug paraphernalia scattered across the desk. The devil had never seemed to stray far from her home, and once again he was back at his devilish ways attempting to disrupt their accomplishments at the most inopportune time.

"No mama! What's going on, what's the problem? You were doing so good! Mama, please don't do this to yourself again," cried Jolisa.

"I'm sorry y'all… it's just I got a sudden urge to give up, I tried," she cried. "The doctor just, just said...," she sniffled.

"Said what?" asked Bo.

"That Jai'Myiah had a seizure last night," she stated, not being able to utter another word, she broke down, crying profusely.

Bo and his sister went and hugged their mother tight at that moment, embracing in a group hug as they rocked back and forth. When Wanda's cry softened, she explained that she didn't exactly partake in the mini smoking session she had planned for herself, but probably would have, had they not shown up in the nick of time.

Bo recommended that she go home and get some rest. He assured her that he would take care of the store for the remainder of the day, and also check on his sister before the night was over. Managing to crack a smile before making her exit, Wanda warned her son not to eat all the candy bars in his state of intoxication.

Jolisa followed Wanda home and sat with her until she drifted off to sleep, which didn't take long after popping a Vicodin. Writing a note demanding that her mother call as soon as she woke, Jolisa sat it on the dresser in plain view before leaving to handle the rest of her so-called business.

As Wanda slumbered, she had a dream, or rather a nightmare, of her previous life as a stone cold junkie.

The summer of 1999 marked Wanda's ninth anniversary since falling victim to the crack plague that flooded the streets of her hometown. She was damn near at the point of no return. She

A Hutlaz Dream

had gone weeks without bathing and dirt hung on her skin causing her complexion to darken. The dirt and ash clung to her bony frame and she looked like a cancer patient. She ate only when she ran out to dope, which was very rare. The hustler in her wouldn't let her sleep until her body just shut down on her. This would happen from time to time, especially when she would go on 30 day missions.

    She received aid for three of her four children at the time. Jolisa was nine, Jai'Myiah 14, and Trish 17; even though Trish packed her bags and relocated a year prior from being fed up with the lifestyle her nuisance of a mother was leading. Wanda still received welfare for the girl due to the fact that Trish hadn't yet turned 18. Bo, 19, slept there periodically, but for the most part bounced around from house to house staying with different females. Wanda made sure to tax him on the nights he did sleep over.

    Jai'Myiah was only 14 when she officially got her feet wet in the cold game of the streets, but it was not by choice. She just wasn't able to accept always going without. The checks that Wanda received always went up in smoke, and Jai'Myiah hated to hear her younger sister cry from hunger pains, or kids making crude remarks because her clothes were a size too small and dingy.

    Jai'Myiah and her best friend Zariah hustled up $125 between themselves and bought a quarter ounce of crack and took it to San Francisco where they heard that the most money was. Zariah's situation was identical to Jai'Myiah's, being that their mothers were good friends.

    Wanda paced a trail in her living room carpet one night awaiting Jai'Myiah's return from the city. She had found out about her daughter's recent activities by searching through her room on a quest for loose change. She found a box of sandwich bags and a razor filled with residue on a dinner plate. She later questioned Jai'Myiah on the need for the items, but she already knew the reasoning. The girl knew her mother was on crack but far from a dummy, so she admitted her actions.

Instead of looking at the big picture, which was that her baby girl was risking her safety in the treacherous streets of the Tenderloin, all she saw were clouds of smoke hovering above her head.

2:30 a.m., Saturday morning, Jai'Myiah and Zariah walked in looking tired and worn out.

"Baby girl, can a 'Fin' get me in?" sang Wanda, hoping her child wouldn't turn down her five dollar bill for a piece of crack.

"Dang mama, you ain't got at least ten? I feel like I'm hustling backwards dealing with you. Every time I come in here, you want to spend four and five dollars and expect to receive a gram or better, that ain't cool."

"Baby hear me out," Wanda pleaded. "I've been walkin' and squakin' all night trying to get a couple more dollars together for you. I tied my hustling shoes on tight, but for some reason they keep sliding off. Come on baby, my hat band is on tight, I need you right now. I just need a little something to lay down."

'This lady always has some type of excuse or something crazy to say', thought Jai'Myiah. "Here," she said handing her mother a dime. She had been outside for the last few hours and all she wanted to do was shower and catch some z's.

Seizing the drug, Wanda hurried off to her room smiling like Ed McMahon had just rang the doorbell with a check with her name on it. Three hours later, the monkey was on her back like Godzilla, beating on her chest like Tarzan. She went and woke up a sleeping Jai'Myiah.

"What?" asked Jai'Myiah, sleepily.

A Hutlaz Dream

"Baby, I need a wake up."

"A wake up?" she asked, irritated. "How you gonna need a wake up and ain't never went to sleep, mama? I ain't got it right now. Please leave me alone, I'm tired."

"Ain't that a bitch?" quizzed Wanda. "I done brought you in this world, and you're going to deny your own mother?"

This fake guilt trip had been placed on Jai'Myiah's ears a number of times, but she didn't bite into it this time. Jai'Myiah turned her back on mother dearest and let sleep consume her. Being that desperate times called for desperate measures, Wanda called her ace boon coon Sandra, and (when it was convenient for her) her boyfriend B. Davis to go bundle hunting. 'Bundle Hunting' was to scour dope spots looking for dope dealers cocaine packs that they had stashed in bushes or camouflaged with litter on the ground. Just in case the jump out boys hit, they wouldn't catch possession charges for having the sack on their person.

They hit two spots that day, the first being a success on 89th and A St. The young grinder was engrossed in a conversation with a girl when B. Davis spotted the bundle right in front of the back tire of a black 5.0 mustang. Bending down as if tying his shoe he snatched the sack and they moved to the nearest cut to blaze up.

Walking up on 90th Ave, they managed to pan-handle enough money to get a much needed pack of Bugler's cigarettes and the cheapest liquor the store sold. They stopped at Booker's liquor of 90th and Plymouth. There was a bunch of commotion in the parking lot. A bunch of teenagers frequented the place to mingle, conduct business and show off their newly purchased possessions.

Wanda, attempting to be incognito, witnessed a small drug deal going on, while Sanda and B. Davis were inside grabbing the goods. She saw that a youngster dropped a bundle between two milk crates on the side of the store and walked off. Being greedy and thinking she was slicker than thick grease, Wanda made a dash. The youngster saw her move and gave her a swift back hand that caught her in mid stride. B. Davis saw the altercation after exiting the store and ran over to try to be of some assistance, Sandra following suit. Needless to say, they all got beat like gang initiation.

Wanda sprang awake in a cold sweat, breathing hard and wondering where she was before realizing it was indeed her comforter that she was wrapped in. Grateful that God had saved her from herself once again, she knew that she was her own worst enemy.

Chapter 9

"Wake up baby, your phone is ringing," said Omari.

"Damn bitch, you just fucked up my wet dream," said Zeh'Shon in a groggily voice as he elbowed the woman out of his face. "Never mind my phone, why don't you come over here and put them wet lips and tongue on this wood."

More than willing to accept his invitation, she made her way to his mid area and took the juicy meat into her moist opening. She was sucking him so good that his toes began to curl. She made way to his sacred jewels and juggled them in her mouth like she was auditioning for a leading role of a circus act. Just when he thought that she had given her best job, she lifted his testicles and flicked her tongue over the tender perineum.

He found himself beginning to climb the walls, the feeling sent him into another zone, a zone he'd never traveled. The euphoria had him floating, but then he got scared. He had to push Omari's head off of his Johnson to hold in the 'bitch' moan that would have inevitability escaped his lips had he let her continue. He slid back down to his original spot and pushed himself back in her jaw so she could finish him off. She bobbed and weaved until warm fluid coated her tonsils, she swallowed each and every drop. She put the lady that was featured on Master P's album 'The ice cream man', #9 commercial to shame with that.

Zeh'Shon caught his breath as Omari gazed into his eyes, hoping that he would give her some of that anaconda after a job well done. She was rudely surprised.

"Bitch go get in the shower so we can cut, it's almost check out time," said Zeh'Shon as he reached for his phone on the dresser to check the call log.

'Aint that cold,?' thought Omari, 'After that love I just showed him, he's just going to leave me to play with myself in the shower. He been acting real stingy wit the dick lately, but that's going to have to change. This nigga got my coochie on a strat diet, ass hole!'

As Omari showered, Zeh'Shon went around the room gathering his belongings and placing them in his Louis Vuitton overnight bag. He and Omari had checked into the La Quinta Inn motel off Hagenburger Rd. the day before. Omari and Sharice had been battling each other for his presence lately, so if time would permit, he would spend one night with one, one night with the other. He bounced around the different motels around the Hangerburger area for two reasons, one he wanted to stay close to the airport or freeway just in case business called and had to be sent on a quick flight or a simple meeting with a customer, and two he would never spend the night at one of their apartments since he didn't trust them. There wasn't any telling who they let in during his down time.

He never wasted any of those nights cup caking with either of them, there was always business involved. His reason for having Omari at that particular room was so that she could break down ten ounces of crack cocaine and bag it up in dimes to be distributed to the young block heads that purchased 'double up'. It took her a good eight hours to finish and by the time she was done cleaning off her 'operating table', it was just her luck that Zeh'Shon was asleep, or so she figured. He was actually faking, always keeping one eye opened when he was around his workers, he didn't trust anyone. When he needed sleep, he would simply go home and turn off his cellular.

Sharice was blowing his phone up, but Omari was out of the bathroom getting dressed and he wasn't up for hearing her mouth, so he just forwarded the calls to voicemail. 'These broads are going to have to start getting along.' He thought to himself, 'I'm a holla at Omari 'bout it when we get in the car, and go holla at Reece in a minute.'

"Come on, I'm ready to shake," he announced when Omari exited the shower, her voluptuous body naked under the small towel. Grabbing his things, he walked out of the room leaving the door wide open for the world to see, as if to say, 'hurry up'.

Both seated in the car Zeh'Shon began, "How much you love me, baby girl?"

"I love you to death daddy, why what's up?"

"Check this, I'm the one asking questions. But the reason I asked is because I want you to help me fulfill my fantasy. I want to have a threesome."

"If that's want you want daddy, I'm cool with it," Omari stated. She wasn't really tripping since she had gotten down with girls in the past and with the dedication she had for her man she would have jumped at any of his wishes without question.

"Aiight, I'm 'bout to call Reece and set this thang up for tonight." Omari's face, which seconds ago held a smile, had instantly turned sideways.

"What's the problem?"

"Come on now, her? You know I can't stand that bitch," Omari said vexed.

"Why don't you like her?" Omari shrugged her shoulders and sat there with 'stupid' stamped on her forehead. "How can you not like something or somebody but don't know the reason? That's crazy, but you know what, never mind. I'll just have Sharice get another bitch that already has her feelings tucked in her shoes".

Sharice and Omari were arch rivals and couldn't stand one another if life itself depended on it. Both women feeling that the other was too much competition for the goal they were after.

"Alright, I'll do it," Omari blurted out. She really didn't want to participate, but she'd be damned if she gave her man a pass to do anything with Sharice perceptively. Just the thought of him alone with the girl upset her stomach.

Pulling to a stop in front of Omari's apartment building, he killed the radio.

"Baby girl, go bag that work up in $1,500 bundles. I'll hit you when and where I want it delivered."

"Okay, daddy," she replied closing the car door.

"Baby, what's up wit you?" quizzed Zeh'Shon through the phone.

"Nothing much, waiting on you to come visit," said Sharice.

"Did you finish hittin' them cards?" He asked referring to the credit cards he had her scan in her and Omari's names. He instructed her to remove the numbers that were currently on the magnetic strip located on the back of the card and replace them with numbers he had gotten via email from his hacker friend, Zackary. The embosser and reader writer machine that he'd gotten through the black market made all of his sliders appear legit.

"Yes."

"You at home?"

A Hutlaz Dream

"Yes, daddy."

"I'm on my way, open the door."

When he arrived he checked on his business and made sure everything was in order first and foremost. Once he was satisfied with knowing that things were in order on her end, he broke down the same conversation he and Omari had. He wasn't interested in the sex itself, he actually could've done without the menage a trois, but he thought this would be a good idea to bring the girls closer. Maybe they would have a good time and stop being so jealous of one another. He was tired of all the drama. He wanted his operation to run smoothly without the headache and the job of mediator. He wanted to be able to send them on trips together. That would leave more time for him to fall back even more.

After hearing his request, she looked up at him as if he'd revealed a secret affair with her mother and there was a possibility that he may be her biological father. From her facial expression alone, he knew that was a no go.

"You know I love you," she said, "but I'm not going to be able to do that one."

"What's the problem, sweetheart?" he asked like it made a difference. "I thought you said you were down for me and would do anything."

"Well, I told you that I would do almost anything. For one thing I'm not gay, bi-sexual or curious, strictly dickly. You should know that by the way I ride you like I'm trying to win the gold medal for the next ghetto cowgirl competition. For two, I hate that bitch Omari. I don't even know why you continue to deal with that bum broad, she don't make no money and she aint cute."

'Here she goes', he thought to himself. Every time one of his chicks felt threatened by one of his other's position they started hating.

"Wow, wow, wow, it's alright sweetheart you don't have to go there. I'm glad to know where we stand. It's okay though, I just thought that since you were my baby girl, you would do whatever to make me smile," said Zeh'Shon, attempting to play with her mind as usual, but this time she wasn't budging.

Sharice looked at him with watery eyes and simply stated, "I'm sorry."

"It's good, be ready wit them cards in the morning, I'ma be y'ally'alls chauffeur to the stores. I'm broke need some money," he said as he exited her apartment. Sharice thought to herself, 'You need some money? Yeah right, that's your favorite line with your ballin' ass, I need some money, out of all the dough I touch I just can't seem to hold onto it for too long cuz I always end up handing it all over to your ungrateful ass.'

The night had come and gone seemingly faster than normal and morning had arrived before Zeh'Shon knew it. He met up with Zo to borrow his Escalade truck, because he had plans for his workers to fill it up immediately, so they could meet back up in enough time to discuss their plan before moving into action. Pulling up at Sharice's spot, Zeh'Shon got in the back seat. He planned to be the driver at first but decided against it. He knew there would be an issue about whoever got to sit in the front with him. The women were above legal age, but when it came down to him they acted like high school students.

"Drive babe," he called out redirecting the steps that were approaching the passenger side of the vehicle. Like a navigation system, he directed her block for block all the way to Omari's

A Hutlaz Dream

house. Sharice played the dumb role like she didn't know how to get there, when all the time she knew exactly which turns to make.

She had to pay big bad ass Omari a personal visit once upon a time. It was early on in her dealing with Zeh'Shon and she wasn't the type to get ran off when it came to something she wanted. Omari tried to play the bold role and called Sharice's phone making threats after finding out a new chick had been initiated into the money team. To prove she was no punk, Reece went to the house and knocked on her door, but after not getting an answer, she knew Omari didn't really want it with her, and she went on about her business.

Sharice was a feisty little lady when provoked. She was calm and collected for the most part, but if you wanted to go there, she'd take it there as well. It was always amusing to watch when she felt froggish, because she'd most definitely leap. She was only 5'1", and 115 pounds soaking wet, so a lot of females had her under estimated, but she was actually a mini beast.

After picking up the 'scally-wag', as Sharice referred to her, they headed out to San Jose to hit a couple stores up that way. The big city of dreams is what Zeh'Shon called it. San Jose had always showed him love no matter what hustling hype he'd gone out there on. From pimping to selling cream, he won every time. Now the game God was allowing him to proper with the credit card scam. Nearing the end of their hustling trip, they stopped at a Best Buy in the city of Fremont. All the cards were maxed out except for the one Omari had that was still paying. She was instructed to get a high priced lap top and a few CDs to listen to on the ride back. Like an obedient child, she went in.

Sharice had to use the restroom and figured she'd better go there, because Oakland was at least twenty minutes away. She didn't anticipate holding it that long, plus Best Buy had pretty clean bathrooms. While Reece was in a stall relieving herself, she heard the door to the restroom open. She thought nothing of it being that she was in a public place, it could've been a shopper or an employee taking a break. Soon she was found to be sadly mistaken.

"Yeah bitch, come up outta that stall so I can holla at you really quick," said Omari aggressively. She thrived off stirring up shit.

'Damn why this bitch had to go there with her scary ghetto ass here? Knowing we're both dirty with all these fraudulent credit cards,' thought Sharice. "Why don't you just hold that thought 'till we get back to Oakland with yo ratchet ass," stated Sharice while walking out of the stall. As soon as she stepped within reach Omari gave her a solid two piece combo to the chin. The move right there instantly released Sharice's inner dragon. She started wailing on her like Floyd Mayweather did Manny Paquiao. Omari being the bigger of the two kept struggling to put Reece in a choke hold, Sharice was too quick on her feet for that move. Omari swung two wild ones and missed while Reece ducked and came up the middle with a rock-hard upper cut to the chin. This blow dazed Omari, causing her to stagger towards the back wall. Seeing this as an opportunity Sharice grabbed Omari by the head and ran her head into the full length mirror that hung to the left of the sink.

The loud bang alerted the store's security so they rushed in to investigate. The girls were locked together like rams as the guards attempted to pry them apart. They were persistent in the battle trying to prove who was the toughest. The tussle would've probably continued for hours had someone not said the police were en route. Running from the store, they both jumped in the truck.

"What the fuck?" questioned Zeh'Shon in utter disbelief. Sharice, who had a cute short hairstyle upon going to the restroom, came back looking like she had just taken her finger out of an electrical socket. Omari's face was lumped up like she just got stomped in the head by a bull, plus her forehead had blood leaking out of an opened wound.

Zeh'Shon waited for an explanation. Reece continued driving as if he was speaking a foreign language and Omari was staring out of the window like she wasn't a resident of the Bay Area and she was taking in sights for the first time. He honestly thought that they got into it with someone who'd worked in the store, maybe an employee figured they were up to something slick and went above and beyond their minimum wage salary and went to investigate. He never would have guessed the story he heard.

As Sharice continued to drive she said to herself, 'I'm through, I give up, I see this nigga really don't give a fuck about me, why should I try to hang onto something that will never fully be mine. That would just be plain dumb. I'm not going to continue to get my heart walked on, and then have to beat up his other bitches in the process. Ohh no, I'm too good for that. Plus my hustle is way too advanced to keep settling for these crumbs this boy dishes out to me, I'm good... Since he's continuously taken my love for granted, I gotta move on... Maybe one day he'll recognize my worth, maybe not, either way it's too late.'

"Hello, do you bitches understand the words that are coming outta my mouth?" He yelled.

Omari started her side of the story while Sharice continued to push the whip through traffic. No sense in trying to defend herself from the fabricated story that crossed her ears since she had already made up her mind about throwing in her towel and giving up the chase.

"Are you bitches retarded?" Zeh'Shon asked," I mean seriously though, that was hella stupid! Do you see all this stolen merchandise we got in this muthafucka. Not to mention all the cards, and me, y'all go really stoop that low when not only were y'all putting y'all's freedom in jeopardy , but mine also, for what? For some bullshit. This is ridiculous. Matter fact, hurry up and drop ya selves off, I need to get somewhere and collect my thoughts. You hoes never cease to amaze me, but this here, is unbelievable. When y'all gonna get a grip?"

The remainder of the ride to Omari's spot was noiseless. Nothing could be heard in the large sports utility vehicle besides the faint sounds of 106.1 KMEL, the Bay's favorite radio station. Turning right on 80th Ave., Zeh'Shon told Omari to get out and go in the house and patch herself up. He would call her later, were his parting words. She tried to protest, but he closed the door in her face and told Sharice to pull off.

The silence continued until they neared Reece's block.

"Baby girl, what seems to be the big issue?" Reece continued to drive staring blankly out of the window as if trying to get her thoughts together. The voices in her head were fighting one another, but this time she was going with her gut for once. The truck came to a complete stop in front of her apartment complex before she spoke.

"I want you to know that I love you. For some reason, I just can't control the feelings that I have for you, but I'm done, gotta call it quits," she stated tearfully.

"Quits? What you mean by that? I'm not letting you go nowhere. Now I don't know what beef you and Omari got going on, but y'all need to get it together..."

"I can't do it no more baby, I'm sorry. I've tried, believe me I have. But it seems like after all these years I have invested with you, I've been running a constant race, but still have gotten

A Hutlaz Dream

nowhere. I was trying to hang but that shit that happened today was the last straw."

Zeh'Shon didn't utter a word he just sat and listened. "All these random bitches you got aint cool in my eyes," she continued, "I tell you all the time, but you steady rub them in my face, bring them around like we are all supposed to be this huge ass happy family, but I'm far from that point. I'll never get that number one spot that I've been trying so hard to obtain, so I'm going to finally stop playing myself. I deserve better, all this drama has taken its toll on me. I'm not doing anything but getting older, and after all these years I haven't accomplished anything... I signed up for school the other day, so I'm going to give that a try for a minute."

"School?" Zeh'Shon chimed in, "I thought I was your teacher?"

Sharice put her head down, but had to follow her first mind. She couldn't continue to be the puppet on his string any longer.

"Well," he continued, "If you leave I'ma retire your jersey and take it off the wall, so it won't be no lookin' back," he stated harshly.

Sharice looked at him with disbelief, hurt etched on her face bringing out every line and wrinkle that had been put there by the person seated next to her. Refusing to shed another tear for this man whom was clearly a cold hearted hustler, she gathered her purse and got out the truck. Zeh'Shon switched seats and said out the window,

"I'll be over here tomorrow to get my shit." The smoke from the burning rubber made her squint her eyes as she watched him disappear out of her life.

Chapter 10

RING.... RING...RING...

"What's up Zeh'?" answered Zo after seeing an incoming call from his folks.

"Where you at? I thought we were going to hook up today and discuss that little business?"

"Yeah I thought we were today, too. But nigga it's 9:30 at night I had to come out here to Sacramento and holla at these Meadow View niggas about some chips. I'll fill you in on the haps when I get back. What's up on yo' end?" Zeh'Shon broke down the day's events to his boy.

"What? That's some wild shit, pimp," said Zo, "But I'ma hit you in the a.m., let's do lunch."

"Aiight, hit me." Zeh'Shon pressed a button and ended the call. Deciding to call it a night, he stopped at Everett and Jones to pick up a plate of BBQ before heading home.

In the meantime, Zo was in Sacramento negotiating prices with two cats that he had done a prison stint with at San Quentin state prison. Zo had the line on coke, and the Sacramento dudes had the line on Mary Jane, they tended to do business on a regular. They respected each other's hustling mind, as well as each other's gangsta. In the midst of doing business over the years, they developed a strong bond and were down for each other in the event somebody had beef, so to speak.

A Hutlaz Dream

"The least I can let a brick go for is $23,500," said Zo.

"$23?" asked baby Trigg, "You tryin' ta tear my head off fa real, huh?"

"Tear ya head off? Nigga it's a drought out here. Niggaz is payin' any where from 25 ta 28 stacks to get they hands on this butta I got, straight up."

Y.B. (young blood) butted in the conversation, "Ay Trigg, the price on that coke shit is up there, 23 is 'bout the best deal you go get right now, and you know this nigga Zo don't touch nothin' but A-1."

"So what's it gonna be?" Zo asked looking from Trigg to Y.B. "You actin' like a nigga is charging an astronomical price, when fa real, fa real I'm just tryin' to make sure all my niggaz bread is buttered, feel me? But anyway we could harp on this subject all night, what's the price on the trees?" he asked right before noticing the call coming through that he'd been expecting. The current conversation took a pause so he could see what was up.

"Dirty Rome, what's the word?"

"Ay, I just got a location on this nigga Kleezy," Rome said into the phone's receiver, "My cousin baby mama just called and said he was next door to her house in the Crest. She said his car been there for 'bout thirty minutes, so you need to hurry up and meet me out there cause it aint no tellin' when the nigga gone dip. I'm leaving Pittsburg now so give me 20 minutes."

"I'm on my way, good lookin' out," Zo hung up. "Ay, I need y'all niggas to take a ride wit me, y'all strapped?" He asked his two partners.

"Most definitely," said baby Trigg.

"Let's do this," said Y.B pulling up his shirt to reveal his pistol.

Even though Vallejo was roughly a forty-five minute drive from Sacramento, the trio made it in thirty minutes flat.

"Where you wanna meet?" Zo asked after Rome picked up.

"Meet me at that Valero gas station right off Fairground Parkway. I'll jump in the car with you."

"We already in this thang three deep."

"Well y'all can hop in with me, I'm in my van. Plus I don't want to ride two cars just in case suspicions arise. I don't want to miss this cat."

"Alright, I'm pulling up."

They got to the cousin's baby mama's house on Hodge St. and went in to get the run down. "Well, the nigga been in there for 'bout an hour. They probably aint doin' nothin' but smokin' hella weed and playin' video games," said Shaina.

"How many people you think in there?" asked Zo.

"Well, the little bitch, Danielle they over there visitin' probably the only female. It's her mama house but more than likely she aint in there. Then I saw Kleezy, Chinese Mike, Key'Mario, and Cator when I went and knocked on the door asking to borrow some sugar."

"Aiight Shaina, thanks for your assistance, but just stay inside until you get a call saying the coast is clear, cuz things might get ugly and I don't want you to get hurt," stated Zo. She nodded. "Okay, you niggaz ready? Let's go in there and lay the house down, but try not to shoot unless necessary. I need the nigga Kleezy to stay alive for a minute. Let my boy Zeh'Shon handle him, it's personal."

After all agreed, they screwed silencers on their guns, crept out of Shaina's house and assumed positions around the small brick home next door. Trigg and Y.B took a side of the

A Hutlaz Dream

house a piece, Dirty Rome headed toward the back and Zo knocked on the door.

"Who is it?" chimed the young ghetto voice of Danielle coming from the opposite side of the beat up wooden door.

"Reggie," said Zo giving an alias while she opened up.

"Can I help you, cuz I sho don't know you."

"Yeah, I was wondering if you had a flashlight, my car broke down and I need to look under the hood."

"I guess, but I might have to charge you." She giggled while in an intoxicated state. Turning around slowly to think of where to locate the flashlight in the midst of the cluttered residence, she continued, "Wait a minute."

No sooner than the last syllable escaped her mouth, Zo sprang into action followed by Y.B and Trigg. Before Danielle had time to understand the situation or give a warning shout to her visitors, Y.B wrapped his enormous hand around her tiny throat and slammed her to the wall as if she were a rag doll, her body slammed so hard the crooked picture of Jesus came crashing down.

Zo stepped into the living room brandishing weapons. In his right hand, he had his favorite Glock 23 and in the other, he held his trustworthy nine milli.

"Everybody lay the fuck down," Zo demanded in a menacing tone.

Two of the four occupants laid it down while the two other's made a run for it, down the narrow hallway they went. Zo let shots off the Glock, aiming at the sprinters. Missing by mere inches, he put two gaping holes in the wall. Trigg took off after them, bucking shots simultaneously. Hearing the mini war erupting, Rome ran from the back in the direction of the front door. Something caught his eye before entering so he blasted. Two figures came darting from the side like they had built-in rockets in their sneakers. Trigg rushed out the front door like a masked bandit. He and Rome proceeded to chase the two targets while letting bullets soar at the same time. They were no competition for the suspects that were running for their lives, so they gave up their pursuit after a block or so. They went back to the house to be of some assistance to the others.

"Y.B make that bitch get you some rope and some duct tape so we can tie these suckas up," ordered Zo. Y.B exited the living room behind Danielle, giving her a hard punch upside the back of the head to hurry her along, and to let it be known that he wasn't playing and that there was plenty more where that came from.

"Now which one of you bitches go by the name of Kleezy?" yelled Zo. The two men lying face down didn't respond. "Let me repeat myself, which one of you suckaz is named Kleezy?" reiterated Zo, giving Chinese Mike an unfriendly kick to the side of the torso.

"Kiss my dick," Chinese Mike managed to utter although the blow knocked the majority of the wind from him.

"What?" asked Zo as he commenced to stomping Chinese Mike's head and upper body area. Rome grabbed his friend and said,

"Not here, we gonna take these cats to the dungeon. There you can do what you want, but if you do it now somebody is liable call the laws. Get a grip for a few more minutes."

Zo agreed with his friend by a simple nod of the head. Y.B and the girl returned with two extra-long extension cords and a couple dingy t-shits.

"We gonna have to work with this," said Y.B as he tossed the items to Zo. They all helped with the task at hand, starting with

A Hutlaz Dream

Chinese Mike. He put up a strong fight but a couple of whacks to the head from Rome's pistol helped compose him.

Next they started in on Key'Mario, he was positioned with his face down on the carpet and arms at his sides. He figured that if he didn't look at the assailants in the face and comply with their orders, he may have a chance to remain breathing. Most hood scenarios consisted of robbers coming in with bare faces and killing everybody, so there'd be no witnesses alive to be able to identify anything in case something went wrong with the heist.

When Key'Mario was turned over to have a shirt tied around his eyes and mouth, he held lids full of tears. Zo knew instantly that he was going to spill the beans and sing like a bird without having to apply much pressure. After the two were bound and gagged, Rome placed a call to Shaina to make sure it was cool to come out. Once given a 10-4, they loaded their human cargo into the back of the van, hopped in and continued to their destination.

They pulled deep into the long driveway of an abandoned house in the Beverly Hills section of Vallejo on Magazine St. They exited and emptied the van of the lames that they'd abducted. As soon as they got settled in the Abandaminium and the defendants were tightly secured to the chairs that were placed in the darkened den area of the home, Zo began his interrogation. He started with Chinese Mike since he seemed to be the mouth of the duo.

Chinese Mike was a black male, age ranging from 21-28 years old. He picked up the name as a child due to his tight chink eyes.

"What's up wit this nigga Kleezy and this shit I'm hearin' 'bout him shooting up a wedding ceremony a few weeks back?" Chinese Mike remained silent. Zo struck him in the face with the butt of his gun, causing Mike's eyes to swell instantly. "Don't make me give you this whole clip," threatened Zo while pressing the pistol to Mike's temple.

"Nigga, I aint my brother's keeper, so how am I supposed to know what that man be into?" said Chinese Mike," I don't know shit, you're going to have to locate that nigga and ask him." Zo looked down at Chinese Mike and interpreted his facial expression. It basically said, 'I'll die before I say a word.' The smug tough guy look got under Zo's skin, so he shot him in both of his knee caps before directing his attention to Key'Mario.

Chinese Mike's outcry from the excruciating pain was quickly muffled as Baby Trigg re-adjusted his mouth muzzle.

"Now you see what can happen when you got a smart ass mouth and withhold the information that we all know you have?" asked Zo while pointing in a squirming Chinese Mike's direction. Just as predicted Key'Mario ran down some vital news.

"All I know is that Kleezy said his cousin, some broad from Oakland, paid him to go shoot up a wedding. Now I don't know the bitch name or none of that. Me and my nigga don't really rock like that, we just from the same hood and get high with each other on occasion."

When Zo pondered what had just been revealed, he cleared his throat and said.

"How I know you tellin' the truth?"

"Man, on my mama, that's the story the nigga been runnin' down to everybody that'll listen."

"Alright, the news flash is appreciated, but I want you to let this nigga know that his head is on the auction block. I'm not going to do nothin' to you, I'ma let your peoples deal wit yo' good snitchin' ass," stated Zo. "Come on y'all, we up."

A Hutlaz Dream

Zo, Baby Trigg, Dirty Rome, and Y.B. Departed leaving the two men for dead and picked up where their night had left off before the call.

On Zo's way back to Oakland from dropping off his two friends that accompanied him to Vallejo from Sacramento, he dialed Zeh'Shon.

"Hello?" he said in a drowsy voice. He had not that long ago drifted off to a deep and much needed, sleep. All the female drama he'd been in lately had drained his psychological and physical being.

"Wake up nigga. I got some important info on this Vallejo nigga."

"What's up?" said Zeh'Shon rose from his position, fully alert.

Zo recounted the events that had recently emerged leaving out not a single detail. Zeh'Shon was ecstatic with his compadres disclosure about the close encounter that he had with the offender, but was confused at the same time with the announcement. He quickly scrolled through his memory's index trying to find out what female he'd come in contact with whom was brave enough to do something as crazy as endangering his life and the life of his loved ones. He quickly ruled out Sharice and Omari thinking to himself, 'Those two bats wouldn't have nerve enough to go against the grain.'

"Man, that nigga was probably lyin'," Zeh'Shon stated, "I just don't think a bitch was involved, that's a little hard for me to believe. I'm not sayin' I'm ruling anybody out, but I need to hear more of the story. We need to find this nigga Kleezy, like yesterday."

"I feel you, but we gonna talk 'bout this some more tomorrow. Get some rest, because for some reason I feel like the shit is 'bout to hit the fan."

"Fa sho, good lookin' my nigga, in a minute."

Exhausted from the adventures of the day, Zo decided to go to his main chick's house and cupcake for the remainder of the evening.

"Hello?" answered Juanita sleepily.

"What you doin' lil' mama?" asked Zo knowing good and well that he'd just brought her back from la-la land.

"Nothing, besides thinking about my man and missing you."

"How much you miss me, baby?" he asked in the sexiest voice that he could muster.

"Ohh baby," she replied in a similar tone, "my body is over here shaking and trembling, in desperate need of your love. My panties are soaking wet just by the power of your voice."

"Is that right? Well keep it like that for thirty minutes, daddy is on the way."

Zo ended the call with a devious smile on his face, reached in the ashtray and picked up his freshly rolled blunt and fired it up. Inhaling deeply then exhaling, he cranked up the volume of the stereo's dial and let 50 Cent and Akon's voice erupt from the four 10" speakers. The song 'Still Kill', was his new found anthem. As the rearview mirror rattled from the bass, Zo sang along feeling every word. "Ohhh, don't even look at me wrong at me wrong when I come thru the hood, aint nothin' changed still holla at my homies, and when I hit the block, I still will kill."

Chapter 11

Zeh'Shon was sound asleep at the time the call came in. But after the recent news was bestowed upon him, his fatigue went out the window. He was now up and amped, in full battle mode ready for war, with the promise of giving the business to all parties involved. The average person would have thought that his thoughts of action were a tad bit harsh. But he planned to bring the pain, pure torture, and show no remorse.

It had been close to two and a half months since the dreadful incident transpired, but at that moment, all of the day's events came rushing back to him as if it had happened yesterday. None of the love he held in his heart for his wife diminished in her absence. If anything, it grew. Even though he chose to carry on in the streets and conduct usual business as if he wasn't hurting, he used his hustle to extenuate his pain, so his mind wouldn't be totally lost. Zeh'Shon thought back and wondered how such a special and beautiful moment could turn into such a bad dream.

'If this world were mine' by Luther Vandross and Sheryl Lynn played softly over the churches surround sound speakers as the audience stood to its feet to welcome the bride. The doors of the chapel opened and in glided Jai'Myiah and her grandfather Earl. She looked as if she were an angel that had fallen from heaven. Whoever designed the wedding dress turned their visual masterpiece in to actuality and created a work of art. The teal/pink color matched her skin to a tee, and hugged her curves like a second skin. The 10 foot train danced in sync with her every movement. A tiara sat upon a head of long, soft loose curls, and shinned brightly giving her a look of pure royalty. Jai'Myiah swayed behind her two flower girls at a slow pace before reaching her post.

Everybody looked so happy for the couple. Trish, Jolisa and Shanell were the bridesmaids, with Zariah being the maid of honor. Zo, the best man followed by Bo, Jamari and Elise as the brides groom were positioned on either side of Zeh'Shon and the pastor, leaving enough room for the queen. Montiece, the little helper in possession of the ring, stood by Zeh'Shon cheesing harder than Chucky at his favorite restaurant on earth.

Jai'Myiah's makeup was immaculately done, bringing out gorgeous eyes that glistened like stars on a cloudless night.

The phone's notification of an incoming caller jarred Zeh'Shon from his thoughts. Glancing at the screen he saw that it was Omari.

"I aint got time for this bitch right now," he said out loud, pressing the 'End' key, sending her directly to the voicemail service. The remaining hours of the night were recklessly spent contemplating who, what, or why. But each avenue he traveled down came to a dead end. A strong migraine settled around his temple area before he decided to rest his eyes. Although putting up a fight, sleep eventually consumed him.

Rising at 11:30, he made a call to Bo and Zo to arrange a one o'clock meeting at 'Ernies' resturant on E.14st. in San Leandro. The plan that he'd come up with was racking his brain and he had to share. When the parties agreed he jumped in the shower and dressed.

A Hutlaz Dream

RING...RING...RING

"Hey mama?" He answered intoned.

"Boy don't you 'hey mama' me. I haven't heard from you in a number of days, what seems to be the problem? I'm still ya mama and won't hesitate to put your big butt over my lap and spank you, don't play," said Niki. Laughing, Zeh'Shon replied.

"My bad mama, I didn't mean to have you worrying." He sounded like a big 'ol kid.

"Don't let it happen again," she joked, "But anyway, Wanda just called and said that Jai'Myiah is slightly improving. She hasn't woke up as of yet, but she is finally breathing on her own." she continued with joy in her voice.

Zeh'Shon's heart palpitated as his entire body was filled with joy and hope.

"You hear me, boy?" said Niki after the line was silent for a few seconds too long.

"Yeah mama, I heard you, I'm just shocked."

"Well you better drop to your knees and thank the Lord, because this is His doing."

"You right mama, but could you thank Him for me?"

"Yes baby," she replied while silently praying that he would come to know God on his own, "Well I'm not going to keep you, I just wanted to fill you in on the good news. I love you son and be safe out there, I'll be praying for both of y'all."

"I love you too mama, I'll be over there to see you soon."

"Bye-bye."

"Bye."

Finishing the conversation he jumped in his Dodge Challenger and started towards 'Ernie's'. While en route he received a cancellation from Zo, stating that they would have to get together later because he had to take his mother to the emergency room.

After greeting with hugs and being seated, Zeh'Shon informed Bo of the situation at hand. Since Jai'Myiah was Bo's baby sister, he was down to ride, and couldn't wait to find this dude to whom all fingers were pointing to. Zeh'Shon considered his own thoughts of revenge to be wicked, but Bo's demented mind was on another level. Severe retribution would be an understatement to narrate his plans.

After the meal was complete, the brothers-in-law decided to hang out a while longer. They rode around East Oakland shooting the breeze and stopping from time to time to tend to business. Omari blew up Zeh'Shon's phone like a suicidal bomber, but not once did he acknowledge her. His mind had become one dimensional and little else mattered at the moment. A bit after night fall, Zo phoned in.

"What's up wit it?" answered Zeh'Shon.

"Shit, shit, chillin', what's up wit the kid?"

"In East Oakland fuckin' around. What's up wit moms? She aiight?"

"Nigga let me tell you, I'm at the hospital, and she act like her visit is G-14 classified and wouldn't tell me why she was there. So I'm sittin' in the waitin' room bored, lookin' through the magazines in shit when they call her name. So you know me, I'm hella nosey. I follow behind her without her knowing and overhear her and the receptionist talking. Nigga come to find out she was there to take a pregnancy test."

Zeh'Shon busted up laughing at his hilarious friend. "Swear?" he asked tight cheeked.

"I swear, my stomach is still rumblin' as we speak, cause the thought alone makes me weak. Moms is old as dirt, hopefully

A Hutlaz Dream

that test come back negative with a capital 'N'. I don't know why she even asked me to be the one to take her, she knew I was going to have hella jokes. The cold part is the tests don't come back for two days. I didn't think moms would still be humping, so I asked her when she decided to get her groove back, and she had the nerve to say it never left. Now that's sickening. But anyways, I'm on Seminary slide thru. I'm thinkin' we should take a Vallejo trip tonight, see what's poppin'."

Zeh'Shon managed to get an, "I'm on my way," out through his chuckle. His side throbbed from laughing so hard but still managed to operate his vehicle smoothly without swerving.

They made it to Seminary in two point two seconds. Zo recommended they utilize his dope fiend rental, just in case they got out there and sparks started to fly, they didnt want anyone writing their licenses plates down and anything getting back to them. The smoker agreed to let Zo borrow the 1994 Astro minivan for the night in exchange for a gram of crack.

After getting in and letting down all the windows for ventilation due to the foul stench of stale cigarettes that permeated the car's interior, they picked up two youngsters from the 'Goon' squad and continued to their destination.

Cruising the I-80 freeway, they smoked a couple of blunts and shared a bottle of Remy Martin while making small talk. They were in no rush to arrive, being that is was only 10:30 p.m. The two bars that they had in mind to visit weren't scheduled to close until 2 a.m. That would give them plenty of time to get there and have a little look-see. Plus they were riding dirty, so they had to obey all state laws. With five niggas rocking dreads, they didn't want to attract any extra unwanted attention.

"I don't think this dude is going to be out here, especially knowin' that he hot. I mean y'all did just try to get at him last night," said Zeh'Shon.

"You never know," said Zo, "we got a hungry bum ass nigga on our hands. He gotta be hungry, cause come on now, from my understanding he got paid to do what he did, and he gotta be a bum for pulling that stunt and bumpin' his gums not knowing who's in ear shot. He must not have ever heard the sayin', 'whisper in the field because the corn has ears'. He seems like a broke cat and you can't stay away from home that long on limited funds."

They approached the first stop on their list for the night, parking a little ways up the street from the 'Coconut Grove'. They sent the goons to see what it looked like on the inside. Bi-Yoow, the eldest of the two had a few cousins from this city and was familiar with a number of its residents. He knew that he would run into someone on the inside that could point him in the right direction.

The remaining men sat in the car sharing their thoughts of their course of action once the guy was found. They felt optimistic about this craziness coming to a head. Above everything, Zeh'Shon needed to know the real person that was behind the play. Not even fifteen minutes has elapsed before they observed Bi-Yoow and Lil' Mason hauling ass toward the van followed by rapid gun fire. They jumped inside seconds before a barrage of bullets penetrated the passenger side of the vehicle. Zo handled the jalopy like a brand new sports car and put distance between them and the 'Coconut Grove' hurriedly.

A safe ways away, Zo pulled over.

"What the fuck happened in there?" demanded Zeh'Shon.

"Man, I go in there and see a little beezy that I know from around this way, so I go holla. I'm trying to pick the bitch brain of

A Hutlaz Dream

any info she had on this cat. I look to my left and see this nigga lil Mason's facial expression and know something 'bout to pop off. He pulled his thumper and I pulled mine out. He let one loose, and then it seemed like the whole place pulled out so we jetted," claimed Bi-Yoow.

"Nigga, this what happened," started lil Mason as he waved his hand in the air, "I see a couple of bootsy lookin' cats by the door rockin' hella fake ass jewels, so I walk up and ask if they know how to get in touch wit a nigga name Kleezy. Hearing the name, one of the dudes starts jumping bad and lifted up his shirt showin' that he was strapped, talkin' 'bout 'That's my cousin, what the fuck you lookin fa him for?' So I turned and acted like I was 'bout to walk off but was really reaching for my pistol. I turned back and said, 'ohh yeah tell him this', and blasted the nigga, and then we had to scoot."

"Y'all little hyphy niggas is crazy" said Zo laughing.

"Shit, I aint crazy, I just felt as though if we put a little action behind our words these dudes will know we serious in our hunt," said lil Mason.

Dirty Rome called earlier giving Zo the address to one of Kleezy's auntie's house that he was known to frequent in the Crest, so they decided to head that way. Even with the van being riddled with bullet holes, that didn't seem to concern them in the least, they were like vampires thirsty for blood and the night was young.

The Crest was as dead at that hour. Making a left on Amellia St, they found the house on the right side. A few lights were on, therefore they figured someone was home. Instead of knocking on the door and asking questions, Zeh'Shon stepped out and shot up the house, his message was sure to arrive sooner that way. Letting it be known to Kleezy that the catastrophe he caused was unacceptable and retribution was ordered.

Twenty or so bullets invaded the home, before Zo once again put his driving skills to use and got them away safely. They found out there were no police in the area with the information on the portable police scanner. He hopped on the freeway heading west bound on the interstate. Making it back to Oakland in one piece the crew dispersed, each going his own way. Zeh'Shon headed home, figuring that there was nothing beneficial in the streets for him at this hour and didn't feel like hanging out.

Chapter 12

Kleezy was hiding out in the notorious 'Acorn' section of West Oakland, in his cousin's apartment on 10th and Filbert. He decided to go around the corner to the 24-hour McDonalds and grab a late night bite since his cousin was a young bachelor and had nothing to snack on. When the Mexican worker opened the window to hand him his order, he said.

"Ay, hook me up with a couple of them apple pies,"

"I can't do that. I don't want to get in trouble," she said evenly.

"Damn bitch, you act like you got stock in this place or somethin', I just asked for an apple pie not the register. Oh, low budget, minimum wage getting ass bitch, you need to quit this shit and come jump on the team." There was no team, but he just loved throwing words out there to portray himself as something he never was. He made sure his best friend Nina Ross's position was accessible (Nina Ross was the name he'd given his gun) in case he had to defend himself against a potential robber before pulling off.

As if he hadn't eaten at all that day, he stuffed fresh out of the grease French fries in his mouth. A couple fell between his legs in the process. Not wanting a stain to form on his new designer jeans, he attempted to fish them out as quickly as possible and was unaware that in the course of his search, he cruised right through a red light. 'Oakland's Finest', which had been parked in the cuts, turned on its siren instantly.

"Aww fuck!" yelled Kleezy. He threw 'Nina' under the seat with speed and cruised a couple more yards before electing to pull over. Not being from Oakland, he decided against taking them on a high speed pursuit. He figured that if he'd just talked to these dick heads like he had a little sense, he wouldn't be detained for too long. He would soon find out that Oakland police must not have graduated from the same academy as neighboring counties, because they didn't play fair at all.

As blueberries and cherries danced from the roof of the police car, a stern voice exploded from the cruiser's bull horn.

"Turn off the car's engine, now!" Kleezy had no choice but to comply.

"License and registration," demanded officer Small from the window. Handing over the paperwork, Kleezy began to sweat like a heathen in a Baptist church. He didn't understand why, maybe it was the officer's voice that had shaken him or maybe it was the squeak of the combat boots as they neared him. After what seemed like an hour, but was only roughly 10 minutes, Kleezy noticed a second cruiser pulling up in his rearview mirror.

"What's going on?" he said aloud. "This can't be good." He thought of turning the key and making a run for it, but as quickly as the thought entered his mind, it vanished upon seeing officer Small and another officer approaching the car with their hands positioned on their holsters. Officer Small neared the driver's window while his partner took the passenger side.

"Step out of the vehicle," said Small.

"Officer, what seems to be the problem?" asked a fearful Kleezy.

"Get the fuck out the car!" Small demanded drawing his weapon.   Pausing for only a mili-second, Kleezy reluctantly submerged and assumed the position to be patted down.

A Hutlaz Dream

When the officer got to his pants pocket, he came across a tiny bankroll and relieved him of a few small bills. "Bingo," shouted Officer Brown after retrieving the 'tucked' pistol from underneath the passenger seat while searching the car.

"What 'cha got there partner?" asked Small, fully aware of the object being a gun.

"Looks to be a 9mm, full clip, one in the chamber," said Brown.

"Looks as if you'll be taking a trip to Santa Rita tonight buddy. Hopefully this doesn't interfere with your plans," Small stated sarcastically.

Kleezy was cuffed and placed in the back seat of the patrol car. He was almost sad enough to shed a few tears, but he held them back. Racking his brain and trying to think of who he could call on to put up money for his bail before his fingerprints came back caused a pain to form in the back of his head. He knew that if he sat in jail too long, he'd be through, fucked with no lubricant.

He'd used that gun in a number of different small heists and knew that as soon as forensics evidence was matched to the serial numbers, he would most definitely be sent up shits creek without a paddle.

After the photo and fingerprinting process was complete, Kleezy was placed in a 6 x 8 cell with a phone that had no cord. In order to make a call, he would have to bend down and place his ear to the wall mounted device. Since everybody he knew had a collect block, he was flustered. The phone made free local calls, but he drew a blank when it came to remembering any for his Oakland associates. He cursed himself for just storing numbers without first memorizing them.

"Williams, follow me," said an Alameda county sheriff's deputy. Upon entering the inmate dressing room, Kleezy was forced to remove his clothing and squat and cough. He was so humiliated that a lonely tear cascaded down his left cheek, which he wiped away before turning back around and facing the deputy once again. After inspection, he was thrown a bag of jail clothes and told to dress. His original clothes were placed in a bag with his name on the front and taken to a back room to be stored until his release.

His skin began to crawl as he held up the pair of dingy briefs that he was prearranged to wear. It looked as though the person who'd worn them before him had literally taken a dump in them instead of the lavatory. He closed his eyes, sucked down a gulp of sour air and dressed.

He was then lead through the outside recreation yard to his housing unit. Being that the booking process took a while to complete, it was roughly four in the morning and other than the seagull soaring over head, the large space was relatively quiet. He thought everybody would be sound asleep at that time, but was mistaken. As he entered the pod he heard loud chatter accompanied with laughter bouncing through the dormitory as if this was where the real party was being held. Not knowing that the inmates had received commissary the previous night, they were wide eyed and amped off multiple coffee shots.

The unit consisted of a large day room with an opened area for eating, a couple dozen metal tables with the built in seats were scattered throughout the rest of the room. Two small televisions held a spot on each side of the unit, and six cages holding up to 28 men in each were in rows, three on the bottom and three on the top tier.

As Kleezy entered the unit, all talking ceased. It was as if Barrack Obama himself had entered the room with news that

A Hutlaz Dream

everyone was to be released post haste. All eyes were on him as the population looked on to see the new arrival.

He was given his designated bed location and made it there quickly. Since he had never been jailed, he knew not what to expect. After making his bed, he layed down, but refused to shut his eyes. All the horror stories he'd heard, he'd be damned if he let a man catch him slipping and try to snatch his manhood. 'No buddy', he thought to himself, he'd be ready.

Chapter 13

BA-BING...DING, went the store's bell, alerting Wanda of a customer.

"Good morning, Kendora, how are you doing? Up and at 'em early aren't you?"

"Girl yes, I'm blessed. How are you holding up?"

"I'm hanging in there."

"Well I just want you to know that Jai'Myiah is in me and my family's prayers."

"Thank you so much, I really appreciate it."

"Listen, when you have time read Mark 11:24, it says 'Everything you ask for in prayer will be yours, only if you have faith." Kendora went around the store and picked up little knick knacks and returned to the counter to pay. "You know I would love for you to visit my church home some time. Here's my number, give me a call when you would like to come, we can ride together." Kendora handed over a piece of paper with her number along with the money to pay for her items.

"I would love that, thank you."

"Have a wonderful day, and be blessed."

"You do the same," Wanda replied. Just as the door was closing following Kendora's exit the phone rang.

"Hello."

A Hutlaz Dream

"Wanda get down to this hospital now." screamed Niki excitedly, "Girl a miracle just happened." Already reading into what was being said Wanda dropped her phone and got on her knees, thanking God for answering her prayers. She closed the store and rushed to Kaiser like a freed bird, all the while dialing her kids and telling them where to meet her.

In the meantime...

Zeh'Shon was home asleep having a very exciting dream. He was a male gigolo, and made money in the adult entertainment industry. Beyonce and Ciara were the biggest customers on his roster, but he didn't discriminate, all money was good money to him in that lifestyle. He was in a fancy hotel room with Ciara, giving her more than her money's worth, but had just gotten off the line with an irate Jay-Z, threatening his career and life if he didn't stay away from his wife. After a quick laugh at the threats, he ended the phone call. He kicked his feet up on the thick mattress and blew out a cloud of smoke from a Gurkha Black Dragon cigar when suddenly there was a knock at the door. On first thought, Zeh'Shon figured it to be Jay-Z coming with his hit men. He grabbed his gun and opened the door. To his surprise, it was Future looking for his baby mama chick. Right as the action was about to take place, his house phone rang rousing him.

"Who is this?" he asked rudely into the phone without first checking the caller I.D. It was 9:17 am and the sun was peeking through his bedroom blinds.

"This is yo mama boy, that's who, get your butt up and get to this hospital, your wife wants to see you," Niki ordered.

"My wife?" Zeh'Shon repeated in shock.

"Yes your wife, or did you forget you got married?" Niki asked, her voice filled with sarcasm. "Now hurry up baby, and come and see God's miracle for yourself."

Zeh'Shon was speechless and frozen in confusion. His mouth was sand dry as it hung to his chest. Niki was overly excited with joy and choose not to hold a silent phone, so she disconnected. When Zeh'Shon came to, he made a mad dash to the bathroom to wash his face and brush his teeth. He rushed to the door so fast and stopped in mid stride, remembering that he didn't put on any shoes. He eyed a pair flip flops by the door and slid into them.

He got to the hospital in twenty minutes flat. Riding in the car pool lane, he paid no attention to the law stating that there had to be two or more passengers per car to drive that lane. He had tunnel vision and all he saw at that moment was his wife's gorgeous eyes.

Pulling up to the hospital's emergency entrance, he stopped his car, jumped out and left it right in there as if Kaiser had curb service. Bypassing the elevator doors, he opted for the stair well, which he took three at a time. He ran the long halls like a mad man in search of the door number once reaching the right floor.

Zeh'Shon's water rapids began cascading down his cheeks as soon as he entered the room. Everyone from their immediate family was in attendance. He was the last to arrive but that didn't concern him. He was just thankful to see Jai'Myiah so full of life again. The last he saw of her was disheartening and he honestly hadn't thought she would survive the battle. When Jai'Myiah saw Zeh'Shon's water works, hers began to run as well.

"Come on y'all," Wanda said to the bunch, "let's let these kids get a minute to themselves. And I do mean a minute." She

A Hutlaz Dream

nudged Zeh'Shon with a heartwarming look, "because we all want to visit." Smiling, she exited as the others followed suit.

 Zeh'Shon inched closer to the bed and just stood there staring. A million things went through his mind, but he couldn't seem to formulate a single word. Grabbing a soft hold of her hand he managed to utter,

 "I love you, Jai'Myiah." Through an extra raspy voice Jai'Myiah responded, "I love you, more." It pained her to speak. Being that she hadn't spoken a word in months, she felt like she needed lubricant for her voice box.

 Fifteen minutes passed as they remained in the same position, quietly enjoying the sight of one another. Wanda finally barged into the room asking if the rest of the family could now come in. Given the green light, Wanda went and rounded up the troops. They were all gathered, laughing and joking when a voice blew over the intercom.

 "Will the owner of a burgundy two door Lexus SC 430 with the license plates H-8-M-E-N-O-W, please move your vehicle from the front entrance immediately, or it will be towed."

 "Ohh shit," exclaimed Zeh'Shon. Catching his mother's eye as soon as the curse word escaped his mouth, he cleared it up. "I mean shoot, sorry mama. I forgot, I just stopped and hopped out, let me go move it."

 "I'll do it," said Jolisa as she snatched the keys and ran out the door before anyone had time to protest.

 She was so excited to drive her sister's car for the first time, because prior to this incident Jai'Myiah acted funny with her wheels, not even letting Zeh'Shon drive.

 "You better have not had my car all around East Oakland, neither." whispered Jai'Myiah's warning, managing a slight smile.

"Girl, you know I don't be in your car, I just drove it up here so you could ride home in your own shit," he said lying through his teeth, since he had driven her whip on numerous occasions. Not that he didn't have plenty of his own toys to choose from, but for some reason he liked the feel of a coupe. It had more get up and go than his big bodies. His next big purchase he thought to himself was going to be a Maserati.

For a few hours the family shared laughs, memories, and praised God for His mercy before leaving, all going their separate ways. They were cheerful that Jai'Myiah pulled through but were starting to get restless in those cramped quarters. Zeh'Shon was the only one to remain, as he vowed to never leave her side again.

They kicked back, enjoying each other's company while the television played. There was so much on Zeh'Shon's mind that he wanted to get off, but chose to keep it to himself until the time was right. His concentration was still cloudy being that there were still questions that remained unanswered. Jai'Myiah had just come out of a coma, and he didn't want to overload her brain with extra drama. Plus, he was pretty sure that she had enough on her brain at the moment.

In between viewing Judge Mathis re-runs, Jai'Myiah's nurse came in with her medication, Nurse Riggins is what her name tag read. She held hood rat chacteristics, and just because she had a good job, it didn't change her character. Zeh'Shon saw ratchetness all in her face when she sauntered through the threshold. She had a body like 'Black Cyna', wearing a pair of pink and gray Old Navy hospital scrubs that were so tight one would wonder how she used the restroom through her shift's period. The bottoms were so snug that if she were to pass gas she probably would have busted the entire seam. The pink and gray Nike Shox she wore went well with the ensemble, as well as her small silver hoop earrings and Tiffany

A Hutlaz Dream

necklace. Her hairstyle was similar to that of Beyonce in her "Drunk in Love" video. The golden highlights complemented her bronze skin favorably.

"How are you doing today Mrs. Banks?" said nurse Riggins. Jai'Myiah gave the lady the thumbs up sign rather than a vocal response. She really didn't care for the woman for a reason she couldn't place her finger on, the woman just wasn't her type of people. The nurse walked around with her nose in the air, which Jai'Myiah didn't fault her for, being that she did also, but Riggins just took conceit to a whole new level.

"Hello, I'm Leeanna Riggins, Jai'Myiah's nurse," she said extending her hand, "you must be a relative, brother, cousin?" she asked seductively.

'Ohh no this hoe didn't', thought Jai'Myiah.

"I'm actually Mr. Banks, Mrs. Banks husband. Nice to meet you," said Zeh'Shon with a sly grin on his face. He had rained on her potential parade instantly, amused with seeing the once lustful stare turn into disappointment.

"Ohh okay, I just assumed you were a brother or cousin since I've never seen you here before today," she stated, trying to start a conflict on the under. Zeh'Shon didn't reply, only looked at her like he wanted to slap fire from her for trying that slick shit.

Carrying on with her task, she changed Jai'Myiah's IV bag, took her blood pressure, dispensed her pills, and jotted down information read on the various machines before heading out.

"Nice meeting you, Mr. Banks. Mrs. Banks, I'll be back with your lunch shortly," Riggins said as she sashayed out of the room, switching unnecessarily hard.

The statement that the nurse made about never seeing him struck a nerve with Jai'Myiah. He could tell by the look on her face, so he spoke on the issue before it turned into one.

"Baby listen, I already know what you're thinking, you aint even gotta say it. I came up here a couple of times right after the shit went down, but seeing you hooked up to all those machines and not knowing what would be the outcome of this situation had me weak. I just couldn't stand to see you like that, it really broke me down. I mean you can ask my mama, yo' mama, I was sick for days straight," he said sincerely.

"It's okay baby, I understand," Jai'Myiah muttered.

She understood that men and women were completely different at every stand point. She knew that if the tables were turned she would've been at that hospital for days on end, it wouldn't have mattered if he was laying with half of his face missing and hooked up to a gazillion machines, as long as he had a heart beat she'd be right by his side, full of hope.

The pain medication started working wonders and a half hour later, Jai'Myiah drifted off into a deep sleep. Zeh'Shon just stared at her; she was still beautiful to him. The gauze that the doctors once had wrapped in layers around her head was absent and the swelling had vanished. She looked almost as normal as she had before the shooting, except she had lost a tremendous amount of weight. Her face was slimmer and her eyes held a darker pigment around them. Her eye sockets had sunk in to some extent and her right ear held a small contusion and needed minor reconstructive surgery, but nothing that time was unable to heal.

The last time that he'd laid eyes on his wife saddened his heart to see her in that state. He honestly thought that she was at the point of no return. But now with the vision of her there in that bed breathing and in living color, he vowed that from that day forth, he was going to do anything and everything to protect her from any danger. He would be on her so hard she wouldn't much less snag a finger nail without him around with clippers.

A Hutlaz Dream

Becoming tired with all the day's activities Zeh'Shon got as comfortable as possible on the pull out recliner stationed in the room and just stared at her. Studying her brought a sense of contentment over him. From that moment on, he decided to cut all of his extracurricular activities and be monogamous for once. The chicks on the side had to go, they'd all served their purposes and their services weren't needed any longer.

His money was up. He'd clearly defeated the odds and surpassed the two million plus mark. The game had truly been good to him, in the sense of seeing the fruits of his labor. He felt it was just time to walk away from it all, and fly right. The obstacle that he'd just encountered and swept under his feet had been a major eye opener. All he wanted from that moment forth was to be a husband to his wife, time to square up and do the right thing. His gazed never left her as he thought back.

February 8, 2008

"Baby, what you doin'? I have a surprise for you," said Zeh'Shon through his cell while driving.

"I'm actually at the store going over the books, what you up to?" replied Jai'Myiah.

"How long is that going to take?"

"About ten or fifteen minutes, I'm almost done."

"Alright, I'm coming to get you to take a ride with me."

"Ohh Lord Zeh', what are you up to now?"

"You'll see!" CLICK.

"I hate it when he does that," said Jai'Myiah out loud.

"Does what, baby?" Wanda spoke, entering the office with a box of supplies.

"Just hang up without saying good-bye."

"You want me to check him for you?" Wanda smiled.

"No mama, I got him. I'm about to leave for the day, you could hold it down by yourself, right?"

"I know you didn't just ask me that. Girl, I'm the one that gave you all the game you got, you better check ya self."

"Okay miss lady. Well, I'll see you tomorrow. If you talk to Bo tell him I need him to change the light bulb in the front of the store for me."

"Bye, baby. I'll tell his little lazy butt, but you might have to run that one by my future son-in-law," She said jokingly as they embraced in a hug before parting.

As Jai'Myiah exited the store Zeh'Shon was already parked and waiting. Anxious to know, she got in and rushed him with inquiries.

"So what's the BIG surprise?

"Don't start with the 21 questions, baby girl. Just kick back and ride," he said turning up the radio and let Plies 'Bust it Baby', play.

Jai'Myiah relaxed in the seat. From time to time, she liked to let him feel like he was 'the man', and that he ran more than his mouth.

So she laid back, rolled herself a blunt, and let the 'purp' take her away.

They had been on the road for twenty minutes and had jumped freeways from 580 to 24 to 680 and Jai'Myiah's curiosity was getting the best of her once again.

"Baby, wh--," she started to ask, but was rudely cut off by Zeh'Shon placing his index to his lips shushing her.

Five minutes after taking a Concord exit, they pulled up at a two story house that wasn't brand new, but wasn't old and decrepit either. The neighborhood was decent, a far cry from those

A Hutlaz Dream

being in the Oakland city limits. Two kids rode bicycles with the proper safety gear, a helmet and knee pads, which were unheard of in the 'hood'. You could be driving down the street and see a miniature two foot child driving an adult 10 speed, standing on the pedal because if they were to sit their legs wouldn't be long enough to pump.

Zeh'Shon pulled up in the driveway and killed the engine. Jai'Myiah was truly concerned now. If Zeh'Shon had her accompany him for a ride of 'business,' he would've left the car running and made the transaction speedy.

"Zeh'Shon, whose house do you have me at?" Jai'Myiah demanded at this point. Zeh'Shon, smiling harder than a kid on Christmas, replied, "Ours."

"Ours?" she took a second to let the word register. "OHH MY GOD, AHHHH!" she screamed.

She jumped out of the car while snatching the keys at the same time. She made a mad dash for the door and made it through with ease. The staircase was the first thing she saw, so she made a run for it. She moved from room to room like a child possessed. Of each of the four bedrooms, she already had perceived what each space would hold. The master bedroom would belong to them; there would be a guest room, a computer room, and an exercise room. Her body was already immaculate, but a tone up wouldn't kill her.

Zeh'Shon made it up the steps as Jai'Myiah was entering a room on the left. Stopping at the window to take in the huge back yard equipped with a swimming pool and Jacuzzi, Zeh'Shon wrapped his arms around her slim waist.

"You like it?" he asked rhetorically.

"Like it? Baby I love it... Thank you so much."

They shared a deep kiss and a hug before Zeh'Shon suggested they check out the house's lower half. They looked from the living room to the family room and the den before entering the kitchen. There on the counter sat a small navy blue velvet jewelry box. She reached out of curiosity then proceeded to open it. Her eyes grew as big as quarters during the view of its contents. She looked up at Zeh'Shon who was now standing directly in front of her, with a look of question.

"Baby girl, will you be my wife?" Jai'Myiah, overwhelmed with joy, let the tears build up in her eyes before answering.

"Yes, baby."

Hunger pains jolting him from his reverie, Zeh'Shon decided to take a trip to the cafeteria to see what was edible on the menu. As he journeyed through the halls, he held his breath as much as possible. For some reason hospitals always smelled like death to him. The pale colors and gloomy looks of people that came and went were nauseating. He couldn't wait to get his wife out of there.

Noticing the string on the left shoe of his new Lebrons was loose he bent down to tie them. As he stood up to his full height, nurse Leeanna Riggins bumped into him purposely.

"Excuse me, I didn't notice you there. I was too busy going over my patient's charts," she lied.

"No problem," he said, "Do you mind telling me where the cafeteria located?"

"Not at all, matter fact I'll show you myself."

The two got on the elevator and she pressed the number 3 button. Zeh'Shon stood in the corner as Leeanna stood directly in front of the doors. He couldn't help but stare at her sensuous derriere. He was a man and just looking, and figured no harm, no foul. As they exited the elevator and entered the cafeteria, Zeh'Shon noticed that Leeanna had put a little extra in her stride. Her back side looked like two basketballs were battling.

"You should try the lasagna, it's hella good." she said as they stood at the counter.

"I aint in the mood for that," he stated as he looked the menu over, "I'ma try the teriyaki chicken bowl," he said to the cashier, "and a large drink." he was reaching in his pocket when Leeanna stopped him.

"I got you," she said before directing her words towards the cashier, "I'll take a chef's salad with no onion and ranch dressing." She flashed her badge for the employee discount before tucking it back in her bra.

"That'll be $8.87," said the cashier.

Zeh'Shon moved out of the way to let her pay since she offered. Where he was from he was taught to turn down nothing but his collar and he lived by that. He grabbed his tray and went to find an available seat in the rear of the room. As soon as he sat down, he found that Leeanna was hot on his heels. Taking a seat across from him she said,

"So how long have you been married?" Zeh'Shon felt as if he had psychic capabilities because he had seen this conversation coming a mile away.

"A few months."

"You faithful?" she asked, being straight forward and very direct.

"Yep," he replied straight to the point.

"Aww, that's too bad," she placed a cherry tomato in her mouth seductively. She then pulled a piece of paper out of nowhere with her name and number scribbled on it.

"If you ever have a problem or need marriage counseling, give me a call," she said before walking off leaving her barely eaten salad.

'Damn,' thought Zeh'Shon, 'from the trap house, crack house, church house, to the sick house, these hoes don't quit.'

He got up to dump his tray after finishing his meal, which was surprisingly quite appetizing. He left the paper holding the number and disposed of it all. He was done dealing with all these random chicks, he vowed to be committed to Jai'Myiah, she at least deserved that.

On the way back to the room, he noticed Leeanna by the nurses' station, eyeing him like a hungry tiger that had just marked her prey. He quickly looked away and put a little pep in his stride. Entering the room, he noticed Jai'Myiah sleeping soundly, so he sat down on his 'bed', and wrapped up in the extra thin blanket that he had been given from housekeeping.

Around 2 a.m., Jai'Myiah awoke suddenly after a bad dream, only to see the love of her life still by her side. She felt instant relief and fell back under.

Chapter 14

Mid-afternoon the next day, Zeh'Shon made a run to JJ's Fish and Chips to pick up Jai'Myiah's favorite, fried oyster and prawn platter, and ordered himself a catfish and chicken plate. When he returned with the orders, he walked in on nurse Riggins fulfilling her daily duties.

As Zeh'Shon placed the food on the table, he heard a light snicker come from Leeanna, but paid her no mind. Jai'Myiah looked from the nurse to her husband, sensing that something was up. Being that for 1, the two didn't exchange pleasantries, and 2, Zeh'Shon hadn't turned from facing the table since he entered the room. Not one to cause a scene, Jai'Myiah decided to wait until the tramp left before checking her man.

As Leeanna gathered her bearings and exited, Zeh'Shon held up the corner wall, looking suspicious so Jai'Myiah started right in.

"So what the fuck is up with you and this bitch?"

"Not a muthafuckin' thang. The bitch tried to pop at me yesterday in the cafeteria, but I shut her ass down quick, told her I was happily married to you. So now I guess the broad is jaded," he said before popping a catfish nugget in his mouth and walking over to place his wife's food on her sliding tray, and wheeling it over to her.

"Well, I don't want that hoe being my nurse anymore. When you're finished eating can you go and have her assigned to another patient? 'Cause I don't want her trying to get me out the way by upping my dosage or poisoning me or some shit."

"I got you baby, but I wish that bitch would try some smirkish shit like that, it wouldn't be wise." He said adding hot sauce to his meal, "Baby I've been meaning to tell you this, I promise you don't have to worry about anything ever. I won't let anything hurt you ever again, and that's on my mama. I'm so sorry you had to go through what you just went through, I've been so messed up..."

"Shhh, baby it's okay I feel you, but you don't have to trip on what happened because I'm here, I aint dead. We're going to make it, it's me and you for forever and always!" she said reassuringly. "Now let me eat before all this good food gets cold, and you have to go back to JJ's 'cause you know I don't do the cold food thing." She smiled.

Zeh'Shon went to alert the proper people of his request for a change of nurse and also asked to see the doctor for an update. Dr. Chan met Zeh'Shon in the hallway by the reception station.

"How are you, Mr. Banks?"

"I'm great now that my wife is awake."

"Yes, indeed she's a trooper. Now, what may I help you with?"

"Well, I have two questions. The first being when do you think I'll be able to take Jai'Myiah home?"

"Well at the rate she's going, she'll be released at the end of this coming week. We just have a couple tests to do, and we also like to keep patients under two week observation just to make sure everything is copasetic."

A Hutlaz Dream

"Okay, that's good news. Now my second question is when do you think it would be okay to have her start walking about?"

"That's a great question. When she is released, she will have to undergo several sessions of physical therapy. It would be good if you would help her stand up and maybe help with a few baby steps at a time. She'll probably be in a bunch of pain due to the fact that she hasn't walked in months, so don't walk her too much. Perhaps a few steps a day, just until she gets back into the swing of things, but make sure you are close enough to catch her if she falls."

"Okay Doc, good lookin', I mean thanks."

"You're truly welcomed. Good luck to the both of you," sung Dr. Chan before walking off and disappearing into a room.

"Baby," said Zeh'Shon getting back into the room. "What's up moms," he said, noticing Wanda sitting on the edge of Jai'Myiah's bed. She must have gotten there as soon as he went down the hall.

"Hey Zeh,'" said Wanda.

"What's up babe?" said Jai'Myiah.

"I got some good news," he said running down the information as it was explicated to him.

"That's wonderful," said Wanda.

"So baby what's up, you ready to take that first walk?"

Jai'Myiah was more than willing to try her old legs out. She was ready to become independent once again. She was tired of having to require a nurse to come and sponge her body and empty her bed pan. he was embarrassed and thought of that job as being truly gross. She could've never been a nurse.

"Yeah, I'm ready, but y'all gotta help me, it feels like I've been laying in this bed for an entire year." She smiled.

Zeh'Shon and Wanda rushed over, each taking a different side of the bed and helped lift her into a sitting position. Jai'Myiah's body hurt like hell to be moved in this manner, but she was a soldier and this had to be done if she wanted to live ordinarily. Zeh'Shon moved her around and gently eased her legs to the ground. Once that was done, he placed his hands under her arms and helped her to her feet, as Wanda held the various machine cords making sure they didn't tangle. Jai'Myiah let out a light whimper.

"You okay babe? You don't have to do this right now, we can just try again another day."

"No I'm alright," she lied. She was in a considerable amount of pain but kept her game face on. She took one step than the next, placing one foot in front of the other. Zariah came in unexpected, with a clap that threw off her concentration on the fifth step. She lost her footing, then stumbled. Zeh'Shon decided that was enough for the day and carried her back to her bed.

"You did great baby," Zeh'Shon whispered in her ear and then kissed her cheek, she smiled.

"Hey moms, what's up?" Zariah said directing her attention to Zeh'Shon and Wanda.

"Hey baby," said Wanda.

"What's up, sis?"

"Nothing much, just came to check on my best friend with her beautiful self," she replied.

"Baby I'm 'bout to shoot to the house and change right quick, and get in the shower. I'll be back in a couple hours, if that's okay with you."

"Yeah I'm fine, go ahead, I'll see you in a little bit." Zeh'Shon gave her a peck and left.

A Hutlaz Dream

He turned on his cell phone and got situated in the car before pulling off. His cellular rang and it was none other than Omari. At first he wasn't going to answer it, but thought he should so he could put an end to their dealings.

"Yeah."

"Daddy, where have you been all this time? I'm getting tired of you pulling all of these disappearing acts," she said in a child's tone of voice.

"Check this, we're going to have to end this little relationship or whatever you want to call it, 'cause shit just ain't working out. So whatever I got at your spot of mine keep it or throw it away, I don't give a fuck. I'm cool on you." 'Not this again' she thought. Right when she was running home from third base, he wants to stop her game plan.

"But why daddy, I got some money for you," she pleaded.

"I don't care about them crumbs, bitch, I'm cool!" Zeh'Shon shouted then hung up.

He then decided to check on his boy to make sure everything was good and to inform him of Jai'Myiah's miracle. The conversation didn't last long at all, because Zeh'Shon wasn't in the talk mood so he hung up and drove home.

Meanwhile in the hospital room...

Zariah, Jai'Myiah and Wanda all sat around and reminisced on the olden days. The few happy moments that they had were worth the look back, even though they were few and far between.

"Ms. Wanda, remember when we was at the Christmas party at your parents' house and everybody was doing the electric slide and you busted out with the chicken head and A-Town stomp? Everybody stopped sliding and watched you get down on the floor," asked Zariah. They all laughed.

"Yeah I remember that, but do you remember when I was staring out of the living room window, peeking at the block's activities and you came busting through the front door? You came in and locked all the locks, jumped in the laundry basket, and covered yourself with dirty clothes. Talkin' 'bout Muhammad was chasing you from the corner store, 'cause you stole some skittles and a Slim Jim?" They all laughed again.

"Well y'all, I had a long day. I think I'm going to mosey on down the road and catch a couple hours of sleep. Tomorrow will be here before I know it," said Wanda, "I love y'all. I'll be back tomorrow evening."

"Love you, too," they said in unison. As soon as Wanda was out of ear shot Zariah began.

"Bitch, Lonnie just got out and he been lookin' for you." Lonnie was Jai'Myiah's first love, before meeting Zeh'Shon, but she ended it with him after he put hands on her during a heated argument. The disagreement was over a female that he'd gotten caught with at the back of Arroyo Park, with his pants down. Weeks after that incident he got indicted on federal gun charges, and sentenced to seven years.

"What he lookin' for me for? I am a happily married woman," said Jai'Myiah holding up her left hand and admiring her wedding ring.

"Girl, word around town is that you're his bitch for life, and he don't care anything about your husband, because he'll kill for his."

"That nigga ain't crazy, he might be a little slow, but naw he ain't crazy enough to go up against Zeh'Shon."

A Hutlaz Dream

"I feel the same way girl, but I just wanted to give you a head's up."

"Good lookin'. Ohh yeah, and I'ma need you to do your homework on a bitch named Leeanna Riggins, she's from South Richmond. The bitch works here, but had the nerve to try to get at my nigga, thinkin' it would be on the under. I ain't having that shit. When I get out this hospital bed, ain't go be no more drama with these broads, straight up."

"Alright, I'm on it."

The talk lasted a bit longer, and Zeh'Shon made it back right before Jai'Myiah's medication kicked in and she fell asleep.

Over the next few days Jai'Myiah's walking had improved and her pain subsided. She was to the point that she could walk the length of the hallway, non-stop. With the fast improvements she made, she was due to get released the following day. She wasn't totally healed, but she was somewhat feeling like her old self again. Minute pain sometimes surfaced, but nothing a Motrin tablet couldn't comfort. She was ready to get discharged and back to her beautiful house.

Zeh'Shon orchestrated a beautiful welcome home gathering for his lady, which consisted of only family and close friends. He went all out. He'd hired a florist, two maids and three chefs. Niki and Wanda insisted on helping cook, but Zeh'Shon told them to kick back and enjoy themselves. Jai'Myiah was ecstatic and everyone had a blast.

ZehShon's phone steadily buzzed off the hook with Omari's name on the I.D. When the battery finally died, he let it remain uncharged because he didn't have time to go back and forth with a desperate slut that didn't know how to let go. Two days later, Jai'Myiah started her physical therapy classes and her husband was with her every step of the way. They were happy for the first time in a long time.

Chapter 15

Three weeks had passed and Kleezy was still stuck in Santa Rita. Out of all the so-called 'friends' he had on the streets, wouldn't none of them put two cents together and help him with bail, or even accept a measly collect call for that matter. He was upset that the people he grew up and broke bread with turned their backs as if he were dead and gone. He told himself that whenever he touched down, he had something for their asses.

Kleezy's charge was possession of a loaded illegal firearm which he was informed by the 'jail house lawyers,' that the feds may pick up since the gun was registered to another state. The thought of the feds indicting him scared him shitless, but he refused to show the emotions on his face and let the entire unit see him for the coward that he really was.

He mingled with the dozens of inmates who were also housed in unit 23. He found out that jail wasn't really like all the war stories that he had heard that had terrified him in his younger years. For the most part it was these stories that steered him away from leading a life of crime. He was also happy that no one knew him, since he was from another county, or so he thought.

While Kleezy was at the spades table gambling for commissary with three OG dudes, K.B and D-rock were positioned by the vending machines engrossed in conversation.

"You see that nigga right there?" D-rock said pointing towards the card players, "The tall light skinned cat?"

"Yeah, what about him?" asked K.B.

"Rumor has it that he's the nigga that shot up Zeh'Shon's wedding."

K.B was Zeh'Shon's younger cousin by four years, he had been housed in Santa Rita for the past 3 1/2 years fighting a murder beef. He had heard about Zeh'Shon's mishap and he was terribly upset that he wasn't out on the streets to help avenge the person responsible. Zeh'Shon was K.B's favorite cousin, well favorite person in the world to be honest. He was the only one that looked out for K.B from the outside world, making sure his lawyer fees were paid and his books stacked. Zeh'Shon had always believed the saying 'visitors make prisoners', so he didn't visit. He sent a couple cute rippers up there from time to time to flash his little cousin a thigh and a titty or something. He also stayed behind a camera's lens and flicked it up to show his cousin how he was living.

Never in a million years would K.B have thought that he would be lucky enough to be graced with Kleezy's presence.

"So that's the nigga right there, huh?" said K.B while gritting his teeth.

"Yeah, but don't do nothin' 'till we lock down. We can catch that nigga slippin' in the pod. We don't want to see the nigga in the dayroom. You know these high priced baby sitters will swarm in here like flies on shit," said D-rock referring to the deputies.

"Ohh fa sho, I'm already knowin'. But on my lil bruh, Will, rest in peace, I got somethin' fa this nigga."

K.B was a small guy with a short man's build. He was 5'6", 165 lbs of muscle and swore he could beat up the world. He had a small peanut shaped head that not even a month before had held dread locks. He opted to cut them off since they weren't growing

A Hutlaz Dream

evenly. He would one day start them over, but for now he rocked a bald fade that had him resembling a brown skinned shaved bird. He did go hard in the paint, and gave anyone that chose to underestimate him a run for his money.

In the meantime at the table.

"Y'all set?" yelled Kleezy as he slammed the big joker on the table, enabling him and his partner to take their eighth book, their opponent's bid was six. "Game over," he continued to taunt while pocketing half of the commissary on the table, leaving the other half for his partner. When he too gathered his winnings, Kleezy rose from the table with a shit eating grin.

"Say youngblood, you just go leave like that? You ain't gonna give me a fair chance to win some of my candy bars back?" said the older competitor.

"Not right now OG, I'ma give you a minute to practice," laughed Kleezy, "Naw, but seriously, I'll come see you later, I have to make a few phone calls before they lock us down."

"Yeah, whatever nigga," huffed the OG, mad that he'd just lost $20 worth of canteen. Kleezy picked up the receiver and dialed his cousin's number.

"Hello," said a female voice.

"You have a collect call from 'Kleezy', an inmate at an Alameda county jail, to accept press 0." Zero was pressed, "Thank you for using evercom, your call is being connected."

"What's up cousin?" Kleezy said excitedly. He hadn't been able to get in contact with anyone since he got locked up.

"What's up?" replied the female in an aggravated tone. Not feeling her attitude but at the same time not wanting to get the dial tone, in a humbled voice Kleezy got right to the point of his call.

"Cousin, I need you."

"Tell me something new, everybody needs me."

"I'm serious. My bail is only $50,000, all I need you to do is take Bad Boys $2,500 and they'll get me out."

"Only $50,000? Well if that's the case bail yourself out, I ain't got it."

"Come on now cuz, I really need you right now."

"What happened to the $1,500 I gave you?" said the chick.

"I spent it," replied Kleezy.

"Well tough luck."

Kleezy had enough of her mouth; "Check this out, it's because of you that I'm in this muthafucka, and shooting that bitch at that wedding was worth way more than $1,500," screamed Kleezy forgetting he was on a monitored phone. "I need the rest of my issue."

"Don't call my house trying to check me. It's your dumb ass fault for holding onto that hot ass pistol. You should have gotten rid of that instantly, Einstein. You ain't got shit coming from me, 'cause I'm broke. You better call uncle Shady, we all know he banked up. Maybe he'll have pity for yo' soft ass, not me!" CLICK, the phone went dead.

"Ain't this a bitch?" Kleezy asked himself while staring at the phone in his hand not believing the conversation that had just transpired. "I got something for yo' trifflin' ass, just wait," he slammed the phone on the wall and walked to his pod.

Hours later, Kleezy was in the shower rinsing off the day's residue that filthy place ejected. Cleanliness has been his greatest attribute, so he was sure to get every crack and crevice twice, but just as he lathered his face with soap he felt a sharp pain in his lower back that broke him down to his knees. That whack, plus the sudden soap in his eyes burned massively as he tried to blink.

A Hutlaz Dream

Seconds later, he felt himself being dragged out the shower as ten or more fists plummeted his face and torso area. The beating felt as though it had lasted for hours, when in reality it was only five minutes. The avengers had departed as quickly as they emerged, like a shadow, leaving Kleezy laid out naked, bleeding profusely.

K.B stepped in the bathroom to admire the work that his folks had put in for him. Satisfied, he headed toward the phones.

"You have a collect call from..." Zeh'Shon knowing the operated instruction, pressed zero so he didn't have to sit through the entire automated spiel.

"What's up cousin?" asked Zeh'Shon.

"Ay blood, you need to come see me ASAP, it's 9-1-1," said K.B and then hung up. He wasn't too much of a phone person in jail. For one he thought of it as a stress box and he had been down for far too long to worry himself about what was going on beyond the cement walls. And two, he'd witnessed to many dumb dudes catch additional charges from running their mouths on the horn.

Zeh'Shon immediately made plans to see K.B the following day. He knew that it had to be important for him to call like that and make such a demand, knowing that he didn't do the visitation thing. K.B's tone clearly stated that Zeh'Shon's presence was required and not that of one of his flunkies.

The following morning, Zeh'Shon was up bright and early, dressing to leave for the visit when Jai'Myiah awoke.

"Good morning, where are you off to this early?" Jai'Myiah asked looking at the clock which read 6:18 am.

"Good morning sunshine, I didn't mean to wake you up, but I'm on my way to Santa Rita to visit K.B."

"Really?" Jai'Myiah asked suspiciously, she knew that he wouldn't dare go near a jail house, but she gave him the benefit of the doubt. "What's going on with him?" Zeh'Shon felt the insecure vibe in her tone.

"I'm not sure. He just called last night talkin' 'bout come see him. You wanna roll with me?"

"No thank you, tell him I said hello, those visiting lines be too long for me."

"I know that's why I'm 'bout to leave now. Hopefully, I get one of the first visits. Bye babe, be back soon," he said before tapping her lips with a kiss.

The visitation area was packed at 8:50. Luckily Zeh'Shon's visit would start at 9:20, so he didn't have much longer to go. Zeh'Shon and an older gentleman were the only men in attendance. The rest were women and children. Probably baby mamas, wives, and side chicks who came to see their loved ones on lock. With all the women, Zeh'Shon was surprised that no drama had jumped off. As soon as the thought escaped his brain cells, the uproar began.

A tall skinny model looking chick walked up on a lady that was just as beautiful, and was seated holding a baby that appeared to be at least eight months old, in her arms.

"Ain't your name Candance?" said chick 1.

"Donna, bitch you know exactly who I am so cut the crap," said chick 2.

"I know you're not up here to see my husband."

"Your husband? Yeah right," laughed Candace, "I'm visiting Rasheed so he can spend a little time with our son."

"Bitch quit lyin', that ugly ass baby ain't Rasheed's. You need to be visiting the hoe stroll to find ya real baby daddy," yelled Donna. The police rushed in and escorted Donna out since she was the only irate one. "I'ma see you in the streets, hoe," her threat echoed from the hallway.

A Hutlaz Dream

'Dumb ass bitch,' thought Zeh'Shon, 'you should have just waited to confront her in the streets in the first place. Now you won't be able to see ya man'. He smiled and shook his head, women were so predictable at times he thought, instead of understanding there was a time and place for everything, they just seemed to be driven on emotions.

What irritated him most about the wait was the amount of chicks that kept coming in his face trying to holla, knowing they were up there to visit their peoples. If it would've been a couple of months ago, he would've popped back, but was done dealing with loose women.

Zeh'Shon was in the first group to be called when visiting started. As soon as he saw K.B, he took a seat in front of him and picked up the phone.

"What's up cuz, how you doin'?" asked Zeh'Shon.

"I'm maintaining," answered K.B, "look Zeh', I know you're a busy man, and I don't want to take up too much of your time. That nigga Kleezy is up in here wit me." A sordid look engulfed Zeh'Shon's facial features and he was ready to speak but was halted by K.B holding his hand up, silently asking permission to finish his story. "Now I didn't get the full details of the story, but I got the basics. The nigga took a slip and fall in the shower last night and he's in the infirmary as we speak. But just know they'll be a banana peel by his bunk waiting for him when he gets back. My welcome committee greeted him with open arms plus the rest of the Santa Rita alumni got the run down and are on point." He spoke in code not wanting to let onto what he was really speaking about, just in case he was being recorded.

"Good looking little cousin, but this is what I need you to do, what's today, Monday?" he asked, then answered himself.

"Yeah," said K.B.

"Alright, he'll probably be in the infirmary at least another day before they bring the nigga back to the unit. I need you to let that boy know that I'll be up here on Friday to pull him out for a visit. If he ain't feeling it, let him know he don't have a choice, feel me? And shoot me a kite with the names and jail info of all the niggas that's on our team so I can bless them with a few dollars. I really appreciate this little nigga."

"Fa sho cuz, anytime. I'll get up with you later," K.B. said before placing his bald fist to the window. Zeh'Shon returned the love.

"Banister, visits over!" announced the officer.

"Suck my dick!" was all Zeh'Shon heard before hanging up his receiver.

"That little hyphy boy is off the hook." Zeh'Shon smirked as he headed for the door.

The next few days for Zeh'Shon were spent at home with Jai'Myiah, catering to her every need. She was in such a rush to get back to work, but he told her to slow down. He wanted her to rest for a few days. One of the things he loved about his wife was her ambitious nature, she always had a plan and was determined to succeed. But as of now he was not letting her out of his sight until he got to the bottom of things.

Zo came over periodically to give Zeh'Shon a cut off of their business dealings. He was a true friend, instead of cutting him out of the equation, Zo kept it lit and held him down in the streets until he got his life together. He was told to take his time and whenever he chose to come back outside to play he still had his seat at the head of the table with his partner in crime.

Zeh'Shon was enjoying the time spent with Jai'Myiah, the only thing that had him vexed through his family time was the constant buzzing of his cell phone that he kept on vibrate. Nine

A Hutlaz Dream

out of ten calls were from none other than Omari. He was tempted to change his number but decided against it since that was his main business line. She would just have to blow him up until she tired herself out.

Friday came swiftly, and Zeh'Shon was up once again at the crack of dawn, readying himself for the meeting with man he referred to as Satan. He had to have some type of demonic spirits in his head to do what he did. Zeh'Shon was not an angel in the least bit. He'd brought heat storms to niggas on plenty of occasions. Since he'd danced with the devil quite a few times, he knew evil recognized evil.

He arrived at Santa Rita and went through the same ritual of signing in and waiting until his name was called. Upon hearing his name called once again in the first group, he lagged a bit so that he could be the last in line. Since he'd never laid eyes on this Kleezy character, he wanted to make sure he was the dude to approach instead of mistaking someone else's visit. When he entered, he saw Kleezy immediately as he was the only one with a face looking like it had been hit by a Mack truck. Zeh'Shon took a deep breath and held it a moment before taking a seat. He wished there hadn't been a thick glass barrier between the two of them or he would rip this young punk's throat out with his bare hands. He told himself to be cool, he didn't want this scary cat to get up and leave. Just looking at the delinquent ran Zeh'Shon so hot that his blood boiled with hatred. He reached for the receiver, Kleezy did the same.

"Feel me on this muthafucka," stated Zeh'Shon, "this is the only chance that I'm giving you to run the information I want, and I do mean everything. You see the stitches you sporting now? Just know they could multiply, or worse, now go."

Kleezy dropped his head but managed to look up at Zeh'Shon through his one good eye. A tear emerged and ran from the one that was swollen shut. 'Aww, this soft ass nigga is a bitch', thought Zeh'Shon. "Speak, I aint got all day."

"I honestly didn't know what I was getting myself into, if I would have...."

"Fuck all that apologetic shit, get to the good part."

"My cousin called me up one day and offered me $1,500 to run up in a wedding and shoot the bride in the head. I was doing bad for a minute, so I agreed. When I asked her what she and the lady's beef were about, she claimed that she had stolen something that belonged to her, and that she had been in the way for years, but she didn't go into details." Kleezy's face was soaking at this point.

"You said your cousin? What's the person's name?" Kleezy took a deep breath. He knew he was selling out by telling on his own flesh and blood, but she obviously wasn't concerned with his wellbeing, so why should he care for hers. Plus knowing that he would possibly be down for a minute, he knew jail living would be pure hell if he didn't cooperate.

"Well the family calls her Yodi, but you might know her by Omari."

The world stopped for a second or two as Zeh'Shon's heart fluttered. 'He couldn't have said who I think he said', thought Zeh'Shon.

"Wha..wha.. what name did you just say?" stammered Zeh'Shon.

"Omari." Zeh'Shon jumped out of his seat letting the phone dangle in the air as he made his way towards the exit.

Chapter 16

Zeh'Shon left the jail house like a man crazed. He ripped down the streets and highway as if his vehicle swallowed jet fuel, getting to 80th and Olive in record time. He got up the apartment's staircase like he had R. Kelly's 'I believe I can fly' on his head, because he sure enough flew.

Not bothering looking for the house key, he gave the door a kick so hard it flew off the hinges. He went through the house shouting vulgar obscenities, his voice roared the apartment interior and echoed into the outdoors. Luckily, Omari had stepped out to pick up a few items from the grocery store, or her ass would've been grass. Zeh'Shon moved expeditiously through the residence damaging anything of value, he booted, punched and flung whatever he touched. Snapping out of his mini blackout, he snatched a photo of Omari off the mantel, rushed down the stairs and got back in the car, leaving before someone called the police.

He rolled around East Oakland, hitting all the spots she was known to frequent, including her families homes. He searched for hours to no avail. Deciding to throw the towel in on his search he did what he didn't want to do, and that was calling her phone. The only time he really wanted to hear her voice was her begging for her life under the death grip he would have around her throat.

"Hello," Omari sang intoned.

"Where the fuck you at, you punk ass bitch?"

"Huh?" she asked dumfounded.

"I'ma kill you when I see you bitch, that's on my mama." He threatened.

"Baby, what are you talking about?" she asked apprehensively.

"Kill that 'baby' bullshit bitch, I know everything and you thought you were so slick. You a dumb ass bitch. I went and seen ya folks Kleezy today." Omari's heart dropped a few inches in her chest when she heard her cousin's name. 'How did he know?' Well obviously Kleezy told him the run down, but how did he find out about her family in Vallejo?' she thought. All these years Zeh'Shon thought he knew everything, but she kept her family in Vallejo a secret just in case she had to use their services on a rainy day. Well instead of halting the rain, her own flesh and blood had brought about a storm.

"What you got to say about that?" Silence. "What Garfield got ya tongue? Bitch, you crossed the line of no return on this one. What gave you the nerve to have a man run up in my wedding ceremony and have my wife shot up? Huh? Bitch, my mama and the rest of my family were there, what if he would've hit one of them on accident? What you thought that if my wife woulda died I would have been with you? If you thought that, then you're even dumber than I gave you credit for. I would never be with you, not in this life or the next. You're a good for nothing hood rat punk bitch!" He continued to roast her as she sat quietly on the other end. "And for the record bitch, I never loved you, not even liked your faggot ass. The only reason I put up with you is cause you know how to make that cash fast, dummy. I love my wife, how you feel now? I knew you had stalker potential from the gate, I was slippin' for not payin' it too much attention, my fault. You better be glad my wife is still amongst the living because if she would've passed, I would've been on a mission at this very moment to kill

A Hutlaz Dream

your whole family, but I'm not even going to take it there, you on the other hand is one gone."

Zeh'Shon paused to take a breather. Wherever Omari was located she must've had a cup of courage juice handy, because she got a bit vocal after hearing Zeh'Shon say the word 'wife' one time too many.

"Nigga, I ain't scared of none of those empty threats your throwin', so knock it off," said Omari lying through her teeth, she was trembling but had to psych herself out. She knew that whatever he was saying to her was more than likely what he planned to do, but she continued, "Yeah, I put a hit out on the bitch. I'm just mad at myself that I didn't do the shit personally, cuz I would a given that home wrecking hoe the whole clip and aired her punk ass out. You were my man. All those years I've invested in your ass, all the money I brought and you wanna up and marry this bitch on some square shit? I don't think so, pimp! You got the game fucked up, what part of the game is that? It must have been misinterpreted to you, 'cause that ain't in the rule book. That one was too hard of pill to swallow, so I didn't even try. But check this out, I'm 'bout to get out the way for a minute, give you enough time to calm down, because I trust and believe we are going to be together one day... And ohh yeah, about that liquor store on 55th and the laundry mat on 82nd ya bitch own, you might as well close shop, cause of right now, it ain't safe."

To Zeh'Shon's surprise, the line went dead in his ear. 'No this crazy broad didn't' he thought. He drove to Jai'Myiah's store to tell Wanda to close up for a couple of days. The cat had gotten out of the bag, and they had a psycho on the loose. He was definitely going to kill Omari as soon as she wound up within arm's reach, but he knew this chick wasn't mentally stable and didn't want to risk the lives of any more of his loved ones. He stopped business at the laundry mat as well.

He headed home to share the news with his wife. He knew that she would be hurt deeply but he had no choice in the matter. This would be a sure test of her 'through thick or thin' vows, because the load he was getting ready to drop on her plate was sure enough extra thick. He prayed that his ride or die chick would remain by his side after his detrimental broadcast. If she didn't stay strong, it was for sure to put a large strain on their relationship.

On the ride home Zeh'Shon racked his brain with ways to break the facts down, but he choose to just be a man and tell her straight up since there was no way to beat around the bush.

After pulling into his driveway, he took his time getting to the door. He gasped deeply before turning the key into the lock and entering his domain. The smell of good home cooked food assaulted his nostrils, so like toucan Sam, he followed his nose to the kitchen where Jai'Myiah rushed about slaving.

"Hey baby," said Jai'Myiah as she opened the oven door to check on the filet mignon she had broiling on the top shelf, macaroni and cheese occupied the bottom rack. On the top of the stove sat a pot of fresh sautéed vegetables to go along with the strawberry cheesecake she had chilling in the refrigerator.

"Hey luv," he replied somberly. Jai'Myiah instantly looked in his direction upon hearing his saddened tone.

"Zeh', what's the matter?" she asked solicitously.

"When you are finished cooking, we are going to have to sit down and have a serious talk."

"No, we can talk now," she said anxious to know what was eating at her mate. She took off her apron and cooking gloves and followed her husband to the living room.

A Hutlaz Dream

Zeh'Shon sat on the love seat and put his head down. Jai'Myiah sat on the full couch directly in front of him and placed her chin in her hand. When he looked up he had tears in his eyes, with one standing on the tip of his eye lid threating to jump. He threw his head back refusing to set the water works free before speaking.

"Myah, you know I love you with all my heart right?"

'Ohh Lord what did this nigga do now' she thought. " Well I assume so, you've been telling me that for a few years, what's up Zeh'Shon?"

"You know the little nothin' ass bitch that I had gettin' money for us, right?"

"Which one? There were so many that were "supposedly" getting money, you have to be more specific," she said sarcastically.

'Damn, she ain't making this easy at all', he thought. "The broad's name is Omari."

"Ohh okay, the one that called my phone a few years back spilling the beans on yall's late night creeps," she said continuing on with the sarcasm, "continue." For some reason she was getting a real kick out of seeing him sweat.

"Well, she was responsible for the shooting," he said and stood taking caution, he had a feeling that a foreign object would be sailing at his head at any given moment.

It was Jai'Myiah's turn to put her head down and collect her thoughts and get her emotions in order. 'What does he mean she was the one responsible for the shooting?' She was silent for a good two minutes before Zeh'Shon chimed in.

"Baby please talk to me."

Jai'Myiah looked up, her face was so wet it seemed as though she had just went bobbing for apples. Zeh'Shon felt a ton of bricks fall on his already loaded shoulder blades. He despised seeing pain in his wife's face, because when she hurt he felt it also.

"You know what? Since I've been awake, I've been trying to run through my memory bank to see if I recognized anyone strange in the audience, or if I got a glimpse of the trigger man, but I kept coming up blank. I also thought that maybe one of your rivals found out about our special day and knew that you would be in a vulnerable position where they could come and get at you easily. I was thinking that you were the target and the shooter just had bad aim, and got me instead." She walked a few feet to the liquor cabinet that they had stationed in the living room and poured herself a double shot of Remy. She threw it back in one gulp like a gangsta, no chaser, and then continued. "…That's how I actually would've preferred the outcome to be. I told you a while ago that I'd die for you, take a bullet jump off a cliff or whatever, because that's how much love I have for you. But that statement doesn't apply when the bitch you fuckin' on the side turns out to be the one firing shots, come on now… Damn, I'm fucked up on this one, I'm not even going to lie." She went back for another shot.

"Baby, I'm so sorry." said Zeh'Shon, thankful that Jai'Myiah was taking the news way lighter than he anticipated, "I've been looking for that bitch all day, and she must've crawled under a rock or something because she's hiding."

"Do me a favor, when you find her make sure I get to holla at her about something. I know you got a couple things in mind for the bitch, but I got a few bones to pick as well. I want you to know that I appreciate you being real with me, I'm not mad. I know bitches just came with the territory when I chose to be with you. Bitches come with the game, unfortunately. I mean I guess this is what I get for dealing with a man of your caliber. But you're going to have to change your occupation if we're going to be

A Hutlaz Dream

together, because your workers are trying to end my life. I need to feel safe in this relationship, and not only that, I've been holding in my jealousy and biting my tongue for too many years, feel me?"

"Baby, you got that, I promise. To keep it real, if I had all the money in the world it wouldn't mean nothing if you weren't by my side, I love you with everything in me."

Zeh'Shon then walked over to her cautiously. She didn't appear resistant so he went in and held her in a strong embrace. He gave her a deep kiss, tasting her Remy Martin flavored tongue. While they were kissing and teasing one another, Jai'Myiah grabbed a hold of his rock hard extra-long member and began massaging it through the fabric of his jeans. Zeh'Shon pulled away hesitantly. Through heavy breathing he whispered.

"Baby we can't yet, I have to call your doctor and see if it's okay to do this so soon.

"Fuck the doctor!" said Jai'Myiah breathing just as hard, "Zeh' I got shot, I didn't just have a baby, now you better get over here and knock the dust and cob webs off this pussy."

He quickly gave in to her demand. He ran to the kitchen to cut off the oven then rushed back to his wife. He swept her off her feet and carried her to their bedroom. They undressed faster than inmates getting released from prison. He laid her down on her back and pinned her arms over her head as he focused on her face. He kissed her forehead right before laying tender kisses on her eyelids, her nose and then mouth. He sucked and nibbled on her earlobe before leaving a trail of saliva from her ear to her breasts, latching on each nipple and savoring the taste as if it were a delicate piece of chocolate. Jai'Myiah shuddered under his touch. Continuing on his journey, he quickly bypassed her mid-section, finding a home for his tongue in his most prized possession that Jai'Myiah held, his treasure box.

He sucked her clitoris like a baby on a pacifier and lapped at her juices like her cream was butter and his tongue was the biscuit. Jai'Myiah's body shook uncontrollably, as if she were having convulsions. It was then that the most pleasurable climax of her young age erupted.

Zeh'Shon rose and slowly entered her missionary style, loving the tightness and warmth of her walls he was gentle as he stroked in and out, relishing the feeling he hadn't felt in what seemed like ages.

"Damn I love this pussy, it feels so good," he moaned.

"Right there, baby, ooohhh," cried Jai'Myiah as she eased herself up a few inches and began to meet him thrust for thrust. They picked up the pace, and she put it down like a porn star. Zeh'Shon tried desperately to keep up, but couldn't. He lost control, busting the biggest nut of the century inside of her glazed walls. The rest of the night they went at it like two hungry alley cats, in every position imaginable, and falling asleep with two exceedingly satisfied grins on their faces.

Early the next morning Jai'Myiah was up and refreshed, like a brand new woman. When Zeh'Shon awoke and went to look for her, he found her on her hands and knees scrubbing the kitchen floor. The entire house stayed immaculate, Jai'Myiah felt that if you kept a messy household, your life was also in shambles. As she cleaned and dusted, Keyshia Cole's 'Just like you' CD played softly in the background. Jai'Myiah was a Keyshia Cole fan, she loved her music, she felt the lyrics to all the songs. Maybe it was because they grew up in the same city and encountered some of the same situations, she really didn't know, she just knew that Keyshia kept it real in her music. Zeh'Shon wasn't a fanatic like his wife, but felt as though he learned all her lines on accident from them being played in his home so much.

A Hutlaz Dream

"Good morning, luv," said Zeh'Shon as he approached his love from behind.

"Good morning babe. You hungry, what do you want to eat?"

"You!"

"You so nasty," said Jai'Myiah slapping his chest playfully.

"Come on baby, let's take a bath, I wanna wash your back," he said with a freakish grin. Jai'Myiah, who was more than ready for round two, raced to the stairway as he ran after her. The bathroom episode was an unforgettable experience as the moans of ecstasy. From there they took it to the bed where they tried to knock a spring out of their Tempur- Pedic mattress.

After the raunchy sex session was finished they lay wrapped in each other's arms and talked.

"So tell me, how did you find out it was Omari behind this disaster?"

"Well, actually Zo was the one who got a name on the shooter, then K.B said he was in jail with him, so I went to see the nigga yesterday."

"Is that right?" Jai'Myaih asked surprised to hear that Zo's name was mentioned in helping out. She never really cared too much for Zo, she considered him an arrogant bastard who had no respect. Not that he ever disrespected her, most likely because he knew that Zeh'Shon would put his size 13 shoe up his ass, but just disrespectful in general. After his name was mentioned for this incident, he won a couple of cool points in Jai'Myiah's book.

"So you went to see the nigga at Santa Rita, and he said that Omari had him do it?" she continued.

"Well come to find out, Omari is the nigga cousin and she paid him to do it."

"That bitch is crazy!"

"Naw that bitch is stupid, I can't wait to get at that hoe," he said steaming, "But this is what I also wanted to talk to you about, both of your businesses are closed down for the time being. I don't want you or your family members in there when this J-cat broad is out there lurking."

"What the fuck you mean? We ain't gonna hide from that bitch!"

"Baby, baby, calm down I know ain't nobody hiding, I'm just being cautious, do this for me, please? It shouldn't take me that long to find this chick."

A minute or two passed before Jai'Myiah finally gave in and agreed to her man's request. She didn't know that he had already placed a few phone calls, and had both businesses on the market to be sold.

A couple months trickled by and Wanda found a new job. Zeh'Shon felt bad about shutting down the store, but it was for her own safety. Since the store brought in most of her income, well that and her social security checks, he paid all of her household bills plus car note. She was grateful but she had to find something to do to keep herself busy. Being afraid that having too much time on her hands could lead back to doing something stupid, she threw herself into her recovery and started attending N.A. meetings and AA meetings religiously. There she met a man named Tom Bowden, who owned and ran a drug rehabilitation center and offered her an administrative assistant job, which she gladly accepted.

During the same time frame, Jai'Myiah found out that she was pregnant. She and Zariah were shopping at Blossom Hill mall, located on Steven's Creek Blvd, in San Jose when Jai'Myiah made a

A Hutlaz Dream

mad dash to the ladies restroom. There she entered a stall and regurgitated all of the food that she'd consumed that day.

"You alright, girly?" asked Zariah as her friend continued to spew her guts. She entered the unlocked stall and rubbed her friends back, "You probably pregnant."

"Fuck you, don't jinx me," said Jai'Myiah.

"Whatever, let's go to the store and get a pregnancy test." Feeling out of it, Jai'Myiah complied to Zariah's suggestion. She wanted to find out ASAP what was going on with her body. She had a strong immune system, she rarely underwent any type of sickness so she wasn't concerned. They put their shopping bags in the trunk of Zariah's 650i BMW, and drove across the street to Safeway grocery store, where they purchased three different pregnancy test brands, and if they all said the same thing, they would go with the result. They picked up EPT, clear blue easy, and first response.

Jai'Myiah then went into the restroom and urinated on each of the three sticks separately. She then handed them to Zariah, not wanting to view the results herself. Three minutes passed, Zariah eyed the tests and confirmed her fear.

"Yep, you got one on the way, mommy." Hearing that, Jai'Myiah broke down and cried. "Man stop it, what's the matter?"

"I'm not ready to be a mama."

"Well you better get ready. I know Zeh'Shon aint going for no abortion shit again. I know y'all been fuckin' like jack rabbits, and obviously y'all don't know what the word 'condom' means, so don't act so surprised," said Zariah keeping it real. "This is a beautiful thing, Myah. You're married to a man that loves you, you're financially stable and you got me and the rest of the family. What you mean you're not ready, how ready do you expect to be?"

"You're right," said Jai'Myaih pushing a smile through her tears.

She called Zeh'Shon and let him know she had to speak with him immediately. He directed her to meet him on 50th and E.12th at his friend's studio. He was in the middle of laying down a beat for one of the local rappers. He wasn't a professional musician, but did have an ear for a good sound, so he dibbled and dabbled every now and then. The guys in the neighborhood suggested all the time that he should pursue producing as a career saying that the music industry needed a cat like him to change the game, and get some of these same sounds off the airways. He brushed their comments off and continued his street business, saying to himself, 'I'm a hood nigga.'

Jai'Myiah arrived at the destination and had him come outside. Zariah parked the car and Jai'Myiah got out. When Zeh'Shon spotted his wife his invisible antennas went up instantly.

"Baby, what happened?" he said after seeing the puff on her eyes.

"I'm pregnant," she blurted out.

The concerned observation that caused his eyebrows to connect quickly vanished and was replaced by a look of pure delight. On the under, he had been trying to impregnate her since she was well enough to have sex again. He felt a child was the only thing missing in his life.

"Swear?" he asked smiling so hard that his cheeks began aching. Jai'Myiah nodded her head and smiled similarly. He picked her up and spun her around in the air, before letting her down and placing a huge wet kiss on her lips.

Zeh'Shon wanted to leave right then but Jai'Myiah insisted that he finish his work, assuring him she was going home to get some rest since she wasn't feeling so swell.

A Hutlaz Dream

During the next month, Jai'Myiah had severe morning sickness to the point where she had to smoke a blunt just to keep the food down. Zeh'Shon was there to wait on her hand and foot, assuring her everything was going to be fine. She was quite irritable in these early stages of pregnancy, and being around Zeh'Shon 24/7 was wearing her thin. What he thought to be an act of love, she considered nerve racking. He put up with her mood swings on the strength of knowing he was officially about to enter into fatherhood. Her family and friends stopped by on occasion, but Jai'Myiah's mouth had turned into a pistol, she fired shots at anyone that came into eyesight so they decided on calling as opposed to visiting. Zeh'Shon couldn't wait for his child to be born so that he wouldn't have to deal with Jai'Myiah's mood swings. He was having to resist the urge he had at times, of wanting to put a sock in her mouth.

Chapter 17

As weeks passed and Jai'Myiah started feeling a little better, she decided to go to Vallejo and spend time with her grandparents for a couple days. Plus she'd felt bad for how she'd been treating her man and decided to give him a break. He'd been in the house babysitting her for quite some time, so she figured he deserved some freedom. She told him to go hang out with his buddies and play in the streets for a little while and that she would be back the following week.

Her grandparents' home was glamorous. It always looked as if it had jumped off a page of a 'Better Homes' magazine, or an episode of extreme make over. It was purely impeccable from carpet to ceiling. She loved her grandparents deeply. Even though they were somewhat up in age, ranging from mid to late sixties, they weren't old school, rocking chair, or crocheting grandparents. They were hip, and she enjoyed their company as much as they enjoyed hers.

Jai'Myiah's grandfather, Earl, was from Shreveport Louisiana, and though he'd been residing in California for the last forty years, he still held on to his deep southern drawl. Her grandmother, born and raised in the heart of East Oakland, moved to San Francisco as a young adult where she gave birth to and raised five kids in the Potreo Hill area. They worked hard for a living and considered street hustlers lazy people who lacked motivation.

A Hutlaz Dream

Out of her sisters, brother, and a host of relatives, Jai'Myiah was no question the favorite grandchild. They adored her beautiful spirit and knew she would be the one to excel in life. After she settled into her room, she went down and had lunch with her grand folks.

"Congratulations are in order I've been told?" smiled Florence, Jai'Myiah's grandmother.

"Yes, thank you."

"Where's that little hoodlum of a husband you have?"

"Grandma, he's not a hoodlum," said Jai'Myiah.

"Well, he is in my book," Florence said with her uppity self. Jai'Myiah would've never believed that her grandma was born and raised in Oakland, had she not seen her Castlemont high school diploma. Then again, Oakland may not have been as gutta as it was now compared to those days.

"Leave that boy 'lone Florence, long as his little ghetto ass don't come 'round here wit that street mentality, he alright with me," said Earl. Earl wasn't as vocal as Florence, but when he spoke everybody within earshot listened.

On the third day of her Vallejo visit, Zariah came down to spend a little time. They were in desperate need of a nail refill and pedicure, so Jai'Myiah called her cousin Myisha to be their tour guide and had her ride with them to the best nail shop, being that she was from there. They ended up at 'Tina's nail salon' on Marin St.

Entering the nail salon, Jai'Myiah saw that it was a far cry from 'Kim's nails' in Oakland where she was a regular. There were only two people patronizing the business, and the service was sluggish. She thought of leaving, but her nails were in dire need of a touch up and she didn't feel like taking that drive to Oakland, so she stayed and waited.

Jai'Myiah was sixteen and a half weeks pregnant, but you really couldn't tell unless you focused on her tummy, she wore it well on her petite frame. Her cheeks were a tad bit chunkier, but if you didn't see her on a daily you wouldn't have been able to tell that either.

In the meantime...

Omari and her friend Chocolate were on their way downtown Vallejo to visit some low budget niggas in the mini projects named the Vistas. They had the music blaring in the small two door black Hyundai, acting real hoodrat-ish, when she noticed something familiar.

"Hold the fuck up," said Omari while slamming on the brakes. Chocolate's dumb ass didn't have on a seat belt so her head bumped the dash board.

"Damn O, quit driving hella stupid like that before you fuck 'round and kill me!" she said rubbing her forehead and feeling the lump that was slowly forming.

"This bitch car right here," Omari said jerking into a parking spot right next to Jai'Myiah's burgundy Lexus.

"What bitch?"

"The bitch I was tellin' you about, let's go," she said and jumped out the car and headed in the shop. Chocolate hurriedly followed suit.

Jai'Myiah, Zariah, and Myisha were thumbing through magazines when the two poor excuses for women stomped through the door.

"What's up, Jai'Myiah?" said Omari.

"Do I know you?" said Jai'Myiah snobbishly, looking up and not recognizing the funny looking woman in front of her.

A Hutlaz Dream

"Ohh you know exactly who I am."

Jai'Myiah then scrolled through her memory bank, recognizing the voice from a conversation that took place years ago. 'Whatever bitch, all I gotta say is watch your back,' echoed the voice in her head.

"Ohh, so you Omari?" said Jai'Myiah with a menacing look on her face but keeping a leveled tone as to not alert the owners. Zariah and Myisha perked up and got in full battle mode, but Jai'Myiah raised her hand to halt them for the time being.

"You are aware that you's a dead bitch right? Your last days are numbered," threatened Jai'Myiah.

"Well, if that's the case bitch let me fill you in on a little something while I'm still breathing," said Omari sarcastically, slapping Chocolate five before continuing. "While you was laid up in the hospital bed, yeah the one I sent you to," she said putting emphasis on the 'I sent you to', "Your, quote unquote, husband was shacked up with me and eating this pussy as if it were the best meal on earth."

Before Omari could utter another word, Jai'Myiah attacked her like that albino tiger attacked his trainer of Roy of Siegfried and Roy, wailing on her non-stop. Zariah and Myisha fought to pull her off of Omari, fearing for the baby's safety. They sat her down and began beating Omari to a bloody pulp, Oakland style. Chocolate, wanting no parts of the squabble and seeing that her friend was getting molly-wopped, hit the door running full speed ahead. All that could be heard besides shoes connecting with Omari's body, was were the voices behind them.

"You no fight here, outside fight," screamed the Asian manicurist. "I call police... outside, you leave now!"

The three women piled into the car with Jai'Myiah in the back. She was so mad that Myisha could've sworn she saw steam coming from the top of her skull.

"Take me to get some weed, now!" Jai'Myiah demanded.

"Cousin, calm down, I don't think weed would be good for the baby," said Myisha genuinely concerned.

"The baby?" screamed Jai'Myiah, "Fuck this muthafuckin' baby, and its daddy. I didn't want this muthafucka no way," said Jai'Myiah, deliriously.

'Ohh yeah, she done really lost her mind', thought Zariah, while asking Myisha the directions to the nearest hospital to get her friend checked out, she wanted to make sure the baby was doing okay. Jai'Myiah continued to rant loud from the backseat.

"This nigga got shit fucked up, while I'm laid up on my muthafuckin' death bed, this nigga is out catting off with the bitch that's responsible, aint that a bitch? Yeah, I got something for his bitch ass too, fuckin' faggot. I should a known his ass couldn't be trusted from the gate. Yeah, that's my dumb ass fault, but never again, you hear me, never a fuckin' gin." They pulled into the hospital's parking lot.

"Ohh good, we at the hospital," said Jai'Myiah, still not all there, "cousin, go in there and tell the doctor to plug up that vacuum they use and get shit ready cause when I get in there I want this muthafucka sucked outta me immediately!"

Zariah shed a few tears for the travesty. In all the years that she'd been Myah's best friend, she had never seen her in such a distressed state. She knew that she must have been hurting deeply for her to be all out of character like she was. She was fearful of her friend's sanity. Myisha walked Jai'Myiah in the hospital to inform the employees that her cousin was having a nervous collapse and

A Hutlaz Dream

was four months pregnant. Zariah got on the phone and called Zeh'Shon.

"What's up, sis?" asked Zeh'Shon after seeing Zariah's name on his caller I.D. Loud music was blaring in the background.

"Zeh'Shon, you need to come out here quick," Zariah said with tears in her voice.

Sensing something was wrong, he turned the music completely off so that he was able to hear her better. "Come again, sis, I didn't hear you."

"I said, you need to come to Vallejo quickly. Jai'Myiah just had a nervous breakdown. We're at Kaiser Hospital, I'm not sure, but I think the street is called Sereno Dr."

Even though Zeh'Shon had two passengers in his car, Zo and Blow, he got directly on the freeway without time to make any drop offs.

"What happened?" he pleaded.

"I'll tell you when you get here, I'm about to go inside and see what's going on," Zariah said and then hung up.

"What's wrong, blood?" asked Zo, noticing his friend's demeanor had drastically changed and they were on the highway going in the opposite direction in which they had previously planned.

"Zariah just hit me saying that Jai'Myiah in the hospital," he said weaving in and out of traffic.

The nurses had Jai'Myiah strapped to the bed checking her vitals and baby's heat rate, as she yelled vulgarities. They tried to calm her, but to no avail. Not knowing what else to do Zariah went outside and called Wanda, informing her of the goings-on that led to this state of affairs. Luckily for Wanda she was in the area at a N.A meeting she had been invited to attend by a friend of hers from back in the day that she used to get high with.

"I'm on the way, I'll be there in ten minutes," said Wanda.

When she arrived, she tried calming down her irate daughter by use of words, but surprisingly they didn't soothe her child. She resorted to giving her a slap on the face to bring her back to reality. Jai'Myiah looked at her mother shocked as Zariah stepped out to answer her ringing phone.

"What's up, bruh?"

"I'm out front. What room y'all in?" asked Zeh'Shon.

"Hold up, I'm 'bout to come out there and warn you about what you're about to step into."

Zeh'Shon standing along with Zo and Blow witnessed Zariah exiting the revolving glass doors; she had both of her hands bandaged up so he knew that something had to be revealed.

"Sis, what's going on?" said Zeh'Shon frantically.

"Well me, Myah, and Myisha was at the nail shop waiting to get our nails hit, and these two dusty hoes walk in talking 'bout 'bitch I was wit yo' nigga while you was laid up in the hospital' and this, that, and the third, when Myah pounced on the bitch. Me and Myisha had to pull Myah off this hoe then me and Isha beat her ass."

"You don't know that broad's name?"

"Yeah, it was that same hoe that called her phone a while back, Omari." Once he heard Omari's name, Zeh'Shon started high stepping toward the revolving door.

"Wait a minute, bruh." He paused and looked at Zariah "She in there flashing, talkin' 'bout fuck you and the baby, so just know what you're about to see ain't no pretty sight." He gave her a head nod and continued walking. Zariah stayed outside with Zo and Blow and smoked a cigarette.

A Hutlaz Dream

Zo and Zariah constantly threw lugs at each other whenever they came into contact with each other. In all actuality, they held secret crushes on one another.

"I don't know why you got your hands all wrapped up, like you was really throwing them thangs. You probably was the one gettin' served."

"You wish nigga. You must have me mistaken for ya bitch." She smiled blowing out a lung full of smoke and flagging him off.

Zeh'Shon entered the hospital room and saw Jai'Myiah bawling on her mother's shoulder. Jai'Myiah must've felt Zeh'Shon's presence when he entered the room because she looked up. Her face was saturated with tears. He knew that she was upset, but he was not at all ready for the tongue lashing that she whipped him with.

"I hate you," Jai'Myiah screamed, "you might as well leave because I don't ever want to see your pathetic ass again."

"Baby, listen," started Zeh'Shon, but was cut off.

"Listen? Yeah right, I'm tired of fuckin' listening. My ears are closed to you. I thought we were better than that, but the shit you did this time, you just can't undo. As a matter a fact, since you were spending so much time with this bitch, the one who put three shots in me, had me hooked up to a fuckin' breathing machine, give that bitch this," she said removing her wedding ring and throwing it at him, "she deserves it. It's OVER!"

Zeh'Shon tried to be empathetic about the situation, but lost his patience by that point and went off.

"What the fuck you mean it's over? It ain't never over, you my wife, we go work this shit out. Know what ever that bitch told you to get all in your head is a lie, so don't believe that. You the one I put a five carat ring on, I wouldn't have gave that hoe a ring if it came out of the Cracker Jack box. But you in this relationship, we fa life ma, believe that. Remember 'till death do us part?"

"Yeah, well that bitch tried her best and almost did part us."

"Check this out sweetheart, I'm not about to keep apologizing about the same things, but I'ma do it this last time, I'm sorry for what that punk bitch did to you. I promise to God, but you're here, almost don't count it because it wasn't your time. Now since I'm done kissin' yo' ass and playing Mr. Nice Guy, this is what you're about to do, you 'bout to leave this hospital when your cleared to go, you are going to go to Berkeley to Zariah's house, Blow is going to take y'all and spend the night to make sure y'all safe and I'm going to find this bitch tonight, understood?"

Jai'Myiah and Wanda looked at each other like, 'no this nigga didn't just lay down the law like this'. But for some reason, Jai'Myiah thought it was sexy, the way he just took charge. Although she didn't want to, she gave in, allowing all of her anger to cease and desist. She hated letting him have that power over her like he did, she'd wished she didn't give in so easily. She had to charge it to her lapse in judgment and not the heart, she just couldn't help it. 'But next time', she told herself that if there ever was a next time, she was putting her foot down and keeping it there.

He placed the expensive ring that she had thrown at him like a piece of trash back on her finger, kissed her forehead and said, "I'll see you as soon as I handle this business." He started to walk out.

"Call me when you find that hoe!"

"Baby, let me hand---," Zeh'Shon's sentence was cut short.

"What did I say?" asked Jai'Myiah seriously.

"Okay mami, you got that." He smiled and left.

A Hutlaz Dream

"That's right a young boss. Got my babies lil' fast ass in check," said Wanda beaming, seeing that Jai'Myiah was in a better mood.

"Whatever mama, he didn't check nothing," she replied smiling.

"Girl aint nothing wrong with it, I had a boss once upon a time also," claimed Wanda, about to tell a story.

"Oh Lord, here we go," said Jai'Myiah.

When Zeh'Shon got outside, he overheard Zariah and Zo going back and forth.

"Yeah nigga, ya money might be long, but I heard you was short down there," she said making a circular motion around her genitals. "Yeah, I heard you pee on your balls when you take a piss," Zariah clowned. Blow had almost busted his side, laughing so hard.

"Naw baby girl, you couldn't have heard that, 'cause my dick is longer than my money and that Diana Ross wig you got on. I've been known to blow the freakiest bitches backs out, and turn 'em on to that Dora the Explorer shit, talkin' 'bout swiper no swiping."

"Y'all need to fuck and get it over with. Y'all too grown to still be fightin' the feelin'," Zeh'Shon said walking up.

"Yeah right, ya boy is used to dealing with cheap hood rat lames, he's not on my level. I'd turn his ass out and he wouldn't know what to do," spoke Zariah.

"Girl please, I'm one of the realest niggas you will ever come across, you should feel privileged to be standing here chatting with me." Zo smiled.

"Whatever," she replied, flipping Zo the middle finger, "What's going on with Myah?"

"She 'bout to stay with you tonight, if its cool. Blow, I need you to be they body guard for a minute."

"Aiight," agreed Blow.

"Zo let's be out, go holla at ya folks and see if he heard of this bitch." He and Zo disappeared into the hospital's parking garage and Blow and Zariah headed back inside to see if the release paperwork was finished.

Chapter 18

"Dirty Rome, what's up wit you boy?" asked Zo into the phone.

"Aww shit, shit, I'm on my way to the hut to go holla at this raggedy ass bitch of mine."

"Before you go in, I'ma need to run a lil' something by you, where you at right now?"

"In the Rich," said Rome referring to Richmond California. "Come slide up to Rudy's, we can have a drank."

"Aiight, I'm on the way."

Zo and Zeh'Shon didn't visit Richmond often 'cause those hot headed youngsters out that way were something else. All they heard about were shoot 'em up, bang bang stories. But they had to give it to them though, in the midst of all the cities beef, they still managed to get that dough. There were a few reputable niggas out the 'Filthy Rich' that were really chewing.

Exiting the car, they grabbed the butt of their guns. Remaining cautious in this unfamiliar atmosphere was a must. They weren't equipped with bullet proof vests, but if anything looked suspicious they'd be ready to shoot first and worry about the answers later.

Entering the bar, they spotted Dirty Rome sitting in the far left corner in a small booth, chomping on a basket of hot wings and sipping a Mai Thai.

"My niggas," greeted Rome standing up and licking the hot sauce off his fingers while giving dap with his elbow. "What can I do you for on this fine evening?" he tried to sound proper with a sly grin.

"I want to know if you ever seen this bitch around Vallejo?" asked Zeh'Shon, handing Rome the picture of Omari he had taken from his pocket.

"Let me see," said Rome taking the picture and walking over to view it over better light. "Yeah, I know this bitch, she in the 'Hot Topix' bike club with my 'lil cousin, Sassy. I just seen the bitch at the bike party they threw in Oakland last week at the Moose Lodge. As a matter fact, she be at them apartments downtown Vallejo. She drives a little black car right?"

"Shit, she probably do now, I don't even know," said Zeh'Shon.

"Let me call Sass and see what she know about this broad, what's her name?" asked Rome.

"Omari."

"What's up with you, big cousin?" answered Sassy, in a born and raised San Franciscan accent.

"What's good loved, one?"

"Shit, shit, chillin', getting ready to go out and meet this ballin' ass Atlanta nigga I met today at the Stone's Town mall. Yeah, the nigga tried to holla at me when I was in Nordstrom's picking up a few outfits. I let it be known that I don't fuck with broke niggas, so the nigga waited until I was done shopping and followed me to the register and cashed out for all my purchases. You know me big cousin, I'm in it for the dough only, niggas gotta pay to play dealing wit me."

A Hutlaz Dream

"I heard that Sassy, baby," laughed Rome, "But look the reason for this call is to ask about the chick Omari in your bike club."

"Now big cousin, you know I'm not hooking yo big pimpin' ass up wit none of my club sisters. I'm not tryin' to be in middle when you take all they money and leave they ass stuck and confused."

"Girl gone with that, it's not like that at all." He grinned. "It's important though, I'll fill you in on the details later," he said trying to get the info from her nosey ass, but not planning on telling her anything else.

"Well since you put it like that, what you wanna know?"

"All I need is her address."

"Aiight, you got a pen and paper?"

"Yeah, shoot."

"She is staying with this broad named Chocolate in the Blue Rock Village apartments on Ascot parkway in number 2422. I don't know how you're going to get in because the complex is gated, and you have to be buzzed in."

"Its good cousin, I got it from here."

"Aight cuz, I don't know what's going on, but just know I got ya back. Hit me if anything smirkish goes down. I love you, one." She hung up.

"Alright y'all, I got the address. Now if you need me to roll wit y'all let me know so I can call this bucket head broad and let her know I'm not coming home yet."

"Naw bruh," said Zo. "Good lookin' on this," he said putting the napkin with the scribbled address in his pocket, "Go 'head and take it in, we don't want you to get in trouble." He and Zeh'Shon shared a laugh.

"What you niggas laughin' at? I run mi muthafuckin' casa."

"Yeah whatever, you square ass nigga," laughed Zeh'Shon, "We'll get up with you later."

They left the bar, laughing all the way to the car. After typing the address into the car's navigation system, they were off and headed back in Vallejo's direction. The traffic was light on this somber night as they reached their endpoint in only twenty minutes. Approaching the buildings, the gate was indeed locked. So Zeh'Shon pulled to the front and parked in an employee stall. He knew that somebody would eventually be coming or going that would have access to unlocking the premises, he would then drive through before the gate shut.

His thoughts served him right, not even ten minutes later somebody pulled in. Zeh'Shon started his ignition and pulled in behind.

"Ay blood, park right there," Zo said pointing towards his left hand side, instructing that they park in the visitor's parking space. "This the 2400 building right here." He pointed toward the brown and beige building on his right. The parking lot was filled with cars, but there was no one in sight.

Walking up on the building they saw a black car parked in the front. Seeing the sign that read 2422 on the upper level, they hurried up the stairs and found the unit to be that of the first to their right.

"I'm a kill this trifflin' ass bitch," Zeh'Shon said in a loud whisper while pulling out his .357 derringer pistol and making sure one was in the chamber.

"Hold on my nigga, we aint gone get active in there, we're just going to run up in there and get the broad. We don't know who is lurkin' out here. Plus, I got a broad that live not too far from here, we can take her over there."

A Hutlaz Dream

"Alright," said Zeh'Shon seeing that his buddy made a lot of sense.

KNOCK, KNOCK, KNOCK.

Zo tapped the door lightly. Moments later, the porch light came on and out bellowed a deep raspy voice from the other side.
"Who is it?"
'Damn, I thought there were only chicks staying here, I shoulda done my homework a little better', he thought, while looking at his friend he placed his hand on his strap. Zeh'Shon sensing trouble was on alert as well.

Locks were heard de-bolting before the door swung open. The sight that stood before him had him at a loss for words. He tried to speak, but had completely forgotten his train of thought. This was by far the ugliest, blackest chick that he had ever laid eyes on. 'Chocolate', he thought back to the name Dirty Rome had given them. She looked like chocolate alright, chocolate tar. Her body was shaped like an upside down pear, which she had the nerve to come to the door with a sports bra and daisy duke shorts on like she worked out on a daily basis and sported a beach body. She had blue/black stretch marks on her already pitched black stomach that looked like large earthworms hanging out on a dark night. He was utterly disgusted, and when his eyes landed on her facial features his stomach bubbled causing him to expel gas on accident, as her halitosis breath lightened his head and caused his sight to become blurry. Zeh'Shon who was on the side of the door out of Chocolate's sight, nudged his partner as if to hurry him along, as he covered his nose with his t-shirt.

"Ohh shit, do you have a cousin or relative named Kenetta?" was all Zo could think of to say, referring to the chick he had hustling for him from San Francisco. They damn near looked like twins, and he knew good and well two ugly people that held that much resemblance had to share the same blood line.

"Kenetta, from Hunter's Point? Yeah, that's my sister on my daddy side."

'Figures,' he thought, "Yeah okay, but anyway, I was wondering if I could use your restroom, I stay downstairs and shit done got stopped up, I had to shit and don't have no plunger."

"Who's that at the door?" said Omari emerging from another room with a terrible limp, holding an ice pack on her eye. Catching sight of Zo's face, she damn near lost her sense of balance as she stutter stepped before completing her foot's full pivot. Zo and Zeh'Shon sprang into action. Zo rushed in and grabbed Omari by the collar causing her to miss her intended step and tumble to the carpet.

Just before Chocolate could fix her mouth to scream, Zeh'Shon put his gun on her lips and backed her into the house, immediately closing the door behind him. Zo picked Omari off the floor and threw her on a nearby grubby couch like a rag doll. Zeh'Shon was not even thinking of attempting to pick up Chocolate. He directed the beastly being toward the same spot. Keeping his gun at a steady aim between the two pitiful ladies, Zeh'Shon threw Zo his car keys and told him to pull it up.

"What's going on?" cried Chocolate, looking nervously in Zeh'Shon's direction and wondering why on earth this disturbed man was holding her and her friend at gun point in her own living room. As she attempted to speak again, Zeh'Shon punched her in the mouth like she was a man. She shrieked in agony. He positioned his fist to strike again, so she swallowed her scream. She was overwhelmed in unbearable pain as she traced the gums of her

A Hutlaz Dream

mouth with her tongue where three of her teeth used be, before passing out.

Omari sat beside Chocolate so afraid that she was literally shaking in her house shoes. The ice pack she once held to her lacerations laid across the room where she flew from, exposing her ugly wound. Her right eye was completely shut and looked as if it had been pumped with helium. There was a cut on her left eyebrow that was so deep you could clearly see the white meat of her head. Her bottom lip was busted open and she was left with a lump the size of a tennis ball in the center of her forehead. Zeh'Shon would probably not have recognized her if it weren't for her colorful quick weave and the tattoo of his name on her neck, which he had opposed before she got it blasted. She looked like a sad sack of shit, and he intended to show no regret.

"Come on, blood," said Zo breathing hard from running up the stairwell.

"Let's go bitch, get up," said Zeh'Shon talking to Omari while trying to lift her from a seated position by the back of the head.

"No! Leave me alone, please, I'm sorry," she yelled. He then snatched her in the air by her neck, clogging her wind pipe, and she gasped for an ounce of air. With a grip of death around her neck, he crouched down to whisper a few threats in Chocolate's ear.

"Bitch, you better not call the police. If you do, I will murder your entire family and leave you alive just to attend the funerals." He wasn't 100% sure if the words registered since she was in a deep snooze, but he would have to keep in mind to follow up with that situation at a later date.

He then dragged Omari in the direction of the door. Her body was weak from the earlier altercation, she relaxed herself as

Zeh'Shon scoped her off her feet and carried her to the awaiting vehicle.

"Hurry up my nigga," said Zo impatiently from the driver's seat as Zeh'Shon took his time stuffing Omari's body in the back seat. "I'm not trying to go to jail on no kidnappin' and beatin' a bitch up charge," he continued. As Zeh'Shon jumped in Zo pulled off before he could close the door.

"Damn nigga, calm down."

"Calm down? Are you serious? You know a nigga be gettin' paranoid at night time." Zo joked. He eased off the acceleration pedal. While gripping the wheel he simultaneously dialed a number on his phone.

RING, RING, RINGGG.

"Hello," said a sweet voice.

"Meka baby... wake up bitch, I'm on my way over there."

"Well hello to you to, with your rude ass. I haven't heard from you in damn near three weeks, what's up with that?"

"Don't question me bitch, you hearin' from me right now. Like I said, I'm on my way, make sure your garage got some space available. I'ma need it."

"What the fuck you need the garage for?"

CLICK.

Ten minutes passed before they pulled up to a blue and white single family home on Carolina St. Zo beeped the horn twice and watched as the garage door elevated. He then backed the car in and watched as the door closed in front of them. Irritation struck Zo as he saw all the clutter of the garage. There were boxes, bikes,

A Hutlaz Dream

and kids toys dispersed around the room. There was barely space to walk, let alone let Zeh'Shon handle his business. Zo opened to door before going off.

"Bitch, what did I ask you to do?" he asked looking around the jumble.

"Boy quiet down some, you know I got kids, and their asleep," Meeka loudly whispered, "Now what you want with this garage?" she asked with a hand on her hip waiting for his response.

"My boy right here needs to holla at his girl for a minute." Meeka approached the car and peeped in the windows inquisitively, her eyes bulged before speaking.

"Aww hell naw nigga, y'all got to take that somewhere else," she said knowing they were up to no good by the look of the beat up girl in the backseat. "Y'all aint 'bout to use my garage as no execution station and have them C.S.I and forensic peoples snooping all around my shit, no sir'ee. Y'all gotta go, I got kids. How dare you?" she said going off. She was always told that Oakland dudes were crazy, but she didn't believe the rumors until now.

"It aint even like that mama, come in the house wit me for a minute."

"Nope, come holla at me when you're by yourself."

"Ohh, so it's like that, huh?"

"Straight like that."

"Well fuck you then bitch, don't call my phone no more with yo scary ass."

"Trust and believe I won't," said Meeka. She wanted him to hurry up and leave so she could lock up and put her alarm on. She wasn't sure what had gotten into him, he may have been on a rampage and she wanted not to be injured in his frenzy. Zo put the car in gear, as soon as the door lifted and burned rubber out of the garage leaving a tire mark by little Meeka's my sized Barbie.

"Where to now?" asked Zo.

"Go to the town," replied Zeh'Shon referring to Oakland.

Halfway through the trip, a small blue light caught Zeh'Shon's attention coming from the back seat. As soon as he turned his head, Omari made a quick movement and hid something under her leg. Zeh'Shon grabbed her face and slammed it onto the seat beside her, causing her body to turn sideways. A small cell phone was revealed which he immediately snatched up.

"Ohhh bitch , you wanna play?" he said pressing the 'End' button before tossing it out on the freeway amongst the dozen or so cars that trailed not far behind them at a legal pace. He then gave her a stern blow to the rib cage with his left fist. "Who the fuck was you callin', Superman? Because he 'bout the only person that can save yo' stupid ass."

Silence...

"Ohh, you tight lipped tonight, huh? Cat got ya tongue? What happened to all that tough shit you was popping not long ago? It's okay, you're about to get taught a real good lesson about disrespecting a pimp," said Zeh'Shon, right before making a phone call.

"Meet me at Mosswood Park," he said, and then hung up. When Omari heard Mosswood, she squirmed in the back seat knowing from that moment on that she was doomed...

Jai'Myiah paced the park's parking lot as Zariah sat on the hood of her car and smoked a cigarette. Blow was standing at the rear of the automobile on his cell phone going off on somebody, telling them not to worry about where he was at, while Jai'Myiah huffed and puffed.

A Hutlaz Dream

"Where the fuck is Zeh'Shon?" Jai'Myiah asked herself, speaking out loud.

"Girl chill out, he just called ten minutes ago. Damn, can he at least get a couple more minutes before you put out an APB?" said Zariah blowing out a cloud of smoke.

"Man, I swear to God, this nigga better be meeting us to share some good news, cause I've just about had it wit him!"

Just as Zariah took the last puff on her Newport and flicked it into a water puddle, a car pulled into the scarcely lit parking lot, with its headlights beaming. Not being able to see the car's make and model due to the lights, Blow instantly grabbed his pistol from his waistband.

"Calm down, killa," echoed Zeh'Shon's voice from the rolled down window, as Zo hit the lights and pulled directly on the side of the BMW. Zeh'Shon got out and reached for the back door handle with intentions of pulling a crying and pleading Omari out. But when he opened the door to his sheer amazement, Omari got out by herself in gangsta mode, with a scowl on her face that said 'let's do this'. Zeh'Shon saw the self-assured look, and the next thing she saw, or rather felt, was his hand coming down on her face as hard as a tire iron. She staggered a bit, but Zeh'Shon caught her by her weave. Regaining steadiness, Zeh'Shon's voice entered her ear like a loud bag pipe.

"Bitch, this my wife right here," he said pointing to Jai'Myiah, "Don't you have something to say to her?"

Punch drunk, Omari held both arms out at her sides as if trying to shake the dizziness. She then spit a mouth full of blood on the concrete, wiping her mouth with her arm she spoke.

"Yeah, I have something to say," she began as everyone stood around to hear what they thought would be an apology, "I want you to know that I am deeply sorry," she coughed, then spit more blood, "excuse me, but I am deeply sorry for... not being the triggerman, cause you would a been dead, bitch!" CRACK.

Zariah hit Omari over the head with an empty beer bottle she saw laying in front of her car, and Omari hit the ground on impact. As soon as her body and head became one with the pavement Jai'Myiah tried to rush her, but Zeh'Shon caught her in mid-kick, and placed her back on solid ground.

"Unt uhh, you aint doing nothing physical, now calm down before I send you home and finish this bitch myself," said Zeh'Shon. Jai'Myiah wanted to cuss him out so bad, but decided to just bite her tongue for the time being.

Zeh'Shon gave Omari's body a nudge with his foot after a couple minutes of watching her lay completely still. She was asleep but Zeh'Shon's shoe woke her game up, and she sat up. Jai'Myiah pulled a .45 caliber pistol with the infa-red beam out of nowhere. She inched towards Omari, deciding that it was time for her to face the music.

Seeing Jai'Myiah's pursuit in her direction with the pistol aimed directly at her and the beam dancing over her body, Omari's one big eye got as big as a silver dollar. She crawled backwards until the metal fence allowed her to move no further. Jai'Myiah bent down to her level, placed the gun to her temple and whispered in her ear.

"Look at all this shit you brought on yourself. Dumb bitch, you should've known from the gate that when I entered the game, shit was getting shut down, there was no longer any competition. You should have just fallen back and played your position, it would never have come to this. I'm your superior bitch, if you would've just recognized and humbly bowed down you could've still had the nigga on occasion, but you chose this. Any last words? I'll give you a minute to say your prayers."

A Hutlaz Dream

"Fuck you bitch, I'll see you in hell," were Omari's words before Jai'Myiah put two in her chest and one in her stomach.

Jai'Myiah got back up and walked to the car with her poker face in place. No one knew what to think or say to Jai'Myiah, so they just let her be. She walked over and got in Zariah's passenger seat with the gun still smoking in her palm. Zeh'Shon walked over to speak to his wife.

"Baby girl, you want to come home?" he said hoping everything was alright.

"Yeah, come get me from Zariah's house when you're finished dropping your friends off," she said with a light smile across her lips. But Zeh'Shon knew that she felt differently than that grin because when he looked in her eyes, he saw a lot of hurt and sadness. He wanted to tell her badly to get in the car with him then and that he would have Zariah take Blow and Zo wherever they were going, but he figured maybe she needed a little time to get her thoughts together and have a little 'girl' talk, so he gave her a kiss on her trembling lips, pried the murder weapon from her grip and walked off with his head down. Zariah got in the car and they rolled out.

When Zariah unlocked her front door, Jai'Myiah went directly to the guest bathroom, shut the door, and turned on the water faucet. She held no barriers as the tears began to flow. She cried hard, not only for what had just transpired, but for everything as a whole. For the years she had invested her all in the relationship with Zeh'Shon. She wept for her non-existant childhood, for the dysfunctional family she was born into, for to have once done bad in order to become successful, for the unknown obstacles she was sure to face, and for the life growing inside of her. She'd remained strong for as long as she could remember, but had finally reached a breaking point. She let the tears flush her face like a downstream current, gripping the edges of the basin to remain standing as she began to hyperventilate. Life wasn't fair to her at all, but yet she remained diligent in her search for peace. It just wasn't her time yet. No surrender, no retreat! After fifteen minutes of pouring out her heart to the man in the mirror, Zariah knocked on the door.

"Myah, you alright in there?"

"Yeah, I'm about to come out right now," she said lathering her hands with soap that was placed on the sink, and then washing her face. After washing up and dropping two drops of Visine in each eye she patted her hair and was ready to make an exit. The cry really helped, leaving her to feel 88% better.

As soon as the bathroom door opened, Zariah stood there teary eyed with her arms spread out, welcoming a much needed hug. "Jai'Myiah, I just want you to know that you are my sister and I love you to death. And just know that whatever you're going through, we are going to make it through this together." Zariah cried giving Jai'Myiah a kiss on the cheek at the end of her sentence, Jai'Myiah couldn't hold back the tears that surfaced once more.

"Z, I love you to death, too, sister I appreciate you for always being there for me and having my back. You've been there since day one, I wouldn't have made it through without you!"

"Likewise..." they hugged for a small number of minutes before Zariah separated herself. "Alright bitch, fuck all this sentimental shit, I need some drank," she said wiping her face, "you want a shot?"

"What you got. Remy?" asked Jai'Myiah.

"Hell naw, you know I fucks wit Patron Silver, and I got some margarita mix, so what it do?"

A Hutlaz Dream

"I'm in, hook it up." She knew that since she was pregnant she shouldn't be sipping, but from her life's recent turn of events, she felt that she needed a pick me up.

On their third drink, Zeh'Shon pulled into Zariah's driveway with Zo in the car.

"What's up y'all?" Zeh'Shon said entering the door.

"Shit, gettin' lit," sang Zariah, "What made you bring back scrappy, I mean, pimpy-doo? What happened, ya bitch put you out again?"

"Never that, I wouldn't give a bitch the opportunity to do such a thing." He smiled, "Hook me up wit whatever y'all drankin, since y'all in here feelin' ya selves." Zo grinned.

"Nigga, I think you left your maid service at the house, you better go in there and hook ya self-up." While Zo and Zariah went back and forth Zeh'Shon and Jai'Myiah talked.

"Baby girl, how you feelin', you aiight?"

"I'm more than alright, the question is, how are you feeling?" she asked slightly inebriated.

"I'm good as long as you're good," he said, mad that Jai'Myiah had been drinking, but not bringing it up knowing she was already hotter than bacon grease.

"I hope you take this as a lesson learned Zeh'Shon," she slurred, "cause the next bitch that call my phone, I'ma pop her ass, too."

'Ohh Lord, I done created a monster,' thought Zeh'Shon, "You ain't got to worry about that happening ever again. It's me and you," he declared.

"Yeah, all that sounds real good. Just remember, I sometimes laugh and joke but I ain't with all the playing no more."

"Aiight gangsta," said Zeh'Shon as they both shared a much needed laugh.

Zo and Zariah joined the couple in the living room with a couple laughs. They got drunk, told jokes and laughed deep into the night before all passing out where they sat.

In the meantime...

A well known drug addict on the Oakland streets, that went by the name of B.G was out and about, amongst the living dead. She had just poked her head out from behind an old broken down station wagon that she used as a shield to block pedestrians view of her as she tongue kissed her first love, the glass dick. Seeing that the coast was clear, she emerged looking like a female version of 'Pookie', from the movie 'New Jack City'. Her eyes bulged from her skull as if she had a hyperactive thyroid problem. Her lips were as white as a Colgate smile and seemed as though the crust had been accumulating for at least a year without any lip balm or Vaseline. Her jaws were sunken in like those of the crypt keeper, looking as though she had just sucked the last drop of juice out of a small straw.

Standing at her full height she looked from left to right nervously. Inspecting the blocks within eyesight, she saw no police patrolling the streets, so she turned up the bottle of her liquid lunch and took the last swig before throwing the bottle behind her. She jumped when she heard it crash on the pavement.

Deciding to roam the streets in search of her next high, she began skipping to her Lou. Already zooted out of her mind and higher than Kuda Brown, she refused to let the buck stop there. She was on one and determined to come up before the sun came out.

"You just a gangsta, I mean you a wanksta," she sang aloud trying her best to recite the lyrics by 50 Cent she had just heard

A Hutlaz Dream

playing from a passing car, "You aint got nuttin',...cop nuttin',....stop fronttin',... yeah that's my boy right there," she said speaking to the air, "That nigga 50 Cent is somethin' else.

She continued singing and dancing to every song that came to mind. Two blocks later, she was singing 'Beat it' by the legendary Michael Jackson, and doing her best imitation of the moon walk. Just as she completed the famous leg kick and swirl, her stomach dropped an inch. She stopped and looked around like a deer caught in headlights.

"Ut oh, doo doo time" she said as she high tailed it across the street to Mosswood park. Spotting a nearby tree, she pulled down her dirty pants and copped a squat, using the tall timber as her personal out house. "Wooow," she said wiping her brow after dropping a funky drug laced load. Realizing that she didn't have any toilet paper, she shrugged her scrawny shoulder. Deciding not to stay in that position all night, she dripped dried and pulled up her already soiled britches.

Making way back to the main street, B.G stopped dead in her tracks after hearing a light moan. She knew she was tweaking hard, but at the same time knew her bionic ears never lied. Due to the crack that she'd just smoked, she swore she could hear an ant's breath.

"Who's there?" she asked looking around tensely. Not hearing a response, she started moving fast. The last time she was in that park geeked up, she got ran out by a tiny green leprechaun during Christmas time, with him yelling, "Where's me pot of gold, Easter bunny?"

As she neared the sidewalk, she heard the moan again by the metal fence, only this time brasher.

"What do you want?" she screamed, turning around in circles with her arms spread in the air. A gargling sound was heard.

B.G then patted down her 1982 wool trench coat in search of her lighter she had "found" on the counter of a corner store earlier that day that was equipped with a mini flash light. She pressed the button on the side; a small luminous light searched the ground as she flashed it in the capacity surrounding her.

As the light found the source of the noises, she inched closer moving her skeletal jaws and gritting her teeth as if chewing a half of stick of gum. Making out the object that laid against the fence looking like nothing more than a clump of maroon dirt, she inched closer.

"What in the fuck?" B.G yelled jumping back. "Aww hell naw, I'm outta here," she began to walk but was stopped short when a barely audible, "Help me...please" entered her ears.

"Alright I'm about to help, I'm a go call the po-po. Be back in a minute." She scurried off in the nearby gas station's direction. At first, she had a thought to keep it moving, but if she didn't at least call for help, her high would be fucked off for the rest of the night.

Approaching the gas station, she darted around the gas pumps and rushed a pay phone that was, luckily, still in service. Her head was discombobulated as she desperately tried to remember the number to 911. Her fingers scanned the numbers like she was reading brail, but just couldn't think of which one came first.

A young teenaged punk rocker came out of the store's entrance with a skateboard under his arm sipping on a bottle of coke. His attire was put together with skinny jeans that had chains hanging from the pocket, an extra small white t-shirt with and opened plaid vest over it with a pair van sneakers decorated with skulls on them. He walked by B.G holding the phone's receiver in a happy go lucky manor.

A Hutlaz Dream

"Hey youngsta," she called out, "what's the number to 9-1-1?"

"9-1-1, dumbass," said the punk rocker as he put down his board and started to scoot. "Crack kills," he shouted behind him.

"9-1-1", said B.G as she dialed.

"9-1-1, what's your emergency?" asked the operator.

"You need to send a police officer to Mosswood Park, NOW!"

"What's the address ma'am?"

"The what? I don't know bitch, just tell them to hurry up, bye, have a nice day." B.G then slammed the phone down and ran back to the park, Dodging cars in the crosswalk since she didn't wait for the walk man to light up on the pole. As her coat flagged in the wind she felt as if she were a superhero wearing a cape. She stopped with a dance right in front of Omari.

"Dut-dut-da-dunt, B.G to the rescue."

Omari laid virtually motionless as B.G being the kleptomaniac she was bent down and patted her pockets. She felt something lumpy so she put her grimy fingers in and swindled Omari out a ten dollar bill.

"Cha-ching-ching," she yelled, with instant dreams of going straight to the dope house and copping a dime shot of crack, putting the whole piece on the pipe and taking a full pull. As she stood, flashing police lights entered the parking lot.

"What seems to be the problem?" asked officer Small after stepping out of the police car.

"What seems to be the problem officer," said B.G clearing her throat, she stood as straight as a light pole with her right hand above her brow saluting the officer, "is there is a dead person or almost dead person over there. You need to call them medical people y'all work with and see if she still got a breath."

Turning his attention to the direction that he'd been pointed in, he turned on his flashlight and began walking over to an incoherent Omari. Officer Small immediately spoke into the radio sitting on his right shoulder.

"One Adam twelve, I need an emergency unit over to Mosswood recreational park immediately, I have a gunshot victim."

"Ten-four."

The ambulance arrived within minutes followed by two other police cruisers. They jumped out and tended to Omari, who was barely clinging to life.

"She has a pulse," said one of the paramedics, followed by a bunch of other medical jargon.

"Ma'am, do you mind telling me what happened here?" spoke officer Small.

"I saw everything and I'll tell you the whole story if you give me five dollars," said a forever panhandling B.G.

"Are you serious?" asked Small.

"As a heart attack." Officer Small reached into his pocket and pulled out a small bankroll, peeling off a five.

'Damn, I shoulda said more,' thought B.G. "Well, I was walking down this here street," she said pointing behind her, "when I stopped cause I noticed something walking from them trees over there. Then here come this big 'ol white man with a knife in his hand, lookin' like Jason. So I took a closer look and I said to myself, I said self where you seen this man at before? And then it came to me, it was on unsolved mysteries, he was none other than the zodiac killer. I got too scared to stick around after that, cause you know what they say, 'curiosity killed the cat', and I aint got no nine lives, so I shook the spot and came back later and here she was."

A Hutlaz Dream

"Okay ma'am, that's enough," said Small walking away as his bullshit detector was going off.

B.G figured that was her cue to be dismissed, hopped along whistling as if nothing had ever happened. Her brain's navigation directed her towards the run down, drug infested motels that lined W. MacArthur Blvd.

Chapter 19

Zeh'Shon woke Jai'Myiah up at the crack of dawn so that they could go home.

"Aww, look at them, they look so cute, don't they?" Jai'Myiah whispered to Zeh'Shon when she saw Zariah and Zo cuddled together on the opposite couch. Zariah was laid out on Zo's chest, his arm wrapped around her lower back.

"Yeah, they aiight. Let's go, I need to go to the house and jump in some water, ASAP."

Sniff, sniff.

"You aint never lied," smiled Jai'Myiah leading the way towards the door, Zeh'Shon playfully slapped her buttocks. After Jai'Myiah locked up using her spare key, they were on their way.

"Home sweet, home," said Jai'Myiah as she walked from the front of her home into the kitchen. She set down her keys and purse then noticed that the light was flashing on the answering machine, indicating a message. She decided not to waste her time at that moment checking them due to the fact that they were more than likely bill collectors or telemarketers. Any one of any importance had her cell number.

"Baby girl, I'm 'bout to jump in the shower right quick," said Zeh'Shon as he headed up the staircase.

"Why don't you take a bath?" said Jai'Myiah, following closely behind him. "Relax some of them big giant muscles that

A Hutlaz Dream

seem to be so tense," she said as she gripped his shoulder blades from behind, giving a miniature massage.

"Only if you promise to wash my back."

"I can do that." She smiled.

As they entered the master bedroom, Zeh'Shon stopped short by the walk-in closet to disrobe as Jai'Myiah continued into the bathroom to draw his bath. She added milk and honey foam bubbles to the water and adjusted the cold and hot water knobs to a temperature she reckoned would be just right for her king. She then lit the aroma therapy candles that were lined around the bathtub, and turned on the jets to medium speed, before heading to the door to fetch his majesty. She pressed play on the restroom's compact disc player and let R. Kelly's 'Black Panties', album play softly in the air.

As she turned toward the door she stopped for a moment to catch her breath. Zeh'Shon stood there in the nude looking like a black god, her knight in chocolaty armor.

"Pick your lips up, baby girl," he said as he lightly brushed her before stepping in the warm water. "The water feels good, why don't you come soak with me?"

She stood still for a moment, as if in deep concentration before replying, "Hold that thought. I'm 'bout to run and check my e-mail, and I'll be right back," she lied. She was really headed to freshen up for the show she had in mind to put on for her man. Disappointed, Zeh'Shon sucked his teeth and flagged his hand as if to say, 'carry on.'

She left the bathroom and closed the door behind her. As she, did the cell phone that Zeh'Shon kept ever so handy vibrated on the counter top.

"Damn," he said not wanting to get out of the enjoyable position he was in. He dried his hand and stepped one foot out the tub to grab the shimming device. As he eased back into the water, he looked at the caller's I.D. Not familiar with the number his first mind told him to send the person to voice mail, but inquisitiveness got the best of him.

"Yeah," he answered.

"Zeh'Shon."

"Yep, who dis?"

"Ohh you don't recognize my voice anymore? It's only been what eight months since our last conversation?" said Sharice.

"What's up Reece?" he said in a cross tone. Knowing he would one day get this call, for the simple fact that he considered himself 'the man' and all his workers eventually wanted to come back home.

"Ohh it's like that, no 'hi, how are you doing?' None of your famous pimp riddles?" she said sarcastically.

"Naw, none of that, but if you got something to say spit it out cause I'm in the middle of something."

"What you in the middle of doing, your wife?"

"As a matter fact I was, now bitch hurry up, my tolerance is starting to wear thin, you have thirty seconds to speak your mind or you're going to have to tell the rest of the story to my cousin Tone " 'Cousin Tone' was slang for dial tone.

"Alright, Mr. Cocky. You have a two week old son, his name is Zeh'Shon Montiece Banks, Jr."

"Wait, wait, wait, hold up bitch run that back one time."

"I said you got a son."

"Bitch, I ain't got no muthafuckin' kids."

"You didn't have any kids, but the reality of this situation is you have a baby now."

A Hutlaz Dream

"You'sa dumb ass bitch and got me totally fucked up, you might as well call the nigga you been fuckin' and tell him the news, cause I ain't claimin' shit."

"Well I'm sorry you feel like that, you'll be getting some court papers in the mail soon. And by the way, you better check your homes answering machine before wifey does, because I called the Maury show looking for you to take a blood test. They told me when they found your number they had to leave a message since they got no answer."

"I'm a kill you bitch!"

"Not before I kill ya pockets, bitch!" said Sharice before hanging up.

"Baby, did you call me?" asked Jai'Myiah peeking her head through the bathroom door.

"No I was on the phone," said Zeh'Shon nervously, hoping his wife didn't hear his side of the conversation, "Baby, can you do me a favor?"

"What's that?"

"Go to the car and get my wallet, I left it in there on accident. I have the card of this car place that I need to call to see if my rims are ready," he said telling a fib. He needed time to check the answering machine.

"Alright." As soon as he heard the front door open he dashed out of the water with urgency. He didn't bother grabbing a towel or drying the water that dripped from his brawny physique.

He grabbed the cordless phone that was placed on the small dresser on Jai'Myiah's side of the bed and dialed the necessary numbers to access the message center.

"Hello," said the automated voice, "you have one unheard message and five saved messages. First unheard message sent yesterday at 2:43 p.m. 'Hi my name is Amy and I'm calling on behalf of the Maury Povich show. We've received a call from Sharice Small requesting a DNA test from you in regard to the paternity of her son. Now I'd like to inform you the test is free of charge, and your airfare, hotel, and meals will be paid in full. If you are in agreement with this request give us a call back at your earliest convenience at 8888-45-maury, hope to hear from you soon, bye.' End of message, to delete this message press '7'. (beep), message deleted. First saved message..."

Zeh'Shon hung up and placed the phone back in its cradle, then tip toed back to the bathtub. As soon as he sat down, Jai'Myiah entered.

"I didn't see your wallet, are you sure it was in the car? You may've left it at Zariah's house."

"Okay thanks, I'll look for it when I get out," he said trying to catch his breath.

"Why's all this water on the floor?" she asked suspiciously.

"I had to take a piss, I wasn't 'bout to go in the tub."

"Yeah, umm hmmm," she said closing the door.

She then went into the guest bedroom to prepare herself for the ground breaking sex that she was going to put on her man. She laid out her sexy negligee that was sure to make Zeh'Shon's eyes bulge. She went into the bathroom to take a quick shower and let the soft fragrance of the body wash seep into her pores. While applying lotion, her cell phone sounded.

"What's up, girly?" she answered.

"Girl, why the fuck I wake up this morning and found myself laid up on Zo's retarded ass? I don't know what was in my drink, I think y'all laced it, but I aint never drinkin' Patron again," said Zariah as Jai'Myiah laughed. "Bitch, I don't see nothing funny, and y'all outta pocket for leaving that nigga over here like that.

A Hutlaz Dream

Zeh'Shon knew they rode over here together, they were supposed to leave together. I had to get up and take his punk ass home. I'm hella mad at yo' ass." Zariah smiled.

"Girl you're alright, you'll get over it. But I'ma hit you in a minute, Zeh'Shon is in the bath tub and I promised to wash his back."

"Aiight, you lil' nasty hooker, in a minute."

They disconnected and Jai'Myiah continued on with the task at hand. She slid into her purple and white thong and matching corset that made her breasts sit up nice and plump like two nice sized grapefruits. She then slid into her clear four inch stiletto pumps, which she referred to as Cinderella slippers. After putting on light make-up, and a couple squirts of her husband's favorite perfume 'J'adore', she wrapped herself in her white satin mid-thigh length robe and headed towards the master bedroom.

As Zeh'Shon sat in the bath tub, he could no longer relax. After that call, his mind raced a mile a minute. 'If it aint one thing, it's some other bullshit', he thought to himself, 'I just can't win for losing'. His thoughts were interjected when Jai'Myiah walked in thicker than a Sunday newspaper and more glamorous than a platinum princess.

"Damn baby, you look hella sexy."

"You like this?" she asked seductively, rubbing her hands from her breasts to the curve of her hips. Zeh'Shon nodded his head like a hungry dog, with his tongue hanging slightly out of his mouth.

"Pick up your lips, baby," she said repeating the words that had been thrown at her earlier.

Prancing towards the CD player, she put in the sex CD mix. When Trey Songz song 'Dive in' began she started to slowly and seductively sway her hips from side to side as she loosened the belt on her robe and let it fall to the floor. Her little baby bump was sexy as it poked out a few inches from her waist line. She did a number of sensuous moves throughout the remainder of the song, but when K. Michelle's 'Pay my bills', came on she went all out. She popped her hips and clapped her ass cheeks like she was double jointed. Zeh'Shon thought for sure that she had taken up gymnastics classes, or became a stripper on the low-low. He didn't understand how she could have so much muscle control to where she could bend over and make one butt cheek bounce and the other stay still, it was beyond him. His dick stood at attention like the arm and hammer man, with the head poking out of the water like a floating missile waiting to be discharged. When she dropped down and popped her pussy to the beat, all he could imagine was her doing that with him inside of her. He couldn't take it anymore; he jumped out of the tub and picked her up, heading directly for the bed. Once again, never minding the towels. He left it up to the air to dry him off.

    Zeh'Shon laid Jai'Myiah on the bed and tried to ease between her legs, but she had other plans in mind. Roughly pushing him down on his back, her lips latched on his nipples, leaving wet circles of saliva before heading down south faster than a flock of birds heading south for the rainy season. She took his dick into her mouth and immediately loosened her throat muscles, bringing him all the way in until her lips rested within his nappy jungle. Between licking and slurping, she sucked him until his toes curled, and just when she felt the head swell, she lifted herself and climbed on top, riding him like she was in competition at a bull riding derby. As she bounced, Zeh'Shon played with her clit, causing her to moan out in ecstasy.

    "Baby, baby. I'm 'bout to ....cum," she shouted.

    "Cum on my dick, baby, cum on my dick."

A Hutlaz Dream

"Ahhhh....fuck," she screamed as she reached climax. She then collapsed down on Zeh'Shon's chest as if she were tired.

"Aww hell naw, wake yo' ass up, we aint finished yet," said Zeh'Shon as he playfully slapped her face. He placed her on her back, straddling her in a female push up position before entering her gradually, making sure not to put his weight on her in fear of hurting the baby. She hummed out in pure bliss as he went to work. He put a hurting on her coochie to say the least, and didn't stop until he beat it up like DMX did his chick in the movie 'Belly'.

Both were exhausted and fell into a deep slumber. Not too long after, Zeh'Shon's loud snoring jarred Jai'Myiah from her great sex induced coma. She stared at his beautiful face for a moment or two, realizing how deep in love with this man she was. As he continued to call hogs, she headed toward the kitchen to prepare a well-earned meal for her boo boo.

As she clanged the pots and pans she thought about the raunchy sexcapade she'd just encountered, and admitted that Zeh'Shon had her dick dizzy for sure. She told herself, if she ever heard of him giving what he had just given to her to another chick, she might just Lorena Bobbit him. But after figuring it would put an end to her back breaking episodes, she quickly abandoned the notion. She knew that Zeh'Shon was a dog in every sense of the word, but she was determined to keep him so full on her loving that he would be less tempted to stray.

As weeks trickled on, and the street convicted shooter was done away with and no longer a threat, Jai'Myiah reopened her stores and resumed normal program. Since Wanda was now fully employed and spending most of her free time with her 'OG Bobby Johnson', she was left to work the two stores until she found somebody trustworthy and dedicated to fill the position. Her sisters were too busy chasing the dreams that ballers sold and gold digging to work a cash register. Her brother Bo, she loved him to death, but knew if he was positioned around a lot of money at one time he would take what he felt he deserved off the top, it wouldn't matter if it was his sister's or not.

She had no problems at all running her businesses, but did feel the need to find a couple helpers in the near future so she could sit back and put the other ideas that she'd seen in her mind's eye into play. She planned on learning the ins and outs to party promoting, since she heard that there was some serious cash to be made in that field, and to start a dog walking company.

When Jai'Myiah shared her future dreams with her husband, he agreed with the first idea, but laughed at the second one. He held a strong dislike for canines since being chased by a Rottweiler as a child. He just didn't understand the love that she had for them. She planned to open the dog walking business in San Francisco where there lived hundreds of wealthy people who loved their pets but simply didn't have the time to do basic tasks such as walking or grooming them. She knew that she'd draw a huge roster of clients, and turn a huge profit.

Realizing that she had a customer by the sound of the door's bell, she landed back to earth from dream land only to be greeted by the same deceitful grin that she'd known so well as a teenager, but wouldn't have cared less if she had never seen it again in life.

"What's up, Bookie?" said Lonnie, calling her by the pet name he had given her years ago.

"My name is Jai'Myiah, but what's up Lonnie?" she said, silently wishing he would disappear at that very moment. At the present he was the last person she wanted to lay her hazel eyes on,

A Hutlaz Dream

plus Zeh'Shon was on the way to bring her lunch, and she didn't need any extra drama in her life.

"It's like that lil' mama, why the cold shoulder? Ain't you happy to see me, it's been what, 7 years?"

"Yeah, it's been a minute. You look like you're doing okay," she sized up the rock hard penitentiary body that her ex now possessed. "So how can I help you?" Lonnie looked at Jai'Myiah's face amazed at how she was getting at him, like he was a sucka or something.

"I just wanted to let you know that during the time I was down, I had a minute to think about all the things that I put you through. Also, I grew up a lot in the process, I want to show you. I was mad at you for a year or so after I got locked up, being that you didn't send a nigga no pictures, a kite, or nothing."

"Hold up, we weren't together when you went to jail. You broke my heart, remember? But that's neither here nor there at this point."

"Here me out, baby" Lonnie interrupted, "I'm a changed man, and I'm ready for you to come home."

"Home?" she said, "I am home, and if you were thinking this gigantic rock on my finger is just for show, it's not boo. I am happily married as if you haven't already heard Mr. 'I am the streets'. I know they've been talking about me and my husband."

"Fuck yo' husband, you my bitch forever, you understand me?" he said taking a step closer.

"Nigga, you better back yo' ass up," said Jai'Myiah as she raised the .38 caliber handgun from underneath the register.

"Ohh, so you go shoot me, after all we been through?" She didn't respond, but merely gave him a look that said 'try me'. "Okay Myah, you know I love your ass still and we go way back. But they say it's a thin ass line between love and hate. Please don't make me hate you, because I can guarantee, you don't want to see my bad side."

"Boy, you can save that drama for somebody that gives a fuck, and them words for somebody that believes em, 'cause I'm not afraid. Your threats don't concern me in the least bit, neither are you pumping any fear over this way. Now what we had back in the day, you need to leave it there. I've moved on, my advice to you is do the same."

"Whatever bitch, fuck you, I'll see you later," he responded like a typical young man that had grown up without any type of home training, and thought that disrespecting and verbally assaulting the females that turned them down made themselves manlier.

"Not if my nigga sees you first," she said with a wink on his way out of the door.

Zeh'Shon arrived with a steak and shrimp burrito from Los Palmas on Fruitvale. She didn't hesitate getting her grub on, so she could calm down the anxious baby that did back flips in her stomach from hunger. She didn't bother telling Zeh'Shon about her run in with Lonnie and the threats he shot her way. She knew he wasn't about that life, he was harmless. Or at least he was before he went to jail.

As they munched down, Zeh'Shon told Jai'Myiah that he had made plans to go to Newport News, Va the following week with Zo to conduct some out of state business. The benefits of the deal were too large to pass up he told her. She wasn't happy, but when he assured her that he would only be gone for three days, she gave him the green light. Plus she didn't want to make him feel that because he said 'I do', meant she'd placed handcuffs on his wrists. He had been made fully aware of the consequences if he did anything outta pocket.

A Hutlaz Dream

The day of the trip came quick. As Zeh'Shon packed the last of his belongings in Zo's car and was ready to head to the airport, Jai'Myiah stopped him by putting a note in his pocket and made him promise not to read it until he was high in the sky. He held up two fingers giving her scouts honor and kissed her before rolling out. She then went inside and packed a small bag of her own, she was going to keep Zariah company until her man returned.

As the airplane ascended into the clear blue sky, Zeh'Shon patted his pockets in search of the pack of gum he purchased at the airport's newsstand to chew in order to keep his ears from popping. During the search, he felt the note left by his wife and decided to read it. Not knowing he should have taken a trip to the restroom to have a little privacy, he unfolded the paper.

Zeh'Shon,
Damn, I love that name. Oh what it does to my pussy every time I say it. It's like when it rolls off my tongue, it puts my body into a seductive state. I can close my eyes, and my mind begins to produce all kinds of images of past sessions that cause me to inhale through clenched teeth. I lick my lips and open my eyes smiling at the sensation you give me. 'Zeh'Shon', I say in a sexy tone. If only your presence was here to touch, to feel, to embrace, to endure the love my heart yearns to give you. Distance and time separates our bodies, but our bond could never be broken. Desire burns in my body creating a need to feel your massive pipe to plunge deep in and out of my sugar walls, until you can hear the sound of my wetness singing in the air. The love we make is explosive, Lil' Kim and Too Short ain't got shit on us. I know I may sound cocky about the way we get down, but we go dumb and games is what we don't play... Damn daddy, it's getting hot in here,

but I'm allowing my imagination to run without limits. I can see you walking up behind me as I stand fresh out the shower, drying the water off me as I place the towel down and gently begin to smooth baby oil all over me. You standing there, admiring the view of my oily ass and the smell of Weekend Burberry that's lingering in the air. 'Come here', you say as you start to rub your dick through your pants. I walk towards you slowly and seductively, rubbing my hands from my thighs to my ass. 'Zeh'Shon', I say rubbing my pussy down causing small waves to ripple through my body. You smile and motion for me to fondle your erection. I walk up to the man I love, place my hands on your piece, look into your beautiful eyes and say, 'Zeh'Shon, I love you', as I kiss your sweet lips softly, I pull your Polo t-shirt over your head and start to stroke that thing that makes my pussy do the river dance. I get to licking and sucking on your neck, and work my way down to your nipples and then to your naval, leaving a trail of my drool on your coco brown edible skin. You grab the back of my hair and tell me to suck your balls, so I help you out of your Polo jeans, to where nothing remains but your socks. I squat down and do as you say while your dick bounces off my face. I hear you moan from enjoyment, but I want to hear you say my name. I release your sac and palm your pipe. I pull the head to my lips and smooth saliva all around it with my tongue. I move my hand to grip your thighs, while you glide in and out my hot mouth. I place two fingers in and out of my sugar walls. You're in another world because the suction from my deep throat action is feeling so damn good. From the way you are gripping my head, you would think you had the winning lotto numbers for $100 million. I can feel you're getting ready to bust from the way your dick is throbbing. I don't stop stroking or sucking until I feel the sweetness of your cum fill my mouth. 'Damn Myah', you say. I smile up at you while I savor the tasty jelly

A Hutlaz Dream

on my tongue. 'My turn', I say as I pull you to the bed by your other head. I lay back and look at you daddy, and smile. 'I love you Myah', you say parting my legs apart. I pull my titties to my mouth and let the jelly roll off my tongue onto my hard nipples. 'I want daddy's dick', I say, but you have other things in mind, 'I wanna taste your sugar walls, mommy', you say, as your looking and admiring my beautiful pussy that's in front of you. You bend down, pin my legs to my shoulders and run your fat, wet, juicy tongue all over my smooth neatly shaven coochie. My temperature rises, and I get to feeling light headed from the way you're serving me up. I grab your head and pull your face to mine because I love the way that I taste. Our kisses are heated from passion. You stick two fingers into my wetness while you play with my clit with your thumb. The feeling is making me go crazy. My wetness turns into a river, my hands grip the sheets, I arch my back, and the sweet creamy cum runs all over your hand. 'Damn Zeh'Shon', I moan. You lay back with your hands behind your head and dick standing at attention, and I'm ready to salute the dick. You say get on top. I position myself backwards, place my hands on your legs for support and lower myself onto your thick long pole. I rock my hips in a hula-hoop motion up and down. Your dick is so deep that I feel it hitting my belly button. As my river starts to flow, you palm my cheeks, grip them, then spread them apart so you can watch your dick plow through the thick sweet cream of pleasure. I lift my head up and continue to straddle the dick. I look over my shoulder at your fuck face and notice the small wrinkle in your brow, and it's telling me that your mind is blown from all the loving. Sweat beads form across my face and neck. You instruct me to lay on my side, I do as I'm told and pull my knee up so you can admire my flexibility and you get to slapping your dick against my clit. You slip it inside me and get to working the middle. Out of breath and in between moans, I say that I want it from the back. You turn me around doggy style, never taking your ship out of my ocean. You wipe the sweat from your face with your back hand and get to pounding my shit. Sounds of explicit sex sings volumes into the air. I reach between your legs and tease your balls, as your dick plunges in and out of my sweet creamy pussy. The motion we are in causes me to cum all over your long thick meat. Our bodies are drenched from the workout, but that aint stopping us. 'Fuck, turn around,' you moan as you pull out, roll me on my back, toss my legs over your shoulders and slide your dick in me, making me go crazy because this position is allowing me to take all your dick. You start rotating your pelvis, causing your dick to go deep. My body is on fire and my head is spinning from all this good dick you're serving me on a platter. Feeding my pussy every inch of your dick, my nipples are like bullets, and my kitty is so wet. I can hear our voices and the sound of flesh smacking together. I can feel your pole swell. From the look on your face, I know you're about to bust. I bite my lip because I'm at that point too. We both let go at the same time, leaving warm sweet cream running outta my ocean all over my thighs and down my ass. Your dick and balls are covered with sweet, sugar cream beneath me. We both catch our breath and you lower my legs, and kiss me softly. Your eyelids gain weight, and sleepiness comes over you. You lay your head on my shoulder and plant kisses on my neck. I wrap my arms around you, kiss your forehead, and we fall asleep. Our love still intertwined.

    I open my eyes, and I'm not where I thought I was. I'm here, but I'm not tripping though, because our bond could never be broken.

    At the end of the letter was a picture of the couple a few years back, holding each other in a warm and loving embrace.

A Hutlaz Dream

When he finished reading the pornographic letter, he had to put his tray table down, due to the large erection that bulged, noticeable through his jeans. He looked over at Zo, who was asleep in the aisle seat. Glad that his friend had popped those three Tylenol p.m.'s before that flight, or he would've been all in his business. He propped his head back on the seat and gazed out at the friendly skies, anxious to land so he could call his baby girl and let her know how the letter made him feel.

Chapter 20

At twenty nine weeks, Jai'Myiah and Zeh'Shon, accompanied by Wanda, headed toward her pre-natal appointment. She was going to find out the sex of her child. She honestly didn't care what she was having, as long as the baby was healthy. Zeh'Shon on the other hand couldn't wait to get the news, he wished for a boy, so he could have a little mini him in the world. He thought that if he had a girl he would have to be around 24/7 to monitor her every move, and as soon as she was old enough to understand, he would let it be known that she wouldn't be allowed to date, or have a boyfriend until the age of 30.

The threesome barely had time to open the first page of a brochure before the nursing assistant called.

"Jai'Myiah Banks." The worker weighed Jai'Myiah and took her vitals before leading the family to the familiar room that she visited once a month to be examined and brought up to date of her fast growing bundle of joy.

"Mama," said Jai'Myiah as they were all seated in the room and waiting for the nurse practitioner to arrive, "Did you hear how much that lady said I weighed? 157 lbs, I can't wait to drop this load. I'ma buy me some green tea pills and go straight on a diet."

"Girl be quiet," replied Wanda, looking around the room nosey as ever, "you gain a couple pounds when you're pregnant, but you aint nothin' but skin and bones. I been meaning to tell you, don't be starving my grand baby trying to be cute." Wanda opened

A Hutlaz Dream

her purse and stuffed a couple alcohol pads. "What the heck is this?" she said aloud holding a few sticks of what resembled a giant Q-Tip. No one answered, she shrugged and dropped them in as well.

Jai'Myiah looked cute pregnant, she still held her shape. The only thing that changed in her appearance was the slight budge in her tummy, which she didn't look to be a day over four months. A slight spread of her nose and her hips widened just a bit, due to her carrying baby Banks in her back.

Her nurse came in, administered her duties and left the ecstatic group with grins plastered on their faces. They had been informed that they would soon be welcoming a baby boy into the world.

Jai'Myiah instructed Zeh'Shon to drop her mother off at home, and then take her to Zariah's to finish the last of her baby shower invitations and get them sent off. He obliged.

"What's up, baby mama?" said Zariah from the couch. She was leaned over the coffee table in the living room filling out party envelopes when Jai'Myiah let herself in.

"I'm having a boy," said Jai'Myiah beaming with pride.

"Shut the fuck up," said Zariah in disbelief, she jumped up and did the cabbage patch in a circle while singing, "I'm going to have a nephew...I'm going to have a nephew." She stopped, realizing that Jai'Myiah was still positioned by the front door.

"Girl you better get yo' big ass over here and help wit some of these invitations. Shit my fingers hurt from all these cards. I don't know why you're inviting all these raggedy hoes anyway. Tasha, we don't fuck with her, Little Lucille we don't fuck wit her, and Quita we damn sho don't fuck wit her," she said going down the list of names that Jai'Myiah put on the piece of paper.

"They alright, don't be like that."

"Them bitches aint alright, but whatever, it's your party," Zariah said as Jai'Myiah took a seat beside her and got down to the dreadful task at hand.

"So tell me about ya hubby, I know he was excited after he heard it was going to be a boy."

"Yes girl, he was. So what you think I should name him?" she said rubbing her round belly.

"Make him a junior."

"Zeh'Shon Montiece Banks, Jr. would be nice," she thought out loud.

The ringing phone caught her attention. She dug through her Gucci bag in search of the drumming device as Zariah made faces while licking the sour strip of the envelope.

"Hello."

"Hey darling, how are you today?" said an older gentleman.

"I'm okay Tom, how are you?" Jai'Myiah said to her mother's male acquaintance. Despite the fact that Tom was old enough to be her grandfather, she accepted him. She was glad to see her mother finally happy, and felt that if mama liked him, she had to love him.

"I'm alright for an old nigga," Tom joked. "Your mother tells me your having a birthday/baby shower in a couple weeks, on May 9th, am I correct?"

"Correct."

"Well, I was wondering if we could add engagement party to the roaster?"

"Engagement party?" Jai'Myiah said flabbergasted.

"Yes, I would like to ask for your mother's hand in marriage, if that'll be alright with you. I can't see a better place to pop the question. I know your mom will be surprised and happy around all of her family members."

"Oh my God, that is so sweet, of course we can add that on the itinerary," she said teary eyed. She was so happy for her mother, plus the pregnancy had her unusually emotional.

"Okay baby, but listen here, please don't let your mama know anything. I just bought her a beautiful ring and I want her to be surprised."

"Okay I got you, step-daddy." She smiled.

"Okay babe, I'll see you soon." They hung up.

"Who was that, got you all cryin' and shit," asked Zariah.

"It was Tom, he's going to propose to my mom at the baby shower."

"Aww, that's so sweet, but I still don't understand what Wanda sees in that old bastard, he probably can't even get his old shriveled up dick to stand up."

"Eww your gross." They laughed together as they finished their duty. Jai'Myiah called for Zeh'Shon to come a fetch her after her and Zariah returned from the post office from mailing off the 50 invitations.

May 9th.

The vehicles that aligned the street of Jai'Myiah and Zeh'Shon's residence were so fly, you would've thought a car show was getting ready to be hosted instead of a baby shower. There were everything from scrappers, Harley Davidson's (hogs), old school Falcon's, to new school Benz' and Lexus'.

Despite the fact that Zeh'Shon liked to keep his home's location a mystery, giving only a selected few the privilege, he let Jai'Myiah have her day. Plus, unbeknownst to her, he had been in the market for a six bedroom. A mini mansion in Fairfield had caught his eye, so he had his realtor looking into it for him. It had a gigantic backyard where his son would be able to run freely, plus a four car garage that would fit all his toys.

The house was jammed packed with barely enough sitting room for the older people. They had to add chairs in all the rooms including the garage and backyard. Zeh'Shon and his folks occupied the family room section of the house, so they could watch TV and hold conversations amongst themselves. Not only that, Zeh'Shon chose that room because it had a perfect view of the stairs so he could make sure no one got the feeling to go on a scavenger hunt and start probing through their personal possessions. He had love for all the fam, but didn't trust any of them.

Minus the few sac chasers that lingered around the family room desperately trying to get a baller's attention, the women hung out in the living room, where their laughter could be heard all throughout the house. They played games such as name that baby food, baby scrabble, guess the mother's belly measurements, etc. They were having a ball.

Niki and Wanda joined with two other relatives threw down in the kitchen. The females hooked up lumpia, shrimp, chicken, and beef, macaroni and cheese, baked beans. They had finger foods on platters, with lunch meat, cheese, pigs in blankets, chips, veggies, and dips, along with cakes, pies and kiddie treats.

Being the best candidate to hold down the grill, Jai'Myiah elected Uncle Guy. His meat was always so tender, and seasoned to the point that every bite caused your taste buds to do a victory dance. They had a plentiful supply of pork ribs, chicken, hamburgers, and turkey sausage links. The alcohol supply was very limited, consisting of only wine coolers and jello shots. Hard liquor

A Hutlaz Dream

was prohibited at the party. Jai'Myiah didn't want any of her recovering kin folks to get the urge to relapse or the alcoholics to shut the party down early from acting a fool.

Jai'Myiah was elated about the party's turn out, all the mothers and brothers were in attendance and getting along fine. Uncle Bee was on the patio keeping the kids entertained with his best Chris Tucker impersonation, Uncle Paul was shooting the breeze with the fellas. Zeh'Shon loved all of his wife's uncles, but just wasn't too fond of Uncle Wee. Everyone had to monitor his alcohol consumption because he was known to get loud and belligerent. For that reason he was left off the guest list for most family gatherings.

"Food's ready," yelled Uncle Guy after slicing the last rib. People swarmed the kitchen area like bees to get a taste of the scrumptious food they'd been anticipating since their arrival. When every plate was fixed, and the prayer said, the home's noise level was extremely low. Only a small amount of chatter and smacking could be heard. After everyone was good and full the party continued.

"Zariah, girl who is that fine ass nigga with the dreads, he got on that brown and white Sean Jean button up," said Lucille, one of Zariah's least favorite people at the party. The girl was fake and confused in Zariah's book. Not only was she known to always gossip and tell everybody's business, she didn't know if she wanted to be gay or straight. She was 23 years old with a cute face, but her body was shaped like that of a 12 year old. She was two pounds away from being considered anorexic, but swearing that she would one day be a model and 'Rock the runway'. But her nose trouble left her no time to think of pursuing her dreams.

"Who Arlonzo?" Zariah asked with a hint of impatience in her voice.

"Yeah girl, hook me up."

"Bitch who I look like cupid, or Chuck Woolery? This aint no love connection, you better hook ya self up," said Zariah right before turning her nose in the air and walking away, leaving Lucille with a 'fuck you bitch' expression on her face.

Not long after the food and opening of the gifts, Jai'Myiah stood to make an announcement, with a glass filled with sparkling apple cider, she clinked her glass with a spoon to get every one's attention. "Umt ummmm," she coughed, getting the attention of those who didn't know that clinging the glass meant shut the fuck up. "I would like to thank everyone for coming out to celebrate with me and more importantly for the gifts." She smiled only half serious.

"Dang, the party over already?" Interrupted Nyree, Jai'Myiah's 15 year old cousin who was positioned in the corner of the room typing on her smart phone.

"No, little girl, but interfere again and yo little butt will be leaving early," she said with a smile. Anyway, I have some one here that would like to make an announcement, come here Tom." As he approached, she continued, "He's a dear friend of my mom's." Everybody was quiet wondering what was going on, and what this man could possibly have to say.

"Hello, I just wanted to take a couple seconds of y'all's time, to let you know that a couple months ago I met a beautiful, intelligent, and strong woman." Everybody was staring at him like 'get to the point',. "Wanda, could you come here please?" He asked holding his hand out to her, she was seated not far from the couch, and she joined him in the middle of the floor. "Wanda, the magic I feel when I'm around you is hard to explain, but I would like you to be a permanent fixture in my life."He then raised his pant leg and got down on one knee. The room was so silent you could hear

A Hutlaz Dream

a mouse pee on cotton as he reached in his pocket. Wanda placed both hands over her nose and mouth and shed a single tear as she knew what was to be said next. "Will you marry me?"

"Yes!" Wanda screamed like a diehard fan. Tom stood up and kissed her passionately and the crowd applauded. As the couple were being congratulated and people returning back to the conversations they had going before the announcement, the doorbell rang.

Jai'Myiah didn't budge, knowing Zeh'Shon was playing the door man on that day. It was probably one of the kids that had been running in and out of the house anyway. She was engrossed in conversation with her Aunt Lori, talking about which carpet cleaning service she was going to use after the party. When Zeh'Shon opened the door, he

expected to be greeted by a party attendee, but was unhappily mistaken. Standing shell shocked by the sight before his eyes, he couldn't move a muscle. There standing with a small baby wrapped in her arms was Sharice. The small child was the spitting image of Zeh'Shon, the only thing that was inherited from its mother was her skin color. There was no denying the fact that he was indeed his seed.

"Bitch, what the fuck is you doing? How you even know where I stay?" Said Zeh'Shon, as he witnessed a black Tahoe truck outfitted with presidential tents, 26" inch rims and chrome grill come to a complete stop in front of his driveway. He gripped the butt of his ever present firearm as he waited for someone to open the door and get out, but they never did.

Zo, while walking from the kitchen area, caught a preview of the unwanted guest and shifted his step in his friend's direction, knowing in advance all hell was about to break loose.

"How I know where you live? That's irrelevant," said Sharice. "I just heard a big party was jumping off over here and thought I'd bring your son over to meet his family."

"I'ma give you four seconds to get away from my door, you and your baby, or I'ma..."

"Or you're going to do what, muthafucka?" Sharice yelled as the window to the Tahoe lowered and four mean mugs came into view. The backseat passenger lowered an AR-15 assault rifle in Zeh'Shon's direction as if to say, 'nigga be easy.'

Hearing all the commotion, Jai'Myiah made her way toward it, followed by damn near the whole house minus the kids that had been promised a whooping if they came outside.

"What's going on Zeh'Shon?" She asked after squeezing her way through the guests to step outside. Looking at the unfamiliar lady holding an infant she asked, "Who is this?"

"Nobody, she was just leaving," he said shooting Sharice a menacing stare.

"Well actually, my name is Sharice, you must be the wife," Sharice said being messy. To put icing on the cake, she extended her hand offering a handshake. Jai'Myiah looked at her like she was crazy, and fixed her eyes on the child. 'No this can't be', she said to herself after seeing the baby's resemblance to her husband.

"Zeh'Shon, what the fuck is going on?"

Zeh'Shon not knowing what to do at the moment, and feeling as though he had been backed into a corner, hauled off and smacked Sharice like she was a grown man. Jai'Myiah's little cousin Loressa reached out to catch Sharice, not wanting to see her hit the ground with a baby in her arms. Before the slap was fully connected, the four doors to the Tahoe flew open and out jumped four guys that looked like stone cold killers, guns in hand. Zeh'Shon's crew drew their fire power simultaneously. After

A Hutlaz Dream

looking at the driver's face, Jai'Myiah stormed into the house and stomped up the stairs like a child throwing a temper tantrum. She was inflamed with anger and totally outdone by the situation. Wanda followed her daughter, concerned for her mental state.

"Come on cousin, go get in the car," said Lonnie taking Sharice by the arm, and leading her in safety's direction. As the standoff remained in progress Lonnie approached Zeh'Shon.

"Nigga you better learn to keep your hands to yourself quickly, because I'm an impatient teacher, and you don't want to suffer the penalties if this happens again."

"Fuck is you?" Zeh'Shon quizzed, "You better take that dumb bitch and your little entourage and get off my property, or the coroner will be on the way to pick up a few bodies."

"Is that right?" asked Lonnie stroking his beard with his index finger and thumb. "I'm tell you like this my nigga. I'ma give you a pass tonight due to you entertaining company and what not, but just know we shall meet again, and when we do I got a hot hollow point with yo' name on it." With that said he turned around and headed towards the SUV.

It took everything in Zeh'Shon to keep his gun cold and the clip filled. He wanted to kill all five of the people involved in disrespecting his home, wife, and family. He just couldn't act on his anger for fear that one of his house guests would become a casualty. He breathed deeply trying to control his anger, as the other three hooligans retreated back to the vehicle.

Just as the truck pulled off, a police cruiser rolled by ever so slowly looking at Zeh'Shon and his home. A member of the neighborhood watch must've witnessed the confrontation and called for service.

"Come on blood, let's go inside," said Zo while tugging at his partner's arm. When they entered, they heard Niki instructing the crowd that the party had come to an end. Basically telling everyone to get the fuck out in a polite manner.

Zeh'Shon's friends were hesitant to leave, wanting to stick around to have their partner's back just in case the black truck decided to backtrack. After being assured that he would be alright, they departed making sure Zeh'Shon was aware that they were just a phone call away. As the majority of the house's occupants filed out and congregated in the front yard to bid their farewells, Zeh'Shon climbed the stairs and headed for his wife, ready to face the music.

Nearing the master bedroom's door, he stopped short to eavesdrop on the conversation that was taking place on the other side of the door.

"Jai'Myiah, you've got to calm down baby," said Wanda.

"What the fuck you mean calm down? Excuse my language mommy, but damn you saw that baby."

"How you know that's his kid?" He heard Zariah say.

"Because I got muthafuckin' eyes, bitch."

Zeh'Shon decided to enter at that point. Wanda and Zariah were seated at the foot of the bed as they watched Jai'Myiah pace back and forth on the plush carpet.

"We'll be downstairs while y'all talk, come on Zariah," said Wanda. The concerned pair made an exit, closing the door behind them. Jai'Myiah continued to pace without acknowledging her husband's presence.

"Baby girl," he said, but she didn't stop pacing. "Can you slow down so I can talk to you for a minute?" He walked up to her and grabbed her elbow.

"Talk," she replied. She snatched her arm away and continued her stride.

A Hutlaz Dream

"Alright," he said nervously, "can you pack a bag and go stay with Zariah until I find out who them niggas was."

"Fuck no, I'm not going to Zariah's house, I'm tired of you always suggesting her house when a problem arises. She's not my fuckin' baby sitter, keeper, or bodyguard," she said stressed, "and fuck that nigga, he's a bitch and ain't gonna bust a crayon at a pre-school riot."

"You know dude?"

"Fuck who or what I know. Why don't you do me a favor and fill me in on what I don't know. What's up with the bitch and the baby? That's your baby, huh?" She stopped walking to look in his eyes to make sure truth was behind whatever he was about to say.

"Okay, I haven't spoken to that broad in over a year, except for a couple of months ago, she called my phone outta the blue, talkin' 'bout she had my baby." He put his head down hating to see the grief in his woman's eyes, especially knowing he was the cause.

"So there is a possibility that you are the father?" She asked already knowing the answer.

"Yes," he whispered, hating the taste that single word left in his mouth he wish there was a way for him to spit it out and never be forced to think of it again. He even had a flashback on the night she conceived, the dreadful night the condom busted.

"Ain't this a bitch? Damn, Zeh'Shon you're just full of surprises, I wonder what's going to happen next. What skeleton is going to hop out of your closet and fuck my world up again?" she said fed up. She felt as though she were on the brink of tears, but just couldn't seem to let them flow. She felt like giving up. "I gotta go Zeh'. Every time, I think we're going to make it shit gets worse. You've been fuckin' me up, not only mentally, but also emotionally, and fa real, I don't think this relationship is healthy. I really tried, I know I'm strong, but damn how much did you expect me to take?"

"Myah, please listen," Zeh'Shon started to plead.

"Save that Zeh'Shon, there is nothing you can say to excuse your actions this time. I mean, she had your baby, that's like disrespect to the 100th power." With that said she went to the bedroom door, and called her mother and Zariah up to help her pack some of her things. As they packed, Zeh'Shon pled his case and said everything he thought would get her to stay.

Wanda and Zariah packed in silence. They took their time as Zeh'Shon continued to spew his heart and soul and they rooted for him, hoping that something in his sincerity would cause Jai'Myiah to have a second thought. They didn't want to see them end like this, but decided to mind their business. After two suitcases were filled Jai'Myiah said that would be all for now and promised to get the rest at a later date. She had Wanda and Zariah take her things to the car.

"I'm sorry Zeh', I'm just tired. I need a little time," she said heading toward the door. Zeh'Shon sat still with his eyes on the floor, not wanting to see his wife go.

"Oh, and about the nigga, I don't know how him and the broad are connected, but he's my ex I told you about a while ago. I guess he just got out of prison."

Zeh'Shon looked up and let the revelation sink in. He watched Jai'Myiah go down the steps and out of his life only for the moment, he prayed. Zeh'Shon didn't chase after her. He would get her back one day, but as for the moment, he had to go see about this nigga that called himself Lonnie and go reprimand that disrespectful bitch ass nigga.

Part 2 coming soon

Also in stores

{ DELPHINE PUBLICATIONS PRESENTS }

DOUBLE BACK

JAMIE DOSSIE

{ DELPHINE PUBLICATIONS PRESENTS }

A SECRET *Worth* KEEPING

A NOVEL BY
LAKISHA JOHNSON

DAVID WEAVER PRESENTS

Trust No NIGGA

TAMIKA NEWHOUSE

AUTHOR OF *KISSES DON'T LIE*